hush

THE BLACK LOTUS SERIES
BOOK THREE

e.k. blair

Hush

Copyright © 2016 E.K. Blair

Editor: Lisa Christman, Adept Edits and Ashley Williams
Photographer: Erik Schottstaedt
Cover Designer: E.K. Blair
Interior Designer: Champagne Formats

ISBN: 978-0-9963970-4-9

To Sally

Because you love him as I do

"It's no use going back to yesterday,
because I was a different person then."

-Lewis Carroll

hush

one

I've come to know illusions well. They're the phantasms I cling to because I'm not ready to let go of the comfort they give me. Most of what brings me solace and peace are nothing more than ghosts of my past, yet I hold tightly to keep them with me in the present for fear that without them, I just might disappear too.

I'm scared to be alone, even though in some ways, I always have been.

A jolt of electricity shoots through the thick blood in my veins. It's the one thing that lets me know the difference between reality and delusion. The spark shocks my system into high alert, forcing my heart to leap out of rhythm as my eyes widen in a storm of a thousand questions my mind can't process.

I crawl to the foot of the bed on my hands and knees, staring at the TV above the fireplace. Declan sits behind me, but I no longer feel him as I struggle to breathe.

"He's alive." It's all I can mutter as I stare at the paused screen of the news report.

"Who?" Declan questions from a million miles away as I stumble off the bed and walk in uneven steps across the room, closer to the TV.

I reach out my hand as I near the image that can't be true, but is. I step onto the hearth, my fingers trembling when I slowly press them onto the screen. The moment I touch him, my heart ruptures, and I cry out. Blood from my wounded soul floods my eyes and spills down my cheeks. My breaths fracture and fill the room.

Strong hands grip my shoulders, and I want to collapse, but I can't look away from the one thing I've been searching for my whole life.

"Talk to me," he says, voice panic-stricken.

Pressing my hand more firmly against the screen, I beg to feel the warmth of him on my skin.

"Who is he?"

"This is real, right?" I ask of Declan. "You and me, in this room, it's real, isn't it?"

"Look at me."

But I can't. I'm afraid to look away for fear that I'll lose him. That somehow he'll vanish from the screen.

"Tell me it's real," I cry.

"It's real, darling. I'm here with you."

And with his words, an ugly sob rips out of my chest, but I catch it quickly when Declan steps onto the hearth next to me. As memories swirl inside, a mixture of foggy emotions fight with each other, and when anger claims victory and swells to the surface, I turn my head to look at Declan. His eyes mirror mine in utter confusion.

"He's dead," I say to him, the words like razors slicing my

vocal cords, but I speak through the pain as tears stream down my cheeks. "They told me he was dead. Why? Why?"

"Who?"

"I saw his grave. I felt the stone where his name was etched," I go on. "Why would they lie to me? Why did he lie to me? Why didn't he ever come for me?"

Declan pulls me into his arms, pressing me tightly against his chest as I wail over and over, crying out for answers that don't find me, screaming for comfort in all of my whys.

"Who?" he questions again, and when I turn my face and bury it into his bare chest, I sob through shattered dreams, broken hearts, and lost souls.

"My dad."

I fist my hands against Declan's chest as his grip tightens around me. His embrace is unwavering and entirely hard as his muscles constrict around my weakened body.

"Why am I so easy to walk away from?"

"Don't do this," he scolds. "Don't you dare blame yourself."

"Why not?" I scream, jerking my body out of his hold, pissed at the world, and for the first time in my life, pissed at my father. Stepping down and away from Declan, I turn back around and lash out in self-pity at the top of my lungs. "What did I do to deserve this life?"

"Elizabeth, please. Just take a deep breath."

"No."

He moves towards me, saying, "The last time you saw him you were only five years old, right? How can you be sure that's even him?"

I step up to him and seethe between my tears, "Because you don't forget the face of the one man you've spent your whole life aching for. There is no doubt that man is my father."

Returning to the TV, my eyes are stoned to the bright blues I remember so vividly. Eyes I thought loved me beyond anything in this world. Eyes I thought bore black six feet under. But he's here, and I've never felt more alone.

"Elizabeth?"

My hands grip the mantel to keep my legs from failing me.

"Elizabeth, please. Look at me."

"Elizabeth?"

His voice is both poison and wine, and hearing it causes my limbs to go ataxic and I crumple to the floor. The familiar smell of clove cigarettes both soothes me and torments me.

"Is it true?" I ask my brother, Pike, but Declan answers first.

"I'll do whatever I can to find out."

"Yes, it's true."

Looking up, I shift my eyes away from Declan to the corner of the room where Pike stands. We both know I shouldn't be looking at him, because Declan thinks I'm taking the pills that kill my hallucinations, but I'm not. I can't say goodbye to my brother yet. Maybe never.

But there he stands, alive, with his dark hair tucked under his black beanie, and his hands shoved into his pants pockets with his inked arms showing. His eyes send love and strength before he nods his head over to Declan, and I follow his cue, knowing I'll lose him when I do.

My throat swells in torment, painfully blistering as I sit here on my knees. It's every dream come true; I just never knew the dream lived within an unimaginable nightmare. No matter all the anger I feel right now, one thing still remains: you can cut me deeply with lies, you can throw me into the flames of life's evils, but I will never give up on what I've always yearned for.

With tears falling down my face in a steady stream of anguish, I painfully choke out the heartbreak of the little girl lost inside of me. "I want my dad."

In two quick steps, Declan is on the floor with me, holding me, rocking me, soothing me, and vowing to do everything he can to find him.

Clinging to him, I take all the comfort he's giving and attempt to steal more, gripping him tighter and pressing my fingers deeper into his skin. If I'm hurting him, he doesn't show it, so I close my eyes and crawl onto his lap just as a child would.

When I open my eyes again, they sting against the fully risen sun, and my cheeks burn with the bite of salt. I'm still wrapped within Declan's arms, and my body aches not only from being in this position for God knows how long, but also from the torture of the past couple days of being held captive.

"I hurt."

Declan stands and scoops me off the floor before laying me on the bed. He hovers above me, looking over my battered face and body with eyes filled with rage and pity.

His expression irks me. "Don't."

"What?"

"Look at me like that. Like you feel sorry for me."

"I'm worried about you. That's all." He then hands me a painkiller that I slip into my mouth.

"I don't understand. I don't understand any of this."

"I don't either. But you've been through a lot lately, so I don't think your mind is capable of clarity. Mine isn't either. So let's focus on one thing at a time, okay?"

"All I can focus on is why my dad's face is on that screen

when it shouldn't be. I don't know if I should be happy or angry," I tell him. "Why didn't he want me?"

Declan doesn't respond as he pulls me against him. I try to fight the haze from the pills that creeps in, but my eyes grow heavy when Declan whispers softly into my ear, lulling me with a comforting, "Shh, darling. I'll take care of you. I'll do what I can to find the answers."

And as I hang on to his words, I give in, releasing a breath before drifting to sleep.

(DECLAN)

ELIZABETH TREMBLES IN her sleep as I hold her. My mind is a god-damn labyrinth as I close my eyes and attempt to process the past forty-eight hours. It's an impossible task as visions race with a hundred new revelations and a thousand new questions. The only thing I do know is that I'm terrified I won't be able to keep Elizabeth from having a full-on mental collapse.

Her face is a canvas of bruises, welts, and lacerations that illustrate the rape and torture she's been through. It pains me to know that I play a part, that some of those wounds were put there by my own hands and the others were put there because I couldn't protect her from that asshole—Richard—the man I murdered.

I didn't even hesitate when I put a bullet in his head after Elizabeth told me he killed my mum. The fact that I could kill so easily scares the shit out of me. It's a grim feeling to be terrified of your own self. I now know I'm capable of anything. I'm a monster created by this woman, whose body is wrapped around mine.

I want an explanation, just as she. Who was Richard? How did he know my mum? Why did he kill her? What part does my father play in all of this? I want to know. I want to understand, but as out of control as I am, she is more volatile than I. She needs strength, so I have to set aside all that haunts me right now and focus on her.

When her breaths even out, I slip out of bed and allow her the rest her body desperately craves. I stop before I walk out of the room and look at Elizabeth lying in my bed as a swell of contentment and anger rushes in a tidal wave under my skin. She's knocked my control off its axis, and I need to steady it back into place to keep her safe—to make sure nothing else happens without my say-so.

two
(DECLAN)

"Christ," Lachlan says with a startle when I slam the double doors to the library, closing us off from the rest of the house.

With my back facing him, my hands grip tightly around the door handles in a lame attempt to control my turmoil. There's rioting in my bones, rattling me into a cold sweat. Pulling back to open the doors slightly, I slam them once more, grunting, hammering my palm into the aged mahogany.

"What can I do?" Lachlan questions from across the room.

A string of answers fills my head and wraps around my neck in a tightening noose. I can't talk as I think about Elizabeth upstairs in a drug-induced sleep. Visions from when I found her last night flash behind my eyes in vivid detail. Her naked and bloodied body, the bruising and lacerations between her legs from what that dickfuck did to her, it brings up sour bile that I fight to swallow back.

All I wanted to give her when she woke this morning was

as much peace as I could, but instead, I watched her world erupt into even more chaos. Chaos she doesn't need. Chaos I'm worried she's not stable enough to handle.

"Declan."

I turn and face my friend, thankful that he stayed the night and is here right now, because there's no way I could sort through my deranged thoughts on my own without smashing my fists through the walls and destroying this house in a blacked out rage.

"How is she?" he questions.

"Sleeping." The word is strangled as it comes out. I walk over to the couch and sit down, lowering my head to meet my clenched fists. My harsh breaths through my nose are audible. I won't allow Elizabeth to see this. She needs to believe I'm in utter control and that she's completely safe with me.

"How is she really?" he pushes for a better answer than the one I just gave him.

I look up and meet his concerned eyes as he takes the seat on the other side of the coffee table.

"She's not good."

I won't go into detail with Lachlan, because what's hers is mine and no one else's.

"Look, what happened last night, what you witnessed—" I start to say but Lachlan cuts in, "It's vaulted."

"It better be," I tell him, my voice glazed in unspoken threats. "You'll never speak of it, not even with her, understand?"

"Without fail," he responds with a nod.

"I need your help," I tell him, shifting the conversation.

"Anything."

"I need you to find someone for me."

"Who?"

"His name is Steve Archer."

With a curious look, he responds, "Why does that name sound familiar?"

"He's Elizabeth's father."

"Her father?" he reacts in surprise. "He's dead. I came across his death certificate when I found her mother."

"I don't know. We were upstairs watching an American news report and she swears she saw him."

"On TV? There's no way."

"She's adamant."

"Declan, her mind has to be a mare's nest right now. I'm sure she's seeing what she wishes to see," he says. "The man is dead."

I shrug my shoulders, releasing a heavy breath. "Pull the news footage and compare the two men."

Lachlan steps over to the desk in the corner of the room, and I follow, directing him to the correct news station webpage. We find the video, play it, and when I see the man who Elizabeth made me pause on, I reach down and stop the video, freezing on his face.

"Him."

It takes a few minutes to find an archived article on his arrest, but Lachlan finally comes across one with a photo.

"There," I say when I see the link. "Click on that."

And with a single click, I know Elizabeth isn't imagining things. It may be an old photo, but there's no way I can argue that it's not the same man.

"Holy shit," Lachlan says as he compares both of the photos.

"That's him. Tell me you're seeing what I'm seeing."

"I'm seeing it."

"Fuck!" Raking my hands through my hair, I pace over to the windows, wishing I never had the goddamn TV turned on this morning. "I can't allow anyone else to hurt her."

"I know."

"Jesus. I mean, she just found out that her piece of shit mother sold her when was just a baby. And now this? I don't think she can take much more."

"Tell me what you want me to do."

She won't let this go. Not that I could expect her to. But I need to keep the upper hand here and remain two steps in front of her.

"Find him. And nothing, not a single piece of information gets past me. Understood?"

"I understand."

"You screwed up once," I berate. "Don't do it again."

He stands, steps over to me, and assures, "You have my word." My glare doesn't waver because what's at stake is too precious to gamble with. Lachlan sees the doubt, grips my shoulder with his hand, and states firmly, "I care about that girl too."

"Then don't fuck this up."

With a curt nod, he squeezes my shoulder before walking away and pulling out his phone.

"I want security too," I call out. "She's not to be alone."

"I'll get on that now."

"You'll do."

"I'm not security, McKinnon."

"You're right. You're a fuckin' dobber when it comes to taking orders. But after last night, you're the only one I trust to keep her safe when I'm not around."

"I'll need to situate a few things in Edinburgh."

"Do it today," I tell him. "You can stay in the cottage next to the grotto."

"The cottage?" He laughs. "You mean the maid's quarters?"

"That's the one, you wanker," I respond with a chuckle. "Oh, one more thing," I add before Lachlan leaves the room, exchanging the banter for seriousness, "Thank you."

"Of course."

I'm willing to go to any length to make sure nothing comes close to touching Elizabeth, but options are limited with the history the two of us carry. Although our time together has been short, it's been riddled with more than enough to land us both in prison. So Lachlan is it for us.

Wandering into the kitchen, I walk over to the security monitor on the wall and check the cameras out front. I flip through them and stop on the gate camera. I'm watching as Lachlan's car drives out onto the main road when my cell rings.

"McKinnon," I answer.

"Good afternoon, Mr. McKinnon. It's Alexander Stanforth from Stanforth and Partners. How are you doing?"

"I'm well," I respond to Alex, the architect that will be working on the London property I recently purchased.

"I hope you don't mind my calling on your cell, but with your interest in expediting the initial meetings, I figured I would bypass your office manager."

"It's why I gave you this number, Alex."

"Good. Well then, I'd like to set up a meeting to discuss the scope of the project, along with schedule and budget. Are you free next week?"

"I can be free. Set it up and call my office to get it on the books, and I'll be there," I tell him.

"Sounds good. I'll get with the team and give your office a call later today."

"Thanks, Alex."

Hanging up the phone, I grab an ice pack from the freezer and make my way up to Elizabeth. She's sound asleep when I enter the room and sit down next to her. The side of her face is swollen; black and blue mar her eye. Gently, I touch the ice to her skin and she flinches.

"Sorry," I whisper when her eyes flutter open. "The swelling is really bad."

Her eyes are dilated dopey black, but she doesn't keep them open long. I watch her lie motionless, soft breaths filling the space around me.

"We used to dance," her hoarse voice murmurs.

"Who?"

"Me and my dad."

I don't say anything when she curls her body over and lifts her head onto my lap.

"Dean Martin was his favorite," she says sleepily, never opening her eyes. "'Volare' . . . that's the song. He'd sing along, and I remember always giggling during the Italian parts."

"He had a good voice?" I ask, keeping the ice on her.

"Mmm hmm," she answers slowly in her listless state. "He'd set me on top of his feet and dance while I hung on to his legs."

She pauses, letting time falter, and I think she's fallen back asleep, but then she begins to blink. When her glassy eyes find me, she whimpers, "Why would he leave me?"

Never in my life have I seen so much heartache in anyone's eyes, and I hate that it's in hers that I see it. She wants answers, but I have none to give her, and it kills me.

"I thought I made him happy."

Setting the ice pack on the bedside table, I turn back to her, and with her face cradled in my hands I assert, "I promise you I'll do everything I can to give you answers. We *will* find him."

"What if he doesn't want me finding him?"

"It doesn't matter what he wants. It's not his choice to make."

This isn't the woman I know. She's something else entirely. She may have been putting on an act to deceive me, but she always had a bold-spirited backbone that a person can't fake. Beneath the lies, that part of her was real, but now it's lost somewhere inside of her violated body.

She takes in a small pain-filled gasp as she shifts her body.

"Why don't you soak in a hot bath?"

"What's the point? Rot is rot."

"That's bullshit," I lash back. "Rot has hurt you, but it hasn't claimed you. And I suggested a bath to help with your pain, not to clean you." My words are half truths; I do want to clean her. Clean all the filth from the sack of shit that did this to her. I want to erase him from her skin because the thought sickens me. I want her covered in me, in my scent, with my hands all over her body. I want her to taste like me, smell like me. It's a feral need to mark her as mine. To own her, every single piece of her.

Pulling her up to me, I press my lips to hers, kissing her softly when I really want to devour her, but she's much too fragile. Her breath on my tongue sparks a shudder through my veins, causing my pulse to race. It takes control not to throw her down, spread her thighs, and bury my cock deep inside her. I want to fuck her so hard she feels me in her bones.

I force myself back, gripping her neck in my hands as I take in a deep breath that I release slowly.

"I've missed having your taste in my mouth," she says, her words not doing much to help me calm myself.

"I want more than just my taste in your mouth, but I can't let myself be that selfish with you right now. I won't be able to control myself, and I'll just hurt you."

Getting out of bed, I go to start the bath before returning to her.

"Give me your hands," I tell her and then help her onto her feet. "Lift your arms."

Moving slowly, I undress her, careful not to hurt her. When I have her naked in front of me, I quickly remove my clothes and then walk her to the bathroom. I step into the tub first and then hold on to her as I help her into the water. She sits between my legs, leaning back against my chest with a grimace of pain.

Her body is hard to look at. The bruises are enough to get my blood boiling. It coils my gut in a retching of turbulent emotions. There's a serrated bite mark on her left breast that I didn't notice last night when I showered her.

"What?" she questions, looking up at me. "What's wrong?"

"What do you mean?"

"Your body tensed up."

"I'm sorry . . . I just . . ." I start, trying for gentle words.

"What?"

But gentle doesn't come easy for me, so I go with honest. "I want to take all these marks away. All the ones that aren't from me."

"I'll always be marked by someone else's touch. I always have been."

"I'd give anything to take them away," I tell her, knowing now that the scars on her back and wrists came at the hands of her foster dad.

"You can't make me into something I'm not, you know?"

"You're not my charity case, if that's what you're inferring," I snap with irritation.

"Was I ever? Even in the beginning?"

"No. You were never a woman I pitied."

"If not pity, then what?"

"There's no easy answer. I don't understand you or your reasoning for all the shit you've done. All I do know is that I must be crazy for loving you, because dammit, I do love you. I've tried not to, I've fought it, but I can't stop."

"But what about what you said last night? You still hate me?"

"Yes."

She drops her eyes, but I bring her back to me, saying, "I love you, Elizabeth."

"Do you really?"

"Of course I do. I've killed for you."

three
(ELIZABETH)

HIS WORDS, HIS truth, they may haunt some people, but for my decrepit soul, they soothe. It's true—he has killed for me—and I have also killed for him. I murdered Pike when I thought he killed Declan. And it's also a murder that I wish every day I could take back. But I can't. The only way I can have Pike is through my mind's trickery.

But aside from Pike, I was a split second away from killing Richard last night, and it would've been all for Declan. In a sick way, it was going to be my gift to him. To rid the world of the man who took my love's mother. Declan wouldn't let me pull the trigger though—he did it for himself, robbing me of the satisfaction. I wanted it selfishly, but if there was one kill Declan deserved, it was that one.

Declan's eyes dig into mine, and I know I've touched a nerve by questioning his love for me.

"I'm sorry," I tell him, running my hands over his, which are tensed around my neck.

"I've never been anything but honest with you."

"I know. I didn't mean to be dismissive of your words."

His grip loosens as he relaxes, resting his shoulders against the back of the tub.

"I'm having a hard time processing everything," I add.

"Then talk to me. Don't hold it in."

Declan made his feelings known last week when I read the file on my mother. He made it clear he wants me to deal with my feelings instead of hiding them and locking them away the way I've done my whole life. I owe him anything he asks of me because of everything I've done to him, but sometimes it's just easier to go numb.

"Maybe later. I'm still really tired from the pain pill." But there won't be a later. I can't cut myself open like that for him because there's nothing that will stop the blood gushing from the wound. Declan's ability to connect me with my emotions scares the shit out of me. There's too much to feel. There's too much termagant despair inside me. I need it to go away and disappear so I can find relief.

I'm in the arms of the man I love, the man I was so desperate to have again, and here he is. Flesh on flesh—every part of me touching every part of him, and here I am—scared and closed off. He's wrapped around me, and I should be content, but in this moment, I crave another man's arms. It's Pike I wish I had right now. He's the only one who can numb me.

He's safety.

He's constant.

He's my painkiller.

"You'll rest better if you get your thoughts out," he suggests.

Leaning forward, breaking the contact, I lie, "I'm really tired. Can you help me back to bed?"

"Don't shut me out, Elizabeth."

"I'm not. It's just the tub is uncomfortable, and I really am exhausted and not feeling well."

I hate lying to him when I swore to him and to myself that I never would, but the alternative is unbearable to even think about. It's best for the both of us if I don't go down that road.

Declan dries me off, brushes my teeth, and dresses me. I give him these things because he needs them. I know him well enough to see that he needs his hands on me, to control and take care. He's always needed that, and I can't even imagine what these past few days have done to him with not knowing where I was and having that authority taken away by another man.

After he applies the ointment to my cuts, he grabs the prescription bottle and shakes out a pill.

"Here," he says, holding the mood stabilizer that was prescribed to me by the doctor who examined me the first night I arrived here.

It's the pill I've been tossing in the toilet because I don't want to lose Pike, and that pill will vanish him from me. I can't say goodbye though. I don't want to. I need him. His smell, his voice, his presence. I'm not willing to let him go.

I take the pill from his hand, and when he gives me a glass of water, I cheek it instead of swallowing.

Another lie.

Another deception I swore I'd no longer partake in.

Another broken promise.

"Good girl."

He walks me back to the bedroom and helps me get into

bed.

"I'm going to run downstairs to get something to drink. Are you thirsty?"

I nod my head and watch him as he strides out of the room. When I hear the creaking on the stairs beneath his feet, I spit out the pill. Being in too much pain to get out of bed to flush it down the toilet, I shove it into my pillowcase until I can throw it away. When he returns, he slips under the covers beside me and pulls me into his arms.

"By the way, Lachlan's going to be staying here," he tells me. "I want security, and with all that he's already seen, he's the only one I trust."

"Okay."

"Are you comfortable with that?"

"Yes," I respond. "From the time I've spent with him, I've come to like him."

"While you were sleeping, I spoke with him about your father. He's working on getting information."

I nod my head against his chest, unable to speak through my tightening throat. I'm sure Declan feels my body tensing up when he bands his arms a little more strongly around me. Closing my eyes, I inhale deeply as he kisses the top of my head.

"I know it's upsetting, but I want to be transparent with you about all of this, okay?"

"You don't think I'm crazy, do you?"

He combs my hair back with his fingers, and I look up at him when he says, "No, darling, I don't. Lachlan was able to retrieve an old photo of your father, and it's the same man from the news."

Declan's face blurs, and I quickly close my eyes before the

tears fall. I can't think about this. It's the worst pain I've ever felt, so I focus on armoring myself against all that threatens to completely eviscerate me.

"You're stronger than your emotions," I hear Pike tell me, the timbre of his voice providing me with the strength I need to take control of my heart.

"Are you okay?"

"Yes."

"There's something else I need to talk to you about."

"What's that?"

"When I was in London, I hired an architecture firm for the new property. Meetings start next week, so you're coming with me."

"London?" I question, pushing myself to sit up. "For how long?"

"For the duration of the build . . . a few years."

"I . . . um . . ." I stammer, unsure of what to say. Then, the realization that I have nowhere else to go hits me, and it all becomes so terrifying. If somehow I lost Declan again, that would be it for me. He is the only person I have, and without him, I wouldn't know where to go. Even though I'm now aware that my father is out there somewhere, it's heartbreakingly clear that he doesn't want me, or else he'd have come for me.

"You don't want to go to London?" he questions.

"No, it isn't that. It's just . . . I don't really know."

My voice cracks slightly, and Declan promptly soothes, "You have nothing to be worried about. I'm here. I'm not leaving you. Wherever I go, you go with me."

I don't respond as he holds me close to him. I'm not sure what to say, because even though he says I shouldn't be worried,

I am.

"I really need you to talk to me," he urges. "Don't close yourself off again."

There's a desperation in his eyes, a neediness that reminds me of our time in Chicago. I played him well, deceiving him to believe I was locked in a violent marriage that I couldn't escape. He held the same desperation then. He tried so hard to help me, to save me, but I was always careful to keep him at a measured distance. I wanted him to believe he had all of me but none of me at the same time.

The game is over though. No longer do I want to see that look in his eyes. It once gave me pleasure to know I had him fooled, but that absconded the moment he crept into my heart. But in order to keep my soul intact, I need to continue to move in calculated steps.

"I *am* worried," I admit.

"About what?"

"About you. If there's no you . . . there's no me."

"You're scared of losing me?"

I nod.

"You're not going to lose me, you hear? It's not happening."

"I lost you once though. It was my fault. Trust me, I know. But I still lost you. I still know that pain, and it scares me."

"I know that pain too. It wasn't just you who felt it." His words drip with intensity. "I felt it in my marrow. That's how deep you run through me."

"So much has happened. I wanted you the second I lost you, and now that I have you, I feel so . . ."

"What do you feel?"

Reaching my hand up to his face, I run my fingers along his

jawline and through his overgrown stubble, listening to it crackle against my palm. "Disconnected," I reveal and then drop my hand along with my head.

"Look at me," he demands, and I do. "It's okay. I'm having a hard time wrapping my head around everything that's been thrown my way these past few weeks, so I understand. I'll take it away, I promise, but it's going to take time. One thing I need you to know is that I'm here. I'll remind you of that every day if I have to. I'm here."

I allow his words to attempt their quieting on my anxiety as I take my hand and cover the bullet wound on his pec, the one Pike inflicted on him with the intent of killing him. My thumb brushes over the raised flesh, and when I look up, his focus is on my hand. Guilt courses its way through my bloodstream. His eyes flick to meet mine, and I ask, "Did it hurt?"

"Not as much as losing you," he responds, wrapping his hand around my wrist while I continue to run my fingers along my betrayal that's now branded on him for eternity.

"I manipulated you. I lied."

"You did. And I hate you for that. I hate you for what your lies turned me into."

"But you missed me?"

"I couldn't unlove you."

Pressing my hand flat against his chest, I feel his heart pumping, and I decide to rip a piece of my own heart off to give to him, exposing a tiny part of what I know I must protect in the fortress of my soul. Declan has always had a way of cutting right through to the core of me. So, I hand over my offering in the form of truth, letting him know, "You scare me."

His heartbeat grows in force, exposing his frustration to my words.

"What about me scares you?"

"The way you break my walls so easily."

"Why do you want walls between us?"

"Because I'm afraid to feel right now. There's so much inside me that I'm fighting off. I'm scared it'll be too much."

He lets go of a hard breath, upset with what I just admitted to him. He drops his head for a moment, and then, with controlled force, he grabs my other wrist and pushes me down onto the bed. I don't resist him when he straddles my legs and sits on top of my thighs. Green eyes scream for obedience, and I give him just that when he rips my top open, tearing the fabric and breaking the buttons to expose my breasts.

The chill of the air hardens my nipples instantly, but it isn't my tits he's after. He quickly gathers both my wrists into his one hand, restraining me, and then takes his other and presses it firmly to the center of my chest.

"This is mine," he professes. "You want me?"

"Yes," I breathe.

"You want to be with me?"

"Yes."

"Then this little heart of yours is mine. It beats for me, and I'll provide its protection. You hear me?"

I nod.

"You need to trust me enough to take care of you. I won't ever let you break."

The rise and fall of my chest hits hard as I take hold of his words, needing them to calm my fears.

"Do you trust me?"

I nod again.

"Tell me."
"I trust you."
Another lie.

(DECLAN)

I LEFT ELIZABETH READING in the library. It's been a few days since I found her, and even though bruises are fading and swelling is dissipating, she continues to be distant. I've yet to fuck her, not that I haven't tried, but I also haven't pushed. Taming the beast inside me isn't something I enjoy while I wait impatiently for her fragility to wane.

Having Lachlan here has helped though. Whatever friendship they forged while she was staying at The Water Lily has dulcified the awkwardness for all of us, leaving just minor remnants. Knowing what Lachlan and I saw that night, the state we found Elizabeth in, doesn't seem to bother her as much as one would presume, as much as it bothers me. I figure her lack of shame stems from her childhood and what she was forced to endure. It was just the other day she admitted that she saw herself as nothing more than rot.

"McKinnon," Lachlan announces, redirecting my thoughts

when I walk through the door of the guesthouse he's staying in. "Sorry I bailed on breakfast this morning, I hope Elizabeth wasn't offended."

"Not at all. Important call?"

"Yes, actually."

I walk farther into the house and take a seat in the living area.

"I got information about Steve from my contact."

"And?"

He sits in the chair adjacent to me and drops a few papers onto the coffee table. "And . . . he's a dead man."

"What?"

"Everything checks out. Take a look for yourself. All the documents, the funeral information with plot and burial. Even the death certificate is there. It's a dead end from that point on. Steve Archer doesn't exist; he's been dead for sixteen years."

I pick up the papers and flip through them, examining the trail of proof that he is indeed dead.

"What's he hiding from?" I ask aloud, not expecting Lachlan to have an answer for me.

"That's what I'm trying to find out."

I set the papers down, knowing damn well they're nothing but bullshit propaganda to support the prevarication of death, and inquire, "What about the passenger manifest?"

"I'm working on it, but we're talking about breaking some strict federal laws. I have a friend putting in a few calls for me, but it might be a long shot. I don't know if anyone is going to be willing to risk their job or compromise their values."

"Values can be bought for the right price, but we need more people on this," I stress with growing intensity. "I want everything my money can buy. Private investigators, hackers, *everything* we can think of."

"I know, and trust me when I tell you, I'm on it." He takes a pause as I let go of a frustrated breath. "On another note, I got everything lined up at One Hyde Park, so the apartment will be ready by the time you arrive."

"I've never been more thankful for buying that property than I am now."

"You should have no worries with Elizabeth's safety there," Lachlan says about the building that I own an apartment in.

It's one of the most secure properties in the world, if not *the* securest. The moment I started considering building in London, I went ahead a snagged up a dual-floor apartment in One Hyde Park. The privacy measures go above and beyond from bullet-proof windows to x-rayed mail.

After being shot in Chicago, I not only transferred Brunswickhill into a private trust, but also moved the London property into one as well. No one will know where Elizabeth and I are except for the people I choose to inform.

"I need to go take care of a few things."

"I'll check in with you as soon as I get an update on the Archer case," he says as I make my way to the front door.

"Don't drag your ass on this one, Lachlan. I need this handled yesterday."

"I'm on it."

On my way into the main house, I peek in the library, but Elizabeth is no longer there. Just the book she was reading, face-down on the sofa.

"Elizabeth," I call out with no answer in return.

I walk down to the atrium where I know she likes to lie on

the chaise and enjoy the sun's heat through the glass. The room is empty though. I stand for a moment, looking out the glass, and eventually movement catches my eye. I watch Elizabeth as she walks aimlessly. She loves taking long strolls outside to explore the grounds.

I make my way out to where she is. "What are you doing?"

"I never knew there was a stream over here."

"There's a lot you haven't been able to see because of the snow," I tell her, pulling her into my arms and pressing my lips to hers.

She quietly moans, slipping her hands under my coat and around my waist.

"You're freezing."

"I'm okay," she responds as I bring her in even closer, strengthening my arms firmly around her body. "What are you doing out here?"

"I want to talk to you, but you weren't inside where I left you."

"Where you left me?" she teases, tilting her head back to look up at me. "What am I? A little trinket of yours that you can place wherever you choose?"

"Something like that." I shoot her an amorous wink and watch her beautiful smile creep in. "Come. Sit with me."

We walk over to a bench perched aside the stream coated in ice.

"I just spoke with Lachlan and wanted to let you know where we are in regards to finding your father."

Blithe ease fades into yearning hope rimmed in years of pain.

"Do you want to talk about this right now?" I ask as her

body language takes on a sudden shift.

"Yes." Her voice is full of anxiety, eager for answers. "What did you find?"

"Evidence of his death."

"But he isn't dead." Her voice pitches with even more anxiety.

"I know that. Lachlan is doing what he can to get a copy of the list of passengers. When we get that, we can go from there."

"Well, how long is that going to take?"

"He's working as fast as he can, but he doesn't have any straight connections with the airline."

Frustration marks her face as I watch her body tense up and fight back against the puddle of tears in her eyes. She's unmoving, and it's taking all her strength to not lose her composure. I wish I could give her the answers she's so eager for. It's a painful sight to see the one I love ache so badly.

I reach my arm around her shoulders, and coax, "It's okay to cry. It won't hurt as bad if you let go of some of the pain."

"I spent my life crying for my father, and it's never lessened the pain," she says, refusing my words.

"Look at me," I demand, and when she does, I continue, "This is not fine. You holding everything in is not fine."

"Why do you want to see me break so badly?"

"You're breaking right now," I rebut. "You, forcing yourself not to feel the hurt. You, pushing me away. You present a stone exterior, but it's just a façade of all your brokenness inside. You're a fool's paradise, but I'm no fool. I see right through you."

"You're an asshole," she bites, pissed that I'm calling her out on her charade, but I won't back down.

"What are you afraid of? My seeing you in a light you're embarrassed of? I've seen you at your worst. Or are you still worried about feeling too much that you'll break apart and be unable to put the pieces back together? What is it?"

"Why are you pushing so hard?"

"If you can't put yourself back together then I'll do it for you."

"Stop!"

"Is that why you won't let me touch you?"

At that, she jerks away from me, but I grip her arms tightly.

"Let go!"

"Why won't you let me fuck you?" I hiss, losing my control and letting frustration and rejection spew out of me. "Answer me, for Christ's sake!"

My voice strains in temper as she fights against my hold, and I eventually loosen my grip and allow her to break away from me. She stands and stumbles back, fuming in pure anger.

"Is that the problem?" she spits. "Your ego is hurt because you can't get in my pants?"

I stand and walk right up to her, chest to chest. "You know damn well that if I wanted what was in your pants, I'd take it."

"Then take it. I don't give a shit. If that's all you want, then have it." Her words taunt, but they infuriate me even more.

"You're so fucking blind. It's not your pussy I want. It's so much more than just that. I want all of you. Every piece. I want to be inside of you because that's the one place you'll be so weak you'll have no choice but to hand all of yourself over to me."

With a slight shake of her head, she looks deep into my eyes, confessing on a whisper, "I just can't."

My hands clutch her face and I speak with fervency, "You can. I need you to try."

"But you have me," she cries out. "I'm here. I'm not running away."

"Stop avoiding."

"I'm n—"

"You're here," I break in, cutting her off. "But you're not really here. You may lie next to me every night, but you're not really there. You're somewhere else entirely. Somewhere deep inside that body of yours, you're hiding away."

There's no response on her part, only glaring eyes that expose just how furious she is.

"How many times do I have to tell you to convince you that you're safe here? That you're safe with me?"

"Let go of me, please," she requests in an even tone.

I drop my hands from her face, and she immediately turns and walks away from me without another word, without ever looking back. I don't say anything to stop her, I just let her go. And before I allow my aggravation grow any further, I too find my way back to the house and up to the third level where my office is.

Needing to relieve my mind of the stress, I busy myself with work. Between phone calls to the office and checking in on my Chicago property, time passes quickly. Lotus is thriving financially and is proving to be one of the most sought after hotels in the city. Exclusivity is key, and that notion is proving itself.

But I can't think about Chicago without thinking about my father. I haven't spoken to him since Elizabeth told me about his arrest. Honestly, I haven't even delved into his involvement with Richard, Bennett, or even Elizabeth's father for fear of what it might stir up inside me. Elizabeth would deem me a hypocrite, and she'd be right, which is why I haven't broached the topic with her yet.

So for that reason alone, I call Elizabeth up to my office, and it takes her only a few minutes to appear in the doorway.

"What's so urgent?" she asks with a hint of agitation that's leftover from our earlier quarrel.

"Come in."

She does, finding a seat in front of my desk. I get up from my chair and walk around to take the seat next to her.

"First, I won't apologize for earlier, except for one thing—I accused you of being afraid of facing your fears when I've been doing the same thing."

"What do you mean?"

"I've been avoiding my father out of trepidation," I admit to her. "But I'm putting that aside, hoping you'll do the same for me."

Her eyes soften.

"So, can you help me?" I ask and she nods, saying, "Okay."

"The night I found you, you told me that Richard and my father were working together, using Bennett's company as a cover for gun trafficking."

"That's what Richard told me," she says.

"You also said that Richard was the one who killed my mum."

She nods.

With my throat constricting as visions of my mum getting shot in the head flash in my memory, I speak on a strained voice, "I need to know why it happened."

She holds my hand in hers, taking her time before she says anything. "He told me Cal was embezzling money into an off-shore account. Richard said he wanted to teach your dad a lesson that would ensure his loyalty."

"So my father knew what Richard was going to do?"

With a hard swallow and eyes full of pity, she nods. "He knew. It was why your dad left town. He didn't want to be there when it happened."

My breathing falters in unsteady breaths as rage explodes in volcanic measures inside my chest. Every muscle in my body indurates in tension, and I let go of Elizabeth's hand for fear I'll crack her delicate bones. I pop out of my chair and it topples over.

"That bastard has spent every day since her death blaming me," I fume. The blades of each word slicing my tongue, filling me with the blood of putrid hate. "He made me believe it was my fault!"

"No matter how it happened, Declan, it wouldn't have been your fault."

I walk over to the window's edge, grip my hands on the sill, and drop my head as I hunch over. It's a battlefield of emotions, to which there is no victor. Outrage and fury fight alongside sadness and longing. I've mourned my mother the way no man should ever have to, but I did. I've allowed the pain to dwell in my heart, embittering it and giving it the power to grow into the man I am today. A man who can't relinquish an ounce of control without being consumed with unsettling fear. God only knows who I'd be if it weren't for this manifestation.

I flinch when I feel Elizabeth's hand on my back. When I turn to look at her, her cheeks are tear-stained, and I wipe them away with my thumbs, asking, "Why are you crying?"

"Because . . . it hurts me to see you in pain."

"I need you to see it though," my voice breaks.

She then reaches her hands up to my face, pulls me to her, and kisses me. She swallows up my ragged breaths, pushing her body against mine, and I instantly grow hard. It's a storm of emotions that begs to be released.

With a growl, I pick her up, and she gasps when I drop her to the couch. She watches intently, trembling as I unbuckle my belt.

"Don't."

"Don't tell me no, Elizabeth," I command.

She jolts up, lurching off the couch in a panic. "I can't."

There's fear in her eyes as she backs away from me, heading towards the door, as if I'm some monster from her nightmares.

"Bullshit! You can, you just don't want to."

She continues to retreat, refusing to connect with me and it's the last fucking stab to my heart I can take! I fucking love her, but she's built this wall around herself to keep me away. It pisses the raging shit out of me, and I explode in a thunderous roar when I watch her leave the room, rejecting me.

"Just give me one motherfucking piece of you!" my scathing voice ruptures, reverberating off the walls.

five
(ELIZABETH)

His VIOLENT SCREAMS echo through the house as I bolt down the stairs to the bedroom, scared that he will take what I'm terrified to give. Not that I don't want to be close with him, but it's the ramifications I'm not ready for. I shut the door, and try to calm myself down.

"What are you doing?"

I look up, relieved to have Pike here with me right now. "Where have you been?" I say breathlessly as I rush into his arms. "I've missed you."

There's never any temperature to his touch, but there's pressure, and it's enough to soothe.

"Just because you can't see me doesn't mean I'm not always here."

"Don't leave," I beg of him. "Stay with me, just for a while."

He strokes his hands through my hair, cradling me close, and I nuzzle my face against his chest. With a deep breath through my nose, I inhale his scent through the fibers of his shirt.

"I'm worried about you."

An overwhelming neediness consumes me, and I finally let the tears fall that I've been holding in for days now. "I miss you so much, Pike," I cry. "It only gets worse as time passes."

"Is that why you're not taking your meds?"

"I won't ever say goodbye to you, Pike. Don't even think about asking me to because it'll never happen. I'm keeping you for always."

"I want you to get better though."

"You make me better. You always have."

We walk over to the bed and slip in. I rest my head in the center of his chest as we lie together, and even though I'm in the arms of a dead man, I feel at home. For the first time since Declan found me with Richard, I feel at peace, in the arms of my brother. He continues to hold me as time passes and the sun sets, darkening the room.

"Can I ask you something?"

"Sure."

"Why are you shutting Declan out after all you've been through to be with him?"

"You know why," I tell him. "You know me better than anyone else does."

"Why are you letting your fear win?"

"I'm not. I'm only protecting myself the way you taught me."

"I taught you to protect yourself against people who hurt you. Declan's not trying to hurt you, but you're definitely hurting him."

Sitting up, I look down to Pike and take in each and every feature, unable to look away.

"What is it? What do you want to say?" he questions, reading my

face and knowing I'm hiding something.

"You'll think I'm crazy."

He smiles, and it's so perfect with the moon casting its glow down upon him. *"I already think you're crazy, Elizabeth. But I'm crazy too. So, tell me what you're thinking about."*

My mind drifts back through our life together. He was always there for me in ways no one else was, giving me what I needed to escape and numb.

"Just say it."

"Take my pain away," I request hesitantly.

He sits up, looking at me as if I've lost my mind by asking him for sex. Maybe I have, but I know what I need, and it's him. He has the power to stop the world from spinning so out of control. If even for just a moment, I crave the reprieve.

"Please, Pike." My voice, filled with so much pain and sadness, pleads as tears drip from my chin.

"I'm not real."

"To me you are."

"Elizabeth," he says cautiously and then repeats, *"I'm not real."*

"But I feel you," I tell him, taking his hand in mine. "I can *feel* you."

"It's not real."

"It is!"

He wraps his arms around me, and I cling to him—desperate for him.

"I'm not crazy. I feel this; I feel your arms holding me. Tell me you feel it too."

"Elizabeth, no. We can't."

"Why not?"

Pike takes my arms in his hands and pushes back to look at me straight on. *"Because of Declan."*

"But he can't give me what you can."

"He can give you something better."

"It's too much though."

"Trust him to know your limits. And trust me when I tell you that he loves you. He'll take better care of you than I did—than I ever could."

"You took perfect care of me."

He takes my face, kissing me softly, and the selfish animal in me moves to wrap my arms around him as tight as I can to keep him close, but my arms slip right through him. My eyes pop open, and I'm all alone. He's gone with a faint shift in the air, whispering, *"I'm never too far from you."*

"Pike!" I cry out, but it's no use.

His scent slowly evaporates as Declan's takes over, replacing the comfort of my past. I'm torn between this polar energy that pulls me from one end to the other—a tug of war. Pike is the easy choice, the safe choice, because with him, there's no pain and no fear. Declan is a different story altogether though. He's a multifaceted enigma with layers, creating an illimitable depth. If I immerse myself in him, I just might fall forever. But if his words are truth, he'll catch me. It's an unknown that's so unsettling it's terrifying.

With every gust of wind from outside, I dart my eyes around the room, hoping Pike comes back, but he doesn't. Unable to sit still, I get out of bed and make my way to the restroom for a drink of water. After downing the tall glass, I set it down with a clink next to the orange prescription bottle. My mood stabilizer, my Pike killer. Shaking out a single pill, I screw the cap back on before walking into the toilet room and flicking it into the water with a tiny *plop*. I watch it disappear after I flush and feel appeased to know that with this deception, I've given another day of "life" to my brother.

Walking back into the bedroom, I notice the door opening and the shadow of Declan as he takes a step in and stops. The room, donned in black, is forgiving on my love's face, casting a muted blue tone to his features. No words are spoken as we both stand and stare at each other while a tornado of words swirls between us.

My earlier conversation with Pike screams the loudest of all. And the possibility of him being right about Declan saws away at the scar tissue of my heart, filling me with sorrow for the way I've treated him. He deserves love, compassion, and obedience, all the things I'm frightened to hand over.

The lines of his face are hard, and when I see his jaw tick, he begins to walk toward me in even steps. My body tenses at the fervor he exudes. In sharp movements, he grabs my face and kisses me with icy control, stealing my breath and marking my tongue with his.

I gasp.

It's desire.

It's sadness.

It's fear.

White-hot fear.

"I won't allow you to be scared of me," he demands when he pulls away.

Breaths hit hard for the both of us, my body trembling as I look into his dilated, lustful eyes.

"I let you build this wall between us because I thought you were too fragile for me to forbid it, but I forbid it now."

His mouth crashes into mine before I can say anything, and he takes my hesitance, swallowing it into his soul, breathing a new life within me. But he leaves a little behind to linger. He leaves it for me to give willingly.

Releasing me from his hold, he steps back and sits in one of the chairs. In full command, he instructs, "Take your clothes off."

The weight of my heart aches painfully in my chest, and the moment I drop my eyes, he takes notice.

"Look at me."

With reluctance, I do.

"Keep your eyes on me."

Every nerve ending is firing inside of me as I unbutton my top and drop it to the floor. I then move to slip my pants off, and watch as Declan grinds his teeth. My stomach turns in anxiety, not knowing what's to come next, but I stand here and try with all I can to believe Pike when he says Declan won't hurt me.

"All of it," he presses as he sits in the night's obscurity, shielding himself in its obsidian.

Cold air trills in goosebumps along my flesh as I unhook my bra and drop my panties to my ankles, exposing the tarnished veneer to my aberration. The bruises have faded, the lacerations are nearly healed scabs, but we both know the garbage I am. I've told him my past in full detail; he knows my life in the closet and in the basement, and yet he grows hard for me as he sits and examines.

He's too good to be a monster like me, too good to be turned on by the grotesque.

"On the bed," he orders. "Lie on your stomach."

"No!" I blurt out at the humiliation that still remains from when he last took me from behind. Although my voice never screamed no, every part of my vitality did as he ripped me apart and violated me beyond boundaries I never thought I had.

"On the bed!" he shouts.

I turn and walk across the room as my eyes prick. Taking a hard swallow, I will the vulnerability away. My back stiffens as I cage my heart in self-preservation.

I can do this.

When I sit on the edge of the bed, he stands, his cock pushing against the fabric of his pants. He walks over to me, taking my knees in his hands and opening me up to stand between my legs.

"Do you trust me?"

"Yes." I'm quick to answer, and he immediately shakes his head.

"I'll punish you for lying, you know I will," he threatens. "Let's try this again. Do you trust me?"

With my neck craned back to look him in the eye, I give him the honesty he deserves. "No."

Declan threads his fingers through my hair, fisting it in clumps, and I wince as it pulls through the scab that's almost healed. The scab he gave me when he ripped my hair out. The scab I kept alive by picking when I thought I'd never have him again.

He keeps his forceful hands on my head, vowing, "I'm going to change that. Right now. Tonight. I won't allow you to fall asleep until I've done so."

His words strangle me.

I panic.

"Take my belt off."

I hesitate.

"Now!"

My fingers fumble as I work quickly to unfasten his belt and pull the leather loose from the loops of his slacks. He then holds his palm open to me, and I hand it over to him.

"Are you scared of me?"

"Yes," I respond with no mask.

With his one hand clutching the belt and the other clutching my hair, he gives his next order, "Take my pants off and suck my cock."

I unhook, unzip, and pull down.

He's raging hard, and when I slide him into my mouth, he releases a guttural moan into the still of the room. My heart races as I suck him deeply. My hands grip around the backs of his thighs while I run my lips up and down the smooth skin of his cock.

"Fuuuck," he groans, and when I look up to him, his head is tilted back.

His hand squeezes around my hair, pulling it even more, ripping the scab when he bucks his hips suddenly, forcing himself to the back of my mouth. I gag slightly, and reflex with a swallow, the opening of my throat clamping around the head of his dick when I do so.

"Jesus Christ." His words claw through the grit of ecstasy as he pulls out of me. In flashes of seconds, he slings his shirt across the room and kicks off his pants.

We're entirely naked.

He kneels down, draping my legs over his broad shoulders and opens me with his hands. The sound of him inhaling deeply takes over me and becomes too much. I pinch my eyes shut, because the sight of him alone is enough to rip me to shreds.

Why does he do this to me?

Soft, wet heat slides through the core of me. It's a single lick through my folds that throws my pulse off beat and I retract.

"Don't!" he barks, and when I open my eyes and look down at him, he continues, "Don't fight me. Don't push me away." And with our eyes linked together, he moves in and closes his mouth around my clit, sucking me gently. My heavy breaths are loud, staggering in rapture as I twist the sheets in my hands. He continues to watch me as his tongue laps and massages, spurring my body to grind against him.

He's soft and deliberate, and then, in an utter contradiction, he bares his teeth and bites my clit, erupting a euphoric scream from deep inside my gut as the pain rips through my pussy and up my spine. I fall back onto the bed, my body now writhing when his lips replace his teeth. Black and white fill my eyes with grey. I want to scream for him to stop and, at the same time, beg him to do it again. I'm hyperventilating when he shoves his tongue inside me, the prickles of his beard chafing my tender skin.

I'm swept away, floating in the air, unable to escape. I hear whimpering, and I know it has to be coming from me, but it isn't sadness my heart feels. I reach down for him, needy for some sort of anchor, and fumble around before he locks a hand to mine, holding it tightly.

His lips are now on mine as his body hovers over me, and he dips his tongue into my mouth. I slide my tongue along his, tasting myself, tasting him. It's a potent cocktail.

"Turn on your stomach," he tells me, and when my eyes widen, he assures, "I won't fuck you like that, not tonight."

I waver for a moment when he begs of me, "Trust me enough to be powerless. I want you weak and depending on me, to know that I'll keep you safe. Give me that power back."

I wanted Pike in that moment. It was a brief need that rushed through me. Pike was always the safe choice; Declan came with so many uncertainties. I feared becoming too exposed with him, and yet I feared becoming too distant with him. I wondered if I kept pushing him away if he would eventually leave me. I couldn't bear that thought. I'd lost him once before and it was the worst pain of my life. Whatever direction I went with Declan, one thing was inevitable: Fear.

I've been told in the past to never make decisions out of fear, but I was at a road block. Turn left—fear. Turn right—fear. I'd rather be scared with Declan than be scared without him. The choice, was clear. Pike faded in that room as I allowed Declan to fill every vacant space.

Turning onto my stomach, I rest my cheek on the bed and make the decision to let all my fears come to life. He takes my arms and crosses the belt around my wrists then turns me over to bring the two straps around my waist, cinching the loop even tighter as he fastens the belt around my stomach.

Bound with no escape. I'm completely his—en masse.

"Are you scared?" he asks, kicking my thighs open.

"Yes."

"Good," he says chillingly. "I want your eyes on me. I want you watching me as I fuck all that fear away."

Before I can digest his words, he slams into me with intense force, rocking my body backwards and kicking the breath right out of my lungs. I have nothing to grab on to as he rears back and thrusts inside me again. Wadding up a handful of the sheets beneath me, I hold on tightly as he begins to pump his scorching hot cock in and out of me.

I move to wrap my legs around his hips, but he stops me, grabbing my knees and pushing them wide open and down into the mattress. His eyes are on fire, molten black.

"Do you feel that?" he grunts. "You feel me inside of you?"

"Yes."

He then grips his hands around my shoulders and buries his cock so deep in me I whimper in ultimate pleasure. He keeps a tight hold on me, never relenting as he pushes himself as deep as he can. It's a searing pain in the tender flesh of my pussy, but so intoxicating.

"Tell me you feel that," his voice strains.

I nod, unable to catch my breath enough to speak.

His cock begins to throb inside of me as he holds himself still, the pressure becoming too much for me to contain. He keeps pushing, deeper and deeper until I can't take it anymore and I burst out in a breathless sob. It isn't from pain though, it's something else. An unyielding need to touch him, to grab him and pull him even deeper. It's a reckless urge for him to permeate me wholly, to rip me open completely. All of him in all of me. My arms ache to be freed, but he has me restrained.

I begin to scream, tears springing from my eyes, needing more.

More.

More.

When I think the pressure can't go any further, it does, intensifying, blinding my vision. My chest bears a thousand pounds of emotion, and I scream out, begging for more.

"That's it, darling. Cry," he encourages. "I want you crying for *me*."

And I am. Every tear is his as I sob for more of him.

He wanted me weak, and here I am, happily weak and desperate. I'm thrashing and fighting the restraint of his belt, but it only makes my muscles burn even more. My whole body is a raging fire, incinerating all my doubts of his love for me.

"I won't let you go!" he yells over my screams. "So stop fighting."

And when I do finally stop tugging against his belt and quiet myself, he leans down and licks the tears that coat my cheeks.

"Are you done fighting me?"

I nod, unable to stop the maniacal emotions from flooding out of me.

"Say it."

"I won't fight you again." My voice, hoarse and cracked.

He slowly releases the pressure, sliding his cock out of me, my muscles aching as I begin to lose him, but he returns with another forceful thrust, claiming, "I own you."

His words provide solace as he fucks me in long, hard strokes. My vision clears, and his face comes back into focus. His body is covered in sweat, every ridge of every muscle flexes and strains as he takes back the control I had been attempting to steal from him. It belongs to him though, so I freely give it.

I watch him move above me, and he takes my hips when he props up on his knees and pulls my ass off the bed. The roped muscles of his shoulders and arms bulge in swollen heat as he takes my pussy. My whole body begins to climb, tingling, sparking, igniting.

"Ask me for it," he snaps, reaching his hand behind my back to hold my hand, as he always does when I orgasm.

I immediately tense up, tightening my core, and he growls as I constrict around his shaft, fighting my release.

"Let me hear you beg."

And I do, pleading for him to fuck me hard, to make me cum, and he does. I shatter, exploding around his cock in pulsing contractions of passion, love, and trust as he squeezes my hand that remains bound behind my back, reminding me that he's here for me, that I'm not alone in the ache we both share for each other. And just as I reach my ultimate peak, live wires spark through my veins, taking my whole body captive. He pulls out and shoots his cum all over my stomach and tits. His hand continues to pump his cock as he empties himself all over me.

Tears paint my face in a piece of art that embodies a love so powerful it can only be ours. It's ugly and beautiful and painful, but it's ours. We are monsters and lovers, animals and killers, but nothing can extinguish what we have when we're together.

He takes his hand and rubs his semen into my skin all over my stomach, breasts, and neck before unlatching the belt buckle, freeing my arms. I immediately sling them around his neck.

"I'm sorry," I cry, tears falling from my cheeks and rolling down his back. "I'm so sorry."

"Shhh, darling," he consoles, whispering into my ear as he holds me tightly. "I have you. You're safe."

He sliced me wide open, and I cry for a long while until the wound slowly mends back together. He holds me the whole time, patient, whispering to me, calming me down.

I lie in his arms, covered in his feral scent, and when he pulls the sheets over our naked bodies, I take his face in my hands, telling him with absolute certainty, "I love you." My heart weeps as I say the words and fresh tears slip out, but I say it again because I want no doubt. "I love you."

He kisses me, and it's tender. Lips brushing lips, sucking and licking. He isn't taking; it's purely giving.

"I don't want you to ever go a day without knowing how much I adore you," he tells me. "You're life-consuming."

With tangled legs, bleeding hearts, and tethered souls, we claw each other throughout the night—desperate for unsurpassable symbiosis.

Six

KARMA IS OFTEN slow to respond, and because of its intimate relationship with destiny, often waits until a future incarnation. I won't have to wait that long though—it's been long enough. Fate became my divinity today when I got a phone call from an old buddy I hadn't heard from in a while. Seems there's a guy who needs to get his hands on an airline flight manifest—the same airline I've been working at for the past decade.

It's not the first time I've been approached to do something that would entail turning my back on the oath of honesty this job requires. But this is the first time I want to turn my back—and I did.

All it took was one name.

Steve Archer.

I first heard that name sixteen years ago when my brother was arrested for smuggling guns over international lines.

I sought my revenge on that man after I found out he ratted out my brother, but it was too late, he was already dead.

Or so I thought.

I hung up the phone and immediately pulled up the manifest for the flight in question. Since I work for the airline's IT department, retrieving the document took mere minutes to do. Steve Archer wasn't on the list though.

But that's okay, because I have the man's name that's looking for him. Lachlan Stroud—he will serve as my map, leading me to fulfill long overdue retribution.

Seven

Waking up this morning is surreal. It's what I used to fantasize about back in Chicago when Declan told me about this estate. And although I've been staying here with him for a couple weeks now, this is the first time I've truly felt connected to him. He's made his feelings known; he's made it very clear that he's not leaving. I've had my doubts, but after talking to Pike last night and Declan forcing me to reconnect and trust him, something has shifted between us.

I'm snug in his arms as I watch the sun bathe the walls. Everything around me glows in warmth. My body sinks into the arms of my prince as we wake in our castle. I try to control my elation, because this world is filled with unknowns that lurk behind the corners of life's winding streets. But for now, I'm at peace.

I watch Declan as he sleeps, and for the first time, I see the stress I've inflicted up close. It's in the extra grey hairs that weren't there in Chicago. It's in his beard that's a few weeks overgrown. It's in the deepening lines at the corners of his eyes. I reach out and run my hand along his jaw, through the bristly hair of his beard. It crackles against my palm, and I smile. He begins to rouse, but I don't stop touching, feeling, studying. Every touch, smell, sight, I cement to my memory. Carving everything about him into the delicate flesh of my heart.

Strong fingers comb through my hair as he wakes, opening his eyes—bright emerald green.

"'Morning, darling." His voice is wrapped coarsely in sleepiness.

"Mmm," I hum softly, nuzzling my head against his chest, and I fall deeper into his hold when he tightens his arms around me.

His body is so warm against mine, and I wonder what I was so afraid of. How did I allow my mind to trick me into believing he was the one to fear? So many questions come to life, and I want to punish myself for doubting him so much, for shutting him out, for not trusting his love.

"Tell me how you feel," he requests, and without any hesitation, I respond, "Safe."

He rolls over on top of me, propping himself up on his hands. I push a lock of hair back that's fallen over his eyes and keep my hand fixed in his thick tresses.

"This is all I wanted, you know? You, here with me—safe."

"I'm here," I whisper softly.

He drops tender kisses along my shoulder, across my collarbone, and over the swell of my breasts. I feel his cock harden against my thigh beneath the sheets, and I open my legs for him to settle against me. His lips move down the length of my body, and his soft kisses intensify when he sinks his teeth into my flesh.

His greedy hunger punctures, and I scream through the pain, but I don't want him to stop.

Blood trickles along my stomach and legs as he continues to bite me between his gentle kisses.

This is how savages love.

With his scent from last night still dried on my body, he now marks me in a different way.

My legs open wider when he buries his head between my thighs. He's a wild beast, fucking my pussy with his mouth. He leaves my hands free to pull and rip his hair as I mewl loudly in sexual delirium. Time no longer exists in this room as he devours me powerless.

He doesn't stop after my body explodes; he keeps going, sending me into a freefall. Every bone in my body aches, both his hands holding both of mine through every orgasm that pounds through my body. It becomes too much, but I don't deny his appetite.

I let him take me higher as my chest seizes in overwhelming paroxysms love. It's only when I lose my breath and begin to gasp for air that he stops. He moves above me, but I can't make out his face. Everything is drowned behind hazy pops of light as I struggle to fill my lungs with its life source.

My body lies limp on the sheets that are drenched in our arousal, sweat, and blood. There's no doubt that Declan is as raw as they come, but that's what I love about him. This love is shamelessly amaranthine.

He's all over me.

I'm all over him.

There's no doubt we belong to each other.

My body is sore as I walk down the stairs with Declan. We're show-ered and dressed and in dire need of food. Walking into the kitch-en, Lachlan says goodbye to whomever he's talking to on his cell.

"Afternoon," he greets when we walk in.

Declan starts pulling out food from the fridge, and I eye Lachlan's cup of coffee and the French press on the table, asking, "Is the kettle still hot?"

"Yes."

I take a teacup down from the cabinet and begin to prepare a cup of hot tea.

"Roasted tomatoes and toast?"

"That sounds good," I respond to Declan as I take my tea to the table to join Lachlan.

It's been nice having him around. When Declan is up in his office working, Lachlan will often take walks with me outside. It's a relief that his treatment of me never changed after what he saw the night he and Declan found me. His banter has been a welcome reprieve from the stress of late.

"Are you hungry?"

He takes a sip of his coffee before responding. "I had a bowl of oatmeal already."

I try to hide my laughter, but he catches me, giving me a questioning glare.

"You eat that every morning."

"It's good."

"It's old man food."

He removes his glasses, and sets down the newspaper he's reading, and teases, "Says the old lady who's about to eat toast

55

for a meal."

"Touché," I admit with a smile, and quickly change the direction of conversation, asking eagerly, "Have you found any leads on my dad?"

"I've made calls to all the contacts I have that have links to the airlines. I'm waiting to hear back."

"Well, how long do we just sit and wait?"

"I know you're anxious," he tells me, "but it's only been a day. I promise you I'm doing all I can, love."

"Lachlan," Declan calls out when he shuts the oven door, taking Lachlan's attention. "What did you decide about London?"

"A hotel would be best."

"A hotel?" I ask. "A hotel for what?"

Declan takes a seat next to me at the table. "Lachlan's coming with us to London."

"Why?"

"For protection."

"I don't need a babysitter, Declan."

"Is that so?"

Narrowing my eyes, miffed, I respond, "Richard's dead. What are you worried about?"

"When it comes to you . . . *everything.*"

I look to Lachlan and tell him, "No offense, but I don't need you looking over my shoulder."

"I agree with Declan on this one."

"We'll be living in one of the most secure buildings in the world," I argue. "What could possibly happen?"

"What about Jacqueline?"

"Jacqueline? Richard's wife?" I practically laugh. "She's nothing. She's a socialite. A housewife. A whore. A—"

"A widow," Declan interrupts harshly. "She knows we killed her husband."

"She doesn't have it in her. She's too weak."

"I wouldn't be so quick to underestimate. She's lost everything, and now her baby has no father."

"Richard wasn't her baby's father," I reveal. "It's Bennett's child."

Declan's brows cinch together in question, and I explain, "He got her pregnant while I was married to him. I didn't know until after he died. That bomb was laid on me when I went to have the will read. Bennett left the business assets to him."

He quickly looks to Lachlan, saying, "Could you give us a minute?"

"Of course."

Once Lachlan leaves the room, Declan continues, "You took his money?"

His accusing voice has a lick of judgment to it, sparking a tingle of rebellion from me.

"Yes," I bite. "I took it."

"How much?"

"Not as much as his bastard child got, but enough."

His teeth grind before he presses further, stressing his words, "How much, Elizabeth?"

My hands grow tense when I think about the number, but I tell him the truth. "One point two."

Declan releases a relieved sigh, and it's then I realize he's assuming fewer zeros, so I clarify, adding, "Billion."

"Billion?" he blurts out.

"Yes, Declan. One point two billion. Surely you knew how wealthy he was. This shouldn't come as a surprise. The only thing that was surprising was how little I got."

My words are snappy, and it frustrates me to see his indignation.

"What?" I question with vexation. "Stop looking at me like that. If you want to say something, just say it."

"You can't take that money."

"Why not? Do you have any idea the hell I went through to get it?"

"But why? For what purpose, really? Because unless you've left out some important detail, Bennett was, by all accounts, an innocent man."

"Innocent?" I yell as heat creeps up my neck. "His lie took my father from me! His lie put me in that foster home! His lie raped me of the life I deserved!"

"He was a child, for Christ's sake!"

"If you want to rationalize this, do it with someone else."

"I saw the way he looked at you, Elizabeth."

"Stop." My voice is cold and hard and blatantly demanding.

"He loved you."

"Stop." I shake my head, blocking his words and refute, "He loved an illusion. He loved *Nina*, the woman who molded herself to be everything he ever wanted in a wife. It was a con, so don't you make me feel guilty."

"But the con is over."

"It may be over, but my feelings about him haven't changed."

"I see that," he finally concludes. "I understand your need to pin the blame for all this, it's just . . . you're blaming the wrong person."

"What does it matter? He's dead. It's not like I can hurt him anymore even if I wanted to."

His eyes are sternly focused on me when he repeats, "You can't keep that money. I killed him; I don't want that on my hands. You may not see this clearly for what it is, but that doesn't mean I don't."

I shake my head, not wanting to lose everything my brother and I worked so hard for.

"It's just money. Money you don't need because you have me."

"That's not the point," I tell him. "And besides that, how do you suggest getting rid of that amount of money without raising suspicion?"

"What about his parents?"

"Are you kidding me?" I exclaim. "His father took my dad out. They worked together and he used Bennett's claim to ensure my dad would be out of the way so he could move up the chain and make more money. Bennett's father hated him!"

Declan lowers his head and pinches the bridge of his nose. I know he's stressed trying to digest all this information I'm throwing at him. It's generations bound by a twisted web of deception and fraud. Everyone is a con in someone else's agenda.

"If I found a way to get rid of the money, would you do it?"

I look at him as my mind goes to Pike. I think about all he gave up for those few years while I worked the scheme with Bennett. I think about his life in that shithole trailer, about the days, weeks, and sometimes months we'd have to be apart. This is as much his money as it is mine. Am I really going to just toss it away as if everything we sacrificed wasn't worth it?

"Tell me your hesitation."

"Pike," I blurt without thinking first.

"Your brother?"

"He earned that money too."

Declan reaches over and takes my hands in his as his eyes immediately soften. "Elizabeth, you're making decisions based on people that are no longer alive," he tells me as gently as he can, but his words still hurt. "When people die, the world changes whether you want it to or not. Your refusal to change with it is doing nothing but hindering the future. A future you deserve. But I'm telling you now, I can't live in the past where you still are."

He motions for me to come to him, and I do. Pulling me onto his lap, he wraps me up in a strong hug, and I hold him close. I need comfort, because I'm not sure if I can continue to carry the weight of my world anymore.

"I need you to let go of the past. I'm not asking you to do it all at once, but you're with me now. I'm your future. Can you do that? At least try to?"

I loosen my arms and pull back to look in his eyes.

"Start with the money," he tells me.

"Don't hang on to this for me. Let the money go. It isn't worth pushing Declan away."

"Okay," I agree with a boulder of reluctance, but Pike is right. I can't take a step back with Declan when we're finally moving forward.

He smiles, repeating, "Okay."

eight

"I GOT THE **address**," *my buddy tells me when I answer my phone.*

I'd be stupid to email, fax, or deliver this manifest in any other electronic way. I don't need my ass getting busted for this breach of security with the FAA. With an address, I can payoff some random Joe to mail this off from any location.

But more importantly, I now have a point of contact.

"Thanks. I'll get this overnighted."

Now, I need to start making a few calls because I need a PI, and quick.

nine

"I'll get you added to my accounts so you can go shopping. I don't want you touching Bennett's money any more," Declan says when I zip up my luggage.

"What are you talking about?"

He eyes my bag, asking, "Those are all your belongings, right?"

"Yes. Well, most of them. I left everything else behind in Chicago. It felt strange to keep them. Those are all Nina's clothes, not mine."

"That's why you need to go shopping."

I take my luggage off the bed and set it on the floor before taking a seat on the mattress.

"Did I say something wrong?" he questions as he walks over to me.

"No, it's just . . ."

He takes a seat on the bed next to me. "Tell me."

"I've never had money," I begin. "I came from white trash.

62

It was one thing for me to spend Bennett's money, because I hated him and it felt good. But . . . I've never . . ." I stumble over my words, unsure of how to say what I'm attempting to and finally conclude, "I don't come from your world, Declan. I can fake it. I can blend in. But at the end of the day, I'm just a runaway street kid. And you asking me to spend money . . . it doesn't feel right."

"Darling."

"I wouldn't even know what to buy. I don't know what I like and don't like. I've never had the luxury of that choice because I wore whatever scraps we could afford from thrift stores and garage sales. It was easy shopping on Bennett's dime because I simply copied what the other women in his circle were wearing." I pause for a moment before admitting, "I know Nina well, but I have no idea who I am because I've spent my life caged up and detached. And when I was with Bennett, I was simply pretending to be what he wanted."

"You have choices now," Declan says. "And you have time. You take all that you need to find yourself. That's one thing I won't rush you to do. But I don't want you feeling guilty for the things I want to give you. You may not have started in my world, but you're here now."

"A part of me still doesn't feel like I deserve to be. I don't doubt you when you say you love me, but it feels undeserving."

"It's not. If I could give you more, I would. Nobody should ever have to face the nightmare that you did." He takes my chin, angling me to him when he states, "You are not trash."

"Some of those choices were mine though."

"Like what?"

"Pike."

His hand drops as he sighs. "I've tried to make sense of

your relationship, and although I hate knowing that side of you two, all I can conclude is that you guys were just two kids trying to survive in a world that was deeper than hell. But you're right, it was a choice you made. Luckily our choices don't define us." He then cradles my face in his hands, saying, "And you, darling, you were never a choice. You were put on this Earth destined to be loved by me."

And with his words, in our continuing need to reclaim each other, he throws me back onto the bed, strips me, ties me up, and fucks me. It's raw and primal and everything else Declan embodies.

LATER THAT DAY, after all our bags are packed and the boys have prepped the property for our vacancy, we are ready to go to London. I feel like a child on her way to Disneyland, and I wear it on my face in an obnoxious smile. Lachlan loads our bags as I sit with Declan in the back seat of his Mercedes SUV.

"You seem mildly excited," Declan teases, giving my hand a gentle squeeze.

I turn my head to him. "Is it that obvious?"

"Insanely obvious. You might as well be skipping instead of walking."

"Skip? I'm not sure I ever learned how to skip. But keep joking with me, and I just might."

"Well, that's everything," Lachlan announces when he gets into the front seat. "Are we ready?"

Declan looks to me, and I give him an approving nod. "I'm ready."

Lachlan drives down the winding road that leads to the gates I used to cling to and cry when I thought Declan was dead. He pulls out onto the main street, and as we get further away, a part of me feels free. Even though I love Brunswickhill, I'm ready for a little distance. So much has happened in the past couple weeks, so many lows, so much anger blended with beatific highs of love and newborn trust. It's a rollercoaster I'm ready to get off because I'm craving the stability of walking with Declan on a solid surface.

Declan never lets go of my hand. It's a simple gesture that reassures I'm safe with him throughout the trip.

"Take her over London," Declan calls out to the pilot who has the cockpit open on his private plane.

The plane's wing dips down as we turn, and Declan kisses me. It's love and avidity, devotion and prurience as he takes ownership of my mouth, forcing me to breathe the air from his lungs. If Lachlan weren't on this plane with us, I'm sure Declan's cock would be buried inside my body right now.

He eventually relents, pulling back, leaving me breathless.

"Look," he says, pointing out my window.

I look down and smile when I see London lit up in the night's darkness, and it's magical. We fly over the River Thames where the Tower Bridge glows brightly above the water. Declan points out the major landmarks as we pass them, and I drink in every word he says. Parliament, Big Ben, and the London Eye are behind us in a blink of a moment as we prepare to land at Biggin Hill Airport.

Once landed, it's another hour drive into Knightsbridge, London. We pass designer store fronts and swanky restaurants that line the brightly lit streets. Everything about this area screams luxury.

"We're here," Declan tells me when Lachlan pulls the car into an underground parking garage that's heavily secured. "You doing okay?"

"Mmm hmm. Just a little tired."

Lachlan finds our designated parking spot and turns the car off. We make our way through the garage, and Declan wasn't lying when he told me how private this place is. I watch as Declan approaches a sleek black box mounted on the wall. He leans his face in, placing his eyes up to the lenses and hits the silver button. A few seconds later, the door clicks and he's able to open it.

"What was that?" I question.

"Iris scanner," he tells me. "It's the only way to get through the first set of doors. We'll get you into the system tomorrow."

I follow him next through the fingerprint sensor that opens another door, and the last door is secured by a key card. Three barriers of security, and we're finally inside the building.

He takes my hand, and with a sexy smile, says, "Welcome home."

"It's practically a fortress."

"Practically," he repeats before stopping at the concierge to drop off the keys to the car and instructing the delivery of all our luggage.

Lachlan stays behind in the lobby as we step onto the elevator. It's one thing for me to be Mrs. Vanderwal, living in the penthouse of The Legacy, but this is on a totally different scale. When Declan told me we'd be living here, I did my research. I knew I'd be living among the world's elite: Ukrainian business moguls, Qatar's former Prime Minister, Russian real estate magnates, among others. We may not be living in the penthouse, but the seventh floor is as intimidating as any penthouse in the United States.

It's a simultaneous finger scan and key card scan to unlock the door.

"After you," Declan says as he motions for me to enter.

I walk through the grand foyer into the impressive living room. Everything is razor sleek lines, clean and simple. Intricate raindrop crystal chandeliers cascade their soft glow over the crisp white walls and white furniture, creating a warmth to the otherwise stark color. The rich mocha woodwork is a pleasant contrast to the white, warming the space even more. It's contemporary design at its most opulent.

"What do you think?"

Turning my head to look over my shoulder at Declan who's still standing in the foyer, I respond with phony condescension, "A bit much, isn't it, McKinnon?"

"You're displeased?"

"It'll do," I tease with an ever-so-slight grin, and he laughs, saying, "Well, it's all yours. Go ahead, darling. Explore."

I look around, opening every door and peeking in every room. The kitchen is outfitted in commercial grade appliances, and the bathrooms are as lavish as those you'd find in upscale spas. Every perimeter is lined with floor to ceiling, wall to wall windows that overlook Knightsbridge. There's an office upstairs that's clearly been furnished by Declan because it's filled with a rich chesterfield couch and chairs, the same as his office in Chicago and his library in Scotland. And both bedrooms, one on each wing of the second floor, have en suites and large, plush beds that stand taller than your average.

"This one is ours," Declan whispers from behind my ear as I stand in one of the bedrooms.

His lips press against my pulse point, sending shivers up my arms.

"It's perfect."

We stand in front of the window, looking down on the lights of the city, and I cannot believe I'm here—in London—with a man who knows my truth and loves me regardless.

"I read an article about this building the other day. They said it was soulless and devoid of life. I know it was referring to the secrecy of its occupants and everything else, but if they only knew what was behind this bulletproof glass."

"And what's that?" he questions, and when I turn around in his arms and look up at him, I respond, "Life."

He leans down, kisses my forehead, and I speak softly to him. "I've never felt so alive as I do with you. Right here, right now. I never thought this was possible, to feel the way I do."

"I never wanted this with anyone else. Even in my darkest days without you, even when I thought I couldn't hate you more, I still wanted you."

Before he can get the chance to kiss me, the ring of the doorbell sounds.

"Bawbags," he fumes in irritation at the interruption, and I can't help but laugh at his Scottish curse.

It really is an ugly language, but the accent is beyond sexy.

I follow him downstairs to the living room, and when Lachlan walks in with two employees with our luggage, I beam with excitement. "Have you seen this place?"

He doesn't respond to me, but instead approaches Declan, asking, "May I?" as I watch in curiosity.

"She's all yours," Declan tells him. "She's about as excited as a lass at her first tea party."

Lachlan laughs, walking straight towards me, and I can't help my own laughter at his demeanor. He grabs me, picking me up as if I were a little girl and gives me a joyous embrace.

"This smile you wear makes dealing with McKinnon's shit-stain moods worth my while."

We laugh as he sets me down, and I'm so thankful for his loyalty to Declan and the friendship he's given me. He's twenty years my elder, and I find comfort in that. As if I can look to him for guidance in a way I can't with Declan. In a way a child might look to a parent. He gives me that feeling, and it's settling.

"Thank you."

"For what, love?"

"Opening my car door the night I first met you."

"Oh yes, our first date," he animates in a shameless attempt to taunt Declan, and Declan doesn't miss a beat when he responds, "Fuck off, Lachlan, and you can get your hands off her now. You got your hug, you're done."

His words are harsh, but they're in jest. These boys go way back to their days at Saint Andrew's, so it's no surprise they fight like brothers, despite their age gap.

"Well, then, if all is in place here, I guess I'll head to my hotel."

"Lachlan, wait."

He takes a step closer to me, and I ask, "Have you heard anything about my dad? Good or bad? Has anyone called you?"

"You've been with me all day," he says, but no matter how content I feel, there's still unsettling anxiety when it comes to my dad.

"I know, I just . . ."

"I promise you I'm doing everything I can, love. We'll find

him for you."

I nod as I feel the weight of the unknown swell in my chest, and Declan immediately senses it. He quickly dismisses Lachlan when I wander over to the windows and stare out.

"This is a good day," he tells me when he moves to stand next to me along the window.

"What if he's down there, right under my nose, among all those people?"

"Then he won't be too hard to find."

My eyes skitter over the men and women walking along the sidewalks, enjoying their night, when Declan pulls me away.

"I'm doing everything I can. We have several people at this point that are trying to find him. The manifest is only one angle of the many we are working on. But you heard Lachlan," he stresses. "He'll call us with any updates."

"I know, I'm just—"

"On edge," he interrupts, finishing my thought, and he's right.

I want answers, and these past few days of waiting are eating me alive.

"Not tonight. I want to see that smile again."

"You act like it's the first time you've ever seen me smile."

"It's the first time I've seen you truly smile from your soul. *You*—Elizabeth. You wear it differently than the woman I knew in Chicago, and I want to see it again," he says and then picks me up, hoisting me over his shoulder.

"Declan!" I squeal out in playfulness. "What are you doing?"

"I'm going to get you naked, tie you up, and then order myself dinner," he teases.

"You're such a romantic asshole."

ten

My first morning here at One Hyde Place was a busy one. No time for lounging in bed until the afternoon. Declan was up early yelling on the phone at a hacker he hired to find out more information on my dad. After that call ended, I sat in his office with him as he proceeded to make more calls about my father, growing more and more impatient as his stress amplified. He's been putting himself under so much pressure to find him, but I didn't want him to get any more worked up than he already was, so I convinced him to step away for a while and take a shower with me to calm him down.

After we were dressed, I met with the head of security downstairs to input all my information, along with my iris and fingerprint scans. Declan then introduced me to a few of the employees that I would be seeing on a daily basis before we returned to the apartment. It wasn't but a few minutes later that the woman who works for the butler service arrived with groceries we requested earlier in the morning.

And now I sit in the living room, reading "A Tourist's Guide to London" that I asked Lachlan to bring over from his hotel. He dropped it off earlier along with a new cell phone that Declan insisted on me having instead of the cheap disposable one I was using since I left *Nina's* phone back in the States. Lachlan input his number along with all of Declan's before heading back out to run a few errands for us. But it's now inching closer to one o'clock, and I'm growing hungry.

I rifle through the fridge, looking for something easy, and decide on a simple grilled cheese. It's practically all I know how to cook, but it's comforting and reminds me of my brother.

"Is the fire extinguisher handy?" Declan jokes when he walks into the room.

I flip the sandwich with the spatula and then flip him the middle finger.

"What a lovely gesture. If we're done with the pleasantries, I'd like to make a request."

Turning the burner off, I slide my grilled cheese onto a plate and walk over to the island bar to sit next to Declan. He hands over an invitation engraved on heavy linen paper with an embossed gold seal at the top.

"What's the Caledonian Club?" I ask, setting the invitation down on the cold soapstone countertop.

"A private Members' Club I've been associated with my whole life. Both my father and grandfather were members."

"Is this one of those male-only chauvinist clubs where you all stand around, smoke cigars, and compete with each other to prove who has the biggest dick?" I badger and then take a bite of my food.

"Something like that, but luckily for you, they started to allow women to accompany members at the social events a few years ago."

"How progressive of them."

"Yes, well, if you're done being stabby, I've RSVP'd our *pleasured* acceptance," he informs me with an appeasing smirk.

"When is it?"

"This evening."

"Tonight?" I blurt in surprise. "Declan, I don't have anything to wear. All my formal attire is back in Chicago."

"Harrods is right across the street," he tells me. "Lachlan can take you."

I drop my sandwich onto the plate, huffing in mild irritation. "Lachlan? Really? So, I'm not allowed to walk across the street by myself, something a child is capable of doing?"

"I thought I made my concerns clear before we came."

"You did, but I didn't think he'd be at my side at all times."

He cups my cheek as he stands, saying, "Must you fight me on everything?"

"Fine," I exhaust. "I'll see it your way this time, but you know he's going to be pissed at you when he finds out you're forcing him to do this particular errand."

"That old man is always pissed at me. I can handle him."

I laugh under my breath, enjoying the lightness of our exchange, and then ask, "What's the attire?"

"Black tie." He then gives me a kiss and starts heading back to his office when he calls out over his shoulder, "I'll call for Lachlan."

"Where is he taking me again?"

"Harrods," he shouts from his office.

I grab my tourist book, flip to the shopping section, and

read while I finish my lunch. I don't have to wait long for Lachlan to arrive.

He's slightly distracted—quiet—as the day moves forward, but I don't push him to talk. Instead, I gather gowns to try on. I'm not sure what Declan's preferences are the way I knew Bennett's. I had more time to learn about Bennett, to study him. So I spend a good amount of time pulling gowns, second-guessing, and shoving them back on the rack.

Thank God for patient sales associates.

Lachlan sits outside the fitting room as I try on the various dresses. One by one, until I finally make my choice when I slip on the Givenchy in kombu green. I decide to take a step out and show Lachlan, but when I do, he's not there. I walk past the empty chair and then hear his hushed voice.

Peeking around the corner, I spot him a few racks down on his cell and quickly retreat when I see him look my way. I strain to hear what he's saying, hoping that it has something to do with my dad, but when I hear his harsh tone barking, "Calm down, Camilla," under his breath, my mind begins to spin.

Camilla?

I step back into the fitting room and wonder why that name sounds so familiar. I trace back and it finally clicks.

Cal's girlfriend.

I met her a few months ago when I accompanied Bennett on a trip to New York City. It was the night Declan showed up unexpectedly at his father's house. But why the hell is Lachlan talking to her? Whatever the reason, he clearly doesn't want me to know. Declan would have his ass if he knew Lachlan left me alone, so whatever he's talking to her about must outweigh the risk.

After I make my purchases, he walks me back home and leaves after I'm safely inside the building.

"How'd it go?" Declan asks when I enter the apartment, and I hold up the garment bag, saying, "I found a dress."

"Good," he says, and my unease intensifies with the knowledge that Lachlan, a man that Declan highly trusts, is corresponding with his father's girlfriend. "Everything okay? You look worried."

I drape the gown over the back of the couch and approach Declan.

"I heard something strange today, and it has me feeling unnerved," I tell him.

"What happened?" he questions with concern.

"It could be nothing, but did you know that Lachlan knows your father's girlfriend?"

"Camilla?"

"Yeah."

"Why? What happened?"

"I overheard him on the phone with her. He sounded mad or maybe annoyed."

"What did you hear him say?"

"Nothing really, he just snapped at her to calm down, and when I heard him use her name, I went back into the fitting room. Something about the tone he used with her and the fact that he'd been distant the whole time I was shopping made me apprehensive."

I see the unpleasant look on his face and ask, "What is it?"

"When we were scrambling to find you, I answered his phone when he wasn't in the room. It was her and she called him *baby*. When she realized it was me on the line, she quickly ended the call."

"Did you ask Lachlan what was going on?"

"He dismissed it as them being old friends. Honestly my mind was completely fucked at the time."

"Maybe it's nothing," I tell him.

"Maybe, but I'll address it with him before I leave you alone with him again."

"Declan . . ."

"Don't contest me. I'm not willing to risk anything when it comes to you."

"You can't control the world."

"No, but I control you and what happens to you," he tells me as he takes my hand and places it on the side of his neck. "Do you feel that?"

I nod as his pulse beats hard into my palm. It's an exorbitant sign of anxiety that he hides well, but it's clearly at war with him on the inside.

"That's you," he says. "You're my pulse. You're the reason it beats and keeps me alive, so don't defy me when it comes to protecting you, because I refuse to be reckless with my quintessence."

He's strident with his words. I know his desire for ultimate control; he's been that way since the day I met him, and he's explained why he is the way he is. Witnessing the murder of his mother has burdened him into adulthood and has shaped him into the man he is today. His demanding ways with me might be harsh for others, but they stem from a loving place.

"I'm sorry. Truth is, you're the first person who's ever gone to the lengths you do to make sure I'm taken care of. I know I give you a hard time, but the rule you have on me feels good."

Before I know it, he has me in his arms, and I'm quick to wrap my legs around his waist as he carries me over to the couch. Tossing me onto my back, he orders me to take my top and bra off, and I do so in mere seconds at the same time he rips off his pants and shirt.

"Hands under your ass," he commands, and when I have them securely beneath me, he straddles my body, pinning me under him. "Spit in my hand," is his next directive, and again, I obey.

His cock is rock hard, and I watch as he beats himself off above me, using my saliva as lube. He's mean and he knows it, teasing me like this. He gives into his desires while forcing me to withhold my own. He refuses to feed my hunger, leaving me without touch as he pumps the length of himself.

I want to touch him, but he's testing my obedience, so I squeeze my thighs together in a lame attempt to create much needed friction for my throbbing clit. I can't contain myself as I watch him stare down at me while he indulges his craving. His breaths begin to stagger unevenly as a sheen of sweat coats his hairline. Every groan that escapes his throat spurs me farther, and I press my thighs together even harder. The moment my body writhes in utter heat, he catches me.

"Open your legs," he barks, and I do.

He then leans forward and locks his free hand around my neck to keep control of me. My pussy aches painfully for him to fill me up, but I know he has no intentions. When I see the muscles of his abs begin to contract, he's getting close. He chokes on a breath of air, his grip around my neck tightening, and then explodes all over me, scenting me in his semen.

His hand leaves my neck, and he kisses me roughly before getting off the couch. I lie here and look up at him when he says,

"Don't clean that off, and don't wear any perfume tonight."

I sit up, and a few drops of his cum roll down between my breasts. "Lucky for me, my dress doesn't have a plunging neck-line," I tease with a smile, knowing he gets off leaving his mark on me.

"I'm going to take a hot shower," he says and then kisses my forehead.

I admire his firm ass as I watch him walk to the bedroom.

While he's in the shower, I take my time doing my makeup and hair. The dress may not have a plunging front, but the back does, so I curl my hair and wear it in a ponytail at the base of my neck so that my scars will be covered. I keep my look simple and clean with no jewelry.

I smile when I look over to Declan who's now fastening his kilt. The Caledonian Club is a private Scottish club here in London, which I was pleased to learn because Declan in a kilt is about the hottest thing I've ever seen.

This is the first event we are attending as a couple, and it feels good to be getting ready and sharing this moment together—a moment we had to work so hard to get to—a moment so many probably take for granted. I slip on my gown and smooth down the fabric that contours closely to my body. It boasts a high round neck, concealing the dried cum that's all over my chest, and flows to the floor in a sweeping, fluted hem. The deep green flatters my red hair, and also complements the green in Declan's plaids.

I stand in front of the mirror and look myself over with restless hands.

"Why are you fidgeting?" Declan asks when he steps behind me. "You seem nervous."

"I am," I admit as he runs his hands up and down the length of my arms.

"Why? You must've gone to hundreds of events like this in Chicago. You're an old pro."

"Yeah, but I was always pretending. I'm a good actress, but this is the first time mingling among the upper crust as *me*. I'm not hiding behind a façade anymore."

He plants a kiss on my shoulder. "The real you is so much better than the lie."

"I don't know about that."

"I do," he says and then turns me around. He looks me over from head to toe. "You're incredibly stunning."

I take hold of Declan's hand to quell my nerves when we arrive at the mansion that was built in the early 1900s. He smiles down at me as we walk to the entrance. When we step inside, my eyes take in the ornate ambiance. The walls are painted ivory with rich gold accents, and heavy ruby drapes fall from the ceiling to the floor. Oil paintings hang from the walls and glow beneath the opulent chandeliers.

The wood floors that lie beneath the carpet creak under my feet as Declan leads me through the club that has a wealth of history here in London. I take in the men dressed in their kilts and fly plaids and the women in their elegant gowns. And suddenly, without my mask, I feel like an imposter—garbage wrapped in silk—and my stomach turns. So, I quickly decide that even though I have no clue who I am, I'll do my best to fake it. The last thing I want is to show Declan any more weakness.

As we walk into the party, I stiffen my spine and feign my place in society with my head held high like I've done for years.

"Declan," a gentleman who looks to be in his fifties calls

out. "It's been a long time since we've seen you."

The two of them shake hands.

"It's good to see you, Ian. How've you been?"

"Busy as ever," he says before turning his attention to me, asking Declan, "And who's this lovely lady?"

"You're a charmer," I lightly flirt and then introduce myself, "Elizabeth Archer."

"Lucky man," Ian notes, to which Declan responds while looking over to me, "Extremely lucky."

We continue to mingle and Declan introduces me to old friends and a few business men and their wives. He drinks his typical Scotch and I sip champagne, we share a few dances, and when Declan can't help himself, he whispers his obscene thoughts in my ear. "I want to take you to another room and suck on that pretty little clit of yours until you cum in my mouth."

I drop my forehead to his shoulder as he speaks to me, my neck igniting in heat with each of his obscenities.

"Just thinking about the taste of your pussy gets my cock—"

"Declan!" a tall woman with long, dark hair says, interrupting our private moment. "I had no idea you were going to be here!" Annoyance rankles me when she pulls Declan in for a hug.

"Last minute move," he tells her, composed as ever.

"Move? You're living here now?"

"I am."

"So I take it you purchased the land to build on?" she asks, and a trill of jealousy creeps alive in me with how much she knows.

"Davina, this is Elizabeth," he introduces.

"Yes, I remember you. You were at the charity gala in Edinburgh last month, right?"

And then I remember. She was Declan's date that night, hanging on his arm and constantly by his side.

"That's right. And you are . . .?"

"An old family friend," Declan answers for her.

"Practically brother and sister," she adds with a big smile. "Although I do fondly remember our wedding. How old were we?"

"Ten. Eleven, maybe."

Watching them go back and forth with such ease turns that jealousy into full blown spite.

"Sounds charming," I interject with mockery, and when I do, I can feel Declan's eyes hurling daggers at me, but I don't engage.

Davina continues to wear her pretentious smile, adding, "The shortbread and jam reception wasn't all that elegant, but it still makes for good memories."

"Well, as much as I'd love to hear more about that humble reception of yours, you'll have to excuse me."

As I walk away from the both of them, I wonder if the feelings swarming inside me are anything like what Declan feels, because if I could put my mark on him like a dog claiming ownership, I would. I want to lock him up and pretend he never had a life before me.

And then I have to question how friendly they've been, because it was only a few weeks ago she was on his arm as his date.

Red heat slithers up my neck, and before I explode, I rush out the doors and into the chill of night. Clouds of vapor escape me with my heavy breathing. Never in my life have I felt threatened and jealous over a man, but then again, never in my life have I been in love. I loved my brother, but in a very different way. I knew he fucked other women—lots of other women, but never did I care. And just to know that this woman has had more time with Declan than I have is enough to ignite this thrashing inside me.

"What are you doing out here?" Declan asks from behind me.

"Did you fuck her?" I seethe quietly so passersby won't hear.

He takes me by the arm and nearly drags me around the building to the parking lot in the back, pushing me against a random car. He isn't happy about my question, but I ask it again.

"Did you?"

"Would it make you mad?"

My anger grows.

"Hmm? Answer me."

"Yes," I spit in hostility.

He presses his chest against mine, fury roiling behind his eyes when he asks, "Tell me how it makes you feel to think about my dick in another woman's pussy."

In a sudden flash, I slap him hard across the face, but he barely flinches.

"Go ahead. Hit me again."

"Go to hell."

"That outrage you feel," he says through gritted teeth. "That rage mixed with passion and jealousy could never amount to what you made me feel. You let me fuck you, fall in love with you, all the while knowing you were fucking your husband. And then I find out you were also letting your brother fuck you. And you have the nerve to question me!" He takes a pause, pinching his eyes closed before opening them again and continuing. "Do I need to remind you of all the fucked up ways you destroyed me?"

"No."

"I didn't think so. And to answer your question, no, I've never fucked her. Never wanted to."

"She was your date."

"Yes," he responds. "She was. Like I told you, she's an old friend. Our families were close and we grew up together. She's attended many events with me in the past so I didn't have to go with random women. But now I have you."

Guilt eclipses jealousy.

"I'm sorry."

"There should be no doubt in that heart of yours that you belong to me. Everyone in that room knows it. My cum is all over your skin, and yet you feel threatened by another woman."

"You just . . ."

"You want to know my past? Because it isn't that interesting. I've never been in love. Not once. I've dated less than five women in my life, but I never loved any of them. Did I fuck them? Yes. Have I fucked others? Yes, but not many. Casual sex isn't really my thing. I've spent my life working hard, trying to live up to my father's expectations. Work was always my main focus. And then there was you. You came into my life and turned everything upside down."

"I don't know what I'm doing," I admit. "I hate that you've seen so many of my weaknesses. I love you, there's no question, but I don't know how to do this the right way."

"You don't fool me. You're the strongest woman I know." He cups my face in his hands, dips his head down to my level, and looks deeply into my eyes, adding, "But you're weak too, and when you let me see that part of you, it only makes me love you more. You and I have been through hell and back, and this isn't going to be easy for either one of us."

I slip my arms around his waist and rest my head against his chest.

Declan presses his lips to my head in a tender kiss. "You have nothing to worry about, you hear me?"

"Yes."

"Come on," he says. "Let's go home."

"We can go back in."

"I've had enough socializing for one night. Let's get out of here."

The drive back to the apartment is a short one, and when we walk through the door, I kick off my heels. Declan gets the fireplace going and we simply hold each other as we lie on the couch. We settle into the silence and darkness, too lazy to slip out of our formalwear. I soak in the heat from his body while he runs his fingertips along my spine.

After a while, Declan's phone rings. I'm edging on sleep when he takes the call.

"McKinnon . . . Yes. Let him up." He ends the call and gently brushes my hair back. "Lachlan's here," he tells me, and I groan, not wanting to get up.

A couple minutes later there's an abrupt knock on the door, and when Declan opens it, Lachlan rushes in.

"I've got it," he announces urgently, holding a sheet of paper.

"What is it?" I question, standing and walking towards him.

He comes straight to me, passing Declan, and hands me the paper. "The passenger manifest."

eleven

"THIS COULDN'T HAVE *gone any better,*" the PI that I hired a few days ago tells me.

"*Were you able to plant the device on him?*"

"*Even better. I followed Stroud from his hotel to a residential building. It wasn't long before he emerged right out the building's front doors with a woman. I trailed them as they walked to a department store,*" he recounts as I sit in my derelict cubical and listen. "*The woman was in the fitting room when he became distracted with a phone call. As soon as the woman walked out to the shopping racks, I figured her phone would have to do since I didn't see a way to get to Stroud's. It only took thirty seconds to find her cell phone in her purse, pop out the SIM card, and replace it with the tracker SIM.*"

"*Why the fuck do we care about some chick? You were supposed to plant it in Stroud's phone.*"

"*This is when you're going to thank me,*" he says with a bout of pride. "*I pulled the data stored on her phone, and that woman is Archer's daughter.*"

"*He has a daughter?*"

"*Elizabeth Archer. She is exactly who we need to be following. It has to be her who's looking for Archer. I looked into her, and it seems she went straight into foster care when Archer was arrested.*"

"*Holy shit,*" I murmur in astonishment.

"*I say we keep quiet and allow her to lead us to our point of contact.*"

"*I agree.*"

"*I'm now adjusting my surveillance off Stroud and onto the daughter. I'll call you with any updates.*"

twelve

Hours have passed since Lachlan delivered the passenger manifest, and I've already completely scoured it. My heart sank a little when I didn't see the name *Steve Archer*. I knew his name wouldn't be on it, but all reasonable thought had vanished in that moment.

Declan immediately pushed Lachlan out when my emotions started getting the best of me. I tried to rein it in as best as I could since Declan is under the impression I'm taking the prescription that's supposed to help these stress-induced meltdowns. But I couldn't deafen myself to the piercing ring in my head. It was painful and sent me into a mild panic.

After I calmed down, Declan suggested I take a break, get a good night's sleep, and revisit the manifest in the morning. But I can't do that. My father is on this sheet of paper, I know it, and I can't sleep until I find which name is his.

Sitting in Declan's office while he's sleeping in the other room, I continue to enter in each name into a people-finder database. I'm not even sure what I'm looking for to guide me in one direction or another, but I jot down any information that pops up for each male passenger. There were one hundred and twenty-two men on that plane. One hundred and twenty-two different paths to follow, but only one will lead me to my dad.

This particular flight was based out of a large hub in Dallas, so the plane is comprised of passengers from all over the States. I star the ones that have a home address in Illinois, but truth is, he's most likely somewhere else if he's hiding out.

My eyes strain against the glow of the laptop in the dark room, but I keep going, entering in the next name: *Dennis Lowery*

"What are you doing?"

Declan's voice startles me, and when he flicks on the lights, I shield my eyes for a moment as they adjust to the brightness.

"I couldn't sleep."

He walks over to me, rounding the desk to see what I'm up to, and when I look up at him, he's annoyed.

"I told you to wait until the morning."

"I know, I—"

"What? Want to give yourself another anxiety attack, because let me tell you something, that episode you experienced earlier . . ." His words falter, and I can tell how much my panic attack affected him. "You can't treat your body like this. You're worn down and sleep deprived."

"Then help me, because I won't be able to sleep knowing that I'm holding his name in my hand. The last time I was this close to him was twenty-three years ago. How am I supposed to sleep? How am I supposed to be patient?"

Raking his hand through his sleep-tousled hair, he releases a heavy breath and succumbs to my eagerness. "Will you start a pot of water for coffee?"

Relieved and grateful for his help, I jump up and let him take a seat, then head to the kitchen to fill the kettle and grind the beans for the French press. I move around the kitchen and gather a few things for the coffee tray. When the kettle whistles, I pour the water into the glass carafe and over the grounds.

I walk back into the office and set the tray down on the desk.

"Come here, darling," Declan says, voice still scratchy with sleep.

He pulls me onto his lap and continues working. I smile down at him, comforted to know his need to be close to me. His fingers type away, entering another name into the search engine, and then he transfers the details into the spreadsheet I've been putting the information in.

"Is there something in particular you've been looking for?" he asks.

"No. I was just getting the addresses and phone numbers and seeing if I recognize any of their listed relatives."

"If he's changed his name and is hiding, I doubt you're going to come across anyone from his past."

"Yeah," I sigh. "You're probably right."

I reach over and pick up a mug from the tray and push the press down to pour his coffee.

"Thanks." He takes a sip and then adds, "There are a few large business-oriented social networking sites for professionals online. We can search all the names through those databases. Most profiles contain pictures."

I grab my phone, anxious to find the man I've been dreaming about my whole life. "Give me the name of one of those sites. I'll search while you're finishing up with the contact information."

Seconds later, I'm on the world's largest business network, punching in the names, starting at the top of the list.

The incessant ticking of the clock greets the sun as it rises behind the cloud-covered sky. I look over from the couch I'm now sitting on to Declan who has just finished the last of his coffee while still at his desk. Sounds of the clock, tapping keys on the laptop, and raindrops plopping against the window are the only noises in the room.

"How are you holding up?"

"There's nothing," I respond in frustration. "Half of these people aren't even on these sites, and the ones that are, half of *those* don't even have a profile picture."

"I'm hitting dead ends myself."

Although I feel defeated, I'm not hopeless, because it's always been my dad who's kept that hope alive when I wanted to give up. Even if it were only a miniscule piece of hope that remained in my heart, I couldn't let it go, and that strength to hang on was always for him.

"I've got to take a break," Declan eventually says, pushing his chair back from his desk. He rubs his eyes, and I can see the reddened fatigue in them. He holds out his hand for me, saying, "Come on. You need a break too."

"I can't."

"Elizabeth, put the phone down. You're going to tire yourself out to the point you'll make yourself sick. If you want to find him, you need to get some rest so your body doesn't give out on you."

"But—"

"It isn't a request, Elizabeth," he states firmly, and it isn't meant to be a test of his authority, but rather a display of concern for me.

It's clear I worry him, so I don't protest again. I take his hand and allow him to lead me back to bed. He curls his body around mine as I lie with my back to his chest, but I never fall asleep. My mind won't quiet down enough for me to relax. Memories flood, playing reels of my past: tea parties, bedtime stories, scratchy beard kisses, and scooter rides around the neighborhood. He's so vivid in my head, his eyes were unnaturally bright, and his smile . . . just the thought pricks my heart in needling pains.

Quiet tears slip out and roll onto the pillow beneath my head, and I wonder if he had been looking for me during the years I wasn't me. Did he just give up when I was living as Nina? Does he know that I devoted so many years of my life to destroying the man who destroyed him? Does he want to find me as much as I want to find him?

"Shh, darling," Declan breathes into my hair, and I'm suddenly aware of my vocal whimpers.

"Do you think we'll find him?" I ask in weak hiccups.

"Yes. It might take time, but I *will* find him for you."

"You know when I was little, after he was taken from me, I spent the first few years being kicked out of every foster home I was placed in," I begin to tell him.

"Why?"

"I would find ways to sneak out in the middle of the night. For the most part, it was me climbing out of my bedroom windows."

"You were only five though. Where did you go?"

"Anywhere. I look back now and feel so bad for the girl I was. A girl so desperate for her dad that she would roam the streets in the middle of the night."

Declan moves to prop up on his side to look down at me and wipes my tears.

"When that foster home realized that I wouldn't stop sneaking out, no matter how much they tried to set up preventions, they'd call my case worker to pick me up and deliver me to the next family who was willing to take me. Eventually, I went through too many homes, and I was sent down to live in Posen, where I wound up staying for good."

"Why didn't you try to leave that house like you did all the others?"

"Because of Pike. Because for the first time since my dad, I had someone who loved me and cared about me," I explain through lamenting pain. "I was more terrified to lose him than being locked away and tortured."

Declan's muscles constrict when he screws his eyes shut. It's an anguished display he can't control, and I suddenly feel guilty for putting that weight upon him.

I reach out to touch his arm and he nearly recoils, causing me to jerk my hand back.

"I'm sorry."

"No," he snaps, blinking his eyes open. "Don't ever be sorry."

"I didn't mean to upset y—"

"I want you to talk to me," he says, cutting me off. "I want you to feel safe enough to unload all your pain, because I want to carry it for you. I want it free from your soul, so I can bury it deep inside mine."

I touch his grief-stricken face and tell him, "I don't want to be your martyrdom. I want to be the thing that makes you happy."

"You do make me happy," he affirms. "You do. I'm happiest when I'm with you—always. Even in our darkness, I'm happier than what I am without you." He drops his head, kissing me, sliding his tongue across my lips. And with my hands tangled in his hair, he looks intently down at me. "You're not my martyrdom. You're my profligacy."

(DECLAN)

I LISTEN TO ELIZABETH as she continues to open up to me more. She tells me a story about the time her father let her put makeup on him. She laughs through her tears as I listen, combing her hair with my fingers and licking away the salts that crystallize her heartache. Each granulated fragment, I take for myself, freeing her a tiny piece at a time.

After a while, her guard is down enough that when I suggest a sleeping aid, she takes it without a fight. I lie with her, watching her lull into a peaceful sleep before going to shower and dress. She still remains in bed, in my sheets. Her red hair splayed over the pillow, her milky skin with faint reminders of her kidnapping, her petite body curled into a ball. One could look at her and never believe the titanic life she's endured.

She poises herself as strong, but it's her cracks that cause me to stumble and fall, making me love her even more. I'm a greedy man, and to know that her weaknesses make her more dependent on me feeds my avarice. But at the same time, I get off on her strong-willed feistiness. She's a mélange that appeals to all my facets and allows me to freely indulge in my nefarious needs that other women would take high offense to. But Elizabeth has this unique way of submitting to me without being submissive in nature.

She's enigmatic.

My phone goes off, pulling me away from the room where my love sleeps. When I answer, it's security needing permission to let Lachlan up. I called him as soon as Elizabeth fell asleep because I need to talk to him about why he's been communicating clandestinely with Camilla.

"'Morning," he greets when I open the door.

"We need to talk," I say and then turn to lead him into the office.

I sit at the desk and he takes one of the seats opposite.

"You look like shit, McKinnon."

"Long night, as you can imagine," I respond.

"How's Elizabeth?"

"Anxious. Stressed. Confused," I tell him. "She's sleeping now, which is why I called you over to talk."

"Let's talk."

"Camilla," I state, and when I do, I note a hint of nerves in Lachlan—restless hands.

"Go on."

"Last week, when I answered your phone, she thought I was you. She called you *baby*. When I confronted her about how she knew you, she told me I should ask *you*. So, as a man I hired because of the implicit trust I have in you, tell me why that trust shouldn't be obstructed by this."

"Like I told you before, Camilla and I go way back." He stops his nervous hands and folds them in his lap. "She's actually the reason I stopped working for your father. We had a long relationship and were engaged when I found out she was sleeping with Cal. She didn't have the nerve to tell me, but the close proximity in which I worked with your father, it was bound to surface."

"Jesus," I mumble under my breath, uncomfortable that I'm having him divulge this embarrassment. But if I'm not only going to put my life and trust into his hands but also Elizabeth's, I need to know everything to make sure there are no hidden agendas.

"Without question, I kicked her out of my home, and it came as no surprise that she went from my house to Cal's," he continues. "That was the last day I worked for him. That is, until a lifetime after all that happened, my phone rang. To my surprise, she was still with the bastard, and an even bigger surprise, I find out he never married her."

"Why did she call you?"

"For help. Your dad had just been arrested."

"Wait," I say, stopping him. "You mean recently?"

"A little over a month ago."

Agitation gets me and I lash out at him. "You knew he was in jail this whole time and never told me? What the fuck, Lachlan?"

"He didn't want you to know. Said you two had some pretty harsh words before you moved back to Scotland from Chicago."

"So explain how it goes from a dissolved friendship to him confiding in you from jail?"

"He needed my help. I gave him over a decade of my loyalty. Bad blood or not, he felt I was his last resort for confidentiality."

"And you just gave it to him? That doesn't add up, Lachlan."

"Perhaps it was curiosity," he defends. "I fucking despised your father and Camilla for what they had done right under my nose. So, imagine my shock when I find out he's in jail and she's left high and dry. Karma had done her job, but I wanted to bask in the wake of her achievement. I humored him and lent him the false comfort of an old friendship."

"Baneful."

"Which is why I didn't tell you."

"Because he's my father?" He nods, and I lean back in my chair, clasping my hands in front of me. "He's a piece of shit," I lash out in hate. "He's spent his whole life virulently criticizing my every move in this world."

"He's a narcissistic bastard, but I had been unaware of any discord between the two of you until he told me about the confrontation the two of you had after you'd been shot."

"Our issues go way back," I say. "That doesn't explain why Camilla is calling you."

"She thinks she can run back to me. She calls, sobs her pathetic story, and thinks I'll take grace on her. She's delusional."

"And your loyalty?"

He leans forward with a leaden stare, stating adamantly, "My loyalty is with you and that girl in the next room."

I then lean forward too, resting my forearms on the desk and brutally threaten, "It better be because if I find out otherwise, I promise you, your head will be the next one I put a bullet in."

My words cause him no hesitation, not even a blink—a steady sign of his integrity. This man knows what I'm capable of—he's seen it with his own eyes—so he's fully aware of the repercussions if I find out there's fault in his word.

thirteen

(ELIZABETH)

THE SMELL OF the black pepper tenderloin Declan's preparing fills the apartment, causing my belly to growl. The past few days I've struggled to eat and even sleep. I keep going over that manifest incessantly. Sometimes I think I'm going crazy, but I can't stop myself. Declan practically had to force-feed me a sleeping pill last night just so I could get some rest. I was pissed and lashing out at him.

"Why aren't you trying harder to find him?" I screamed as he fought to hold me down.

"I'm doing everything I can, but I don't know what he's hiding from or the threat we face when we do find him."

He then pinned me to the couch and shoved the sleeping pill down my throat. In the process of gagging on it, I accidentally swallowed it. When he released my arms, I began swinging at him, irate that he would rob me of the time I could've used to get closer to finding my dad.

I woke this morning after allowing sleep to fuel my body with restored energy and a clear head and apologized to Declan. But the moment he left to go attend a meeting with the architecture firm, I was back at it, dissecting the manifest. It's been five days since I received this list of passengers, and I'm no closer to finding a lead. What's even more discouraging is the fact that both Lachlan and Declan are starting to feel like they've exhausted all avenues aside from traveling all over the States to knock on all one hundred and twenty-two doors. And as much as Declan affirms that he will find him, I don't doubt that he would actually go to those lengths to do so.

While Declan is in the other room cooking, I take my time getting ready. As I'm applying a little gloss to my lips, I hear the buzzing of my cell phone. It catches me off guard since no one aside from Declan and Lachlan has the number. When I walk into the bedroom, I spot the phone on top of the dresser and pick it up.

UNKNOWN, reads across the screen.

"Hello?" I question curiously when I answer the call.

"Hey, kitty."

His voice stuns me for a split second.

"Matt?"

"You miss me?"

God, he's so skeevy.

"How did you get this number?" I bite on a quiet voice as I walk into the bathroom and close the door so Declan can't hear.

"Everyone is traceable. Even you, my dear."

"What do you want?" I snap irritably.

"That's no way to greet an old friend."

"Cut the shit, Matt."

"Fine. I need your help."

"Forget it."

"Do I need to remind you of your place in this equation? You owe me."

He's right. I very well could be sitting in prison if he hadn't covered up Pike's murder for me, so I swallow back my hatred for his slimy ways. "What do you need?"

"Well, it seems I'm in a bit of a bad situation with a loan shark."

"What the hell are you doing business with a loan shark for?"

"Pike's murder being the face of my business wasn't a good look, kitty. No one wanted to be associated with me with the threat of cops watching. I needed money."

"What happened to it?"

"It's gone. I gambled it away in hopes of increasing my profits."

"You're an idiot, you know that?"

"The idiot who saved you from a life behind bars," he reminds with growing pique, and then drops the bomb. "They're gonna kill me." He pauses. "I can't buy any more time from them."

I brace my hand on the edge of the sink and drop my head. I could bail him out, sure, but he'll never leave me alone. The threat of this guy will continue to hang over my head, and how do I have a shot in hell of moving forward in this life if my past is forever following me? Matt is nothing but corrosive—he always has been. Unwilling to allow him the opportunity to one day pull me down with him or to risk him turning me in to the cops for all the crimes I've hidden under my belt, I take back the control.

"You want me to bankroll you?"

"I need you to wire the money. My time is up." Panic seeps through his words the more he speaks. "Pretty soon, there's gonna be a bounty on my head."

"If I do this, will you leave me alone?"

"Yes."

I take a moment to let him sweat a little, enjoying the upper hand and listening to him squirm for my help.

"I don't believe you."

"Elizabeth, what the fuck? Come on!"

"Don't call me again."

"You fucking cunt!"

"Let me tell you who the cunt is," I seethe through my teeth, injecting each word with the poison of my rusted heart. "You don't get to fuck with me anymore. I'm not a toy you get to play with. So this cunt is done with you, you little shit. Let them kill you; it'll do me the favor of dispelling you from my life."

Before I give him an opportunity to respond, I disconnect the call and shut my phone off. With both of my hands clutching the countertop, I look at myself in the mirror and greet the monster that stares back at me, but no sooner say goodbye. I take in a few deep breaths and rein in the beast I've been trying to tame—for Declan—for us.

Minutes pass, and my heart settles into a healthy rhythm. I apply a little more gloss before taking the phone and shoving it down in my purse that's in the closet. I turn to the mirror and give myself a lookover, paranoid that Declan will see right through me.

Walking out of the bedroom, I watch Declan for a few seconds. He's barking at someone on his phone while pots are steaming and boiling. He surprised me with the announcement earlier today that Davina, his childhood friend, is joining us for dinner. I'm not exactly happy about it but refuse to let Declan notice my displeasure. He says that he wants me to give her a chance, that it's time I stop secluding myself from people and put myself out there to make friends. The thought doesn't sit well with me though. I've never had friends. The women I socialized with back in Chicago were merely a charade I put on to appease Bennett and play my part in the whole con. Those women weren't my friends though.

The only two people I've ever truly welcomed into my life are Pike and Declan. I never saw the point in having friends; I still don't. But Davina is part of Declan's life and it's important to him that I get to know her. So with my fake smile, I'll do my best to stifle any jealousy that might arise to placate him.

"Is someone in trouble?" I ask when I walk into the room after Declan ends his call, shaking off the residue of Matt's phone call.

"I think I'm going to have to make a trip back to Chicago to deal with some business concerning Lotus."

"Is everything okay?"

"Yes, everything is fine. *Forbes* is going to be doing a feature on me for an upcoming issue and they want to get photos of me at the Lotus property."

"You're kidding. Declan, that's amazing!" I exclaim. "Congratulations!"

He laughs at my reaction, but I can't help myself. Declan's spent his life trying to measure up to his father's success, so to have a feature in *Forbes* is incredible validation.

I take his face in my hands and look up at him with a huge

smile. "I am so proud of you."

"You are?" he flirts, hoisting me onto the counter.

"Yes. And you should be more excited."

"I am excited." His voice is low and even, teasing me.

"I'm serious. This is amazing."

"You're amazing."

He takes my hands from his face, pins them down on the countertop beneath his, and moves in to kiss my neck. The whiskers of his freshly trimmed stubble tickle me, and I tilt my head to close my neck off to him. Declan disapproves with a groan and forces my neck open with his head. He continues to kiss and nip, and every now and then sinks his teeth into the sensitive skin. I drop my head back with a pleasurable moan and widen my legs to invite him in closer, but before he presses against me, his phone rings.

"Ignore it," I pant, needing more of him.

"I can't, Davina is here."

He steps away from me and takes the call. Sliding off the counter, I clench my thighs together to help relieve the pulsing ache of arousal that's built up inside of me thanks to Declan.

"You're a tease," I say with a nudge to his ribs when I walk past him. "I'm going to get you back for that."

"Is that a threat?"

"No. It's a guarantee."

Soon there's a knock on the door, and when Declan opens it to let her in, the raven-haired "friend" greets him with a much too affectionate hug. They exchange pleasantries before Declan holds his hand out to me, saying to Davina, "You remember Elizabeth?"

"It's so good to see you again." Her smile is too wide as she hands me a bottle of wine. "I figured you could use this since you're living with the most uptight man I know."

"That's nice," Declan says in mock umbrage as he heads back into the kitchen, leaving me alone with her in the living room.

"Thank you," I tell her, shoving my insecurities away for fictitious assurance. "It's extremely thoughtful."

I used to wine and dine the upper crust of Chicago for the satisfaction of Bennett, so Davina should be as easy as selling age-defying pigeon shit facials to haut monde housewives.

"Please, have a seat. Should I pour you a glass?" I ask, holding up the bottle.

"I never turn down wine."

She's much too perky and much too happy, or maybe it's just me being much too judgy. Either way, I grit my teeth as I walk to the kitchen and open the bottle of Sangiovese.

"Declan," she says as she walks over and takes a seat at the island bar. "How long do we have to wait for your new property?"

"Years. We're building from the ground up," he tells her. "I was in meetings all day today going over budgets and schedules. We haven't even started on the design yet."

"How long do you plan on staying in London?"

"Until completion. Same as the Chicago property. So, three, maybe four years."

I hand her the glass of wine and she holds it up. "Well, cheers to new neighbors," and then she takes a sip. "So, Elizabeth, I know you can't be from around here with that accent of yours."

"No, I'm from the States. Illinois," I tell her.

"Where Declan was? Chicago?"

"Yes."

"So indulge me. Tell me how you two met."

As soon as the question is out of her mouth, I feel the tingling in my palms, but I don't stress for more than a second when Declan begins to answer.

"She was at the grand opening of Lotus," he says, plating the food. "I spotted her immediately in this long navy dress. It didn't take me long to introduce myself, and lucky for me, she needed a place to throw an event, and I offered her the space at the hotel." He picks up two of the plates, adding, "The rest is history."

I pick up the third plate and follow him into the dining room. We all sit to eat, and I listen while the two of them share a few funny stories from their childhood with me. I smile and laugh at all the right places in conversation as I tame the covetousness I feel that she's had more time and shares more memories with Declan than I do. She has a deep-rooted past with him, knows his annoying habits I haven't caught on to yet, and can practically finish his sentences for him.

"Elizabeth," she addresses, exchanging her attention from Declan to me. "What is it that you do?"

I swallow the sip of wine I just took, then clarify, "That I do?"

"Do you work?"

"Oh, um, no. Not at the moment." Not ever, unless helping my brother weigh out and bag the drugs he and Matt used to sell on the streets counts as a job. I feel like such a fraud sitting here with her. As if this is my standard of living.

"That's always nice. Have you been to London before?"

"No. This is the first time I've been out of the States, believe it or not."

"I have a lot to show you then," she says excitedly. "Have you done any exploring yet?"

"Not if you consider walking across the street to Harrods," I joke.

"Declan," she scolds. "Why are you keeping this woman locked up? Take her out!"

"Damn! Why are you jumping my case?" he says, charading indignation the way Pike and I often would with each other—the way most brothers and sisters probably do. "We've been busy trying to settle in."

Turning back to me she continues, "Well, you must let me show you around one day next week. I have a few client meetings, but other than that, I'm free."

"Client meetings?"

"Oh, excuse my bad manners. I'm an interior decorator. I'm working on three homes at the moment. Two I'm finishing so my workload will be lightening up soon."

"That sounds like a fun job."

"Anything that involves shopping on another person's dime is fun," she laughs.

When we finish dinner, I stand and collect the plates, taking them to the kitchen so she and Declan can continue to talk. When I put the kettle on the stove to boil water for tea and coffee, I see Davina's phone on the bar where she was sitting earlier light up and vibrate with an incoming call. While I wait for the water to heat, I pick up her phone and take it over to her.

"I think someone just tried calling you," I say when I hand it to her.

"Oh, thank you." She takes the phone and looks to see who called, mumbling, "Bawbags."

"What's wrong?" Declan asks as I sit back down.

"It's William."

"I didn't think you two spoke anymore."

"We don't, but apparently I have a piece of jewelry that belonged to his mother that he's demanding. I've told him there's none in the house that belongs to him and to check his safe deposit box, but he claims it isn't in there. He's keeps hounding me about it."

"Tell him to let the attorneys handle it."

"I did, but the cheap bastard refuses," she tells Declan before turning to me to clarify, "Ex-husband."

"Oh."

"We divorced for religious reasons. He thought he was God, and I didn't."

Out of all her jokes she's made, this is the first where I can't help my laughter.

"Have you been married before?" she asks, and my laughter wanes.

I bite my lip and turn to Declan when I nearly blurt out *yes* without thinking. She's caught me off guard, and when Declan sees, he speaks for me.

"No. She's never been married."

Davina looks between Declan and me with a curious expression upon her face, most likely wondering why her question choked me up and why Declan would butt in to answer for me. She knows something is off, and I thank God for the kettle on the stove as it begins to whistle loudly.

"Excuse me," I say, getting up and rushing off to the kitchen.

I take in a deep breath, sick and tired of all the questions. I've lived so many years pretending to be Nina that she feels like a part of me, and when asked questions, I forget that I'm just Elizabeth and I can't be crossing the two lives.

"Are you okay?" Declan asks in a quiet voice when he joins me in the kitchen.

"She knows we're lying. Did you see the look on her face?"

"She doesn't. It's fine," he says. "Stop worrying."

"Here." I hand him the French press. "Take this to the table please."

He does, and I follow with my tea. The evening winds down as we finish our drinks, and when Davina announces she must be going, I pacify her with a few empty pleasantries before thanking her for coming over, and she reminds me to give her a call.

"We'll go shopping or meet up for a nice lunch," she says, and I respond by lying, "That sounds really nice."

"You can get my number from Declan."

We say our goodbyes, and when she's out the door, Declan says, "That wasn't so bad, was it?"

"No," I fib. "She's very lovely."

He eyes me suspiciously.

"What?" I question.

"You're not still jealous, are you?"

"No, I'm not still jealous," I fib again. "You're awfully full of yourself."

"I like it when you're jealous." He reaches for me, but I dodge his touch. "Get your ass back here."

"You wish, McKinnon. You want to touch me?"

"Always."

"Payback's a bitch," I taunt. "You shouldn't have teased me so much earlier."

"You're sadly mistaken if you think you call the shots around here."

He moves towards me again, but with each step forward, I take one step back, keeping the distance between us. He wears a smile almost as big as mine as I try to contain my laughter. I love this side of us together, a side we've yet to explore with one another. It's young and free-spirited and a rare look inside Declan's boyish charm. There's a joyful glint in his eyes that makes me want to run to him.

But where's the fun in that?

Let him catch me!

fourteen

"I HAVE THE plane scheduled to leave tomorrow afternoon," Declan tells me when he walks into the living room. "What are you doing?"

I lift my pencil from the paper and look at the jumbled letters, realizing how crazy it must look to him. "I have to keep trying."

"I'm not accusing, darling. I'm just curious what all those letters mean."

"I don't know," I admit with a shrug of my shoulders. "I guess I wanted to see if there was something to the names. That maybe if I took the letters and rearranged them I would be . . ." I let my words fade when I'm aware of how nutty I sound. "I just . . . I can't give up."

"I would never ask you to give up, but—"

"Let me exhaust this avenue before you tell me I'm wasting my time."

"Okay." Stepping back from the topic he continues, "So tomorrow afternoon . . ."

"I'll be ready. I don't have much to pack, so it shouldn't take me long."

"I was thinking maybe you could get out of here for a while. Go shopping. You have hardly any clothes."

"You mean spend your money?"

"*Our* money," he disputes. "But if you feel awkward spending it, let Davina spend it. It wouldn't be the first time."

"What does that mean?"

"She once stole my piggy bank to buy herself a rickety pair of roller skates."

I laugh at his farcical outrage. "So, she robbed you?"

"Pretty much, that unforgiveable twit. I'd been saving that money for a long time."

My smile dissolves as envy creeps in.

"What's wrong?"

I take a moment, not sure of what to say when I finally speak. "You really had a happy childhood, didn't you?"

His face levels out in emotion when he sees the harbored sadness in my eyes. He doesn't answer me right away until I push him to.

"Yes. I was a happy kid."

There's resentment that festers within me, but not for Declan. It's for all the people who betrayed me and my dad and Pike. I don't hate Declan because he had a good life, but I'd be lying if I said I wasn't jealous, because I am—because it isn't fair.

"You have all these wonderful stories to share with me, and I have none to share with you."

"Come on, you must have some good memories with your brother."

"Honestly," I start and then pause to grip tightly to the sting of tears that threaten, "it hurts too much to think about."

"It's only been a few months since you lost him. Give it time."

I think of the words he chose: *lost him*. As if Pike were a set of keys I misplaced. My gut sinks when I think of the ugly reality.

I didn't lose him.

I killed him.

I doubt that any amount of time will fade away the agony that torments me because of what I did.

"Hey," he says quietly. "This is why you should get out of the house. You need a break from everything. Fresh air and a little distraction will do you well."

"Are you going to let me go by myself?"

"No."

"I didn't think so." I let out a faint laugh. "I'll call Lachlan."

"Why don't you call Davina?"

I set my pencil and notepad down on the coffee table and exhale heavily. "Can I just call Lachlan?"

"Why are you so afraid to make friends?"

"First off, I'm not afraid. And second, why do I need friends when I have you? I'm not one of those girls who has this incessant need to gossip and chit chat about things I find no importance in," I explain with a shard of annoyance. "Women are vicious and catty, everyone knows that."

"If that were true, what does that say about you?"

I squint my eyes at him, but he just smirks.

"I'm vicious, but I'm not catty."

He shakes his head at me. "Do me a favor. Humor me."

"Why should I?"

"Because she's practically the only family I have," he tells me. "She's a good person. A tad on the bubbly side, but she means well and is trustworthy. I also think it would be good for you to start venturing out—make a friend."

"I've never had friends."

"What about when you were a child and in school?"

"All the girls were too busy making fun of me. I was teased every day." I shrug my shoulders as I remember the shame and embarrassment. "I wouldn't even know how to be a friend to someone."

He takes my hands in his, saying, "Just be yourself."

"Well, there's an idea." My voice edges on soreness. "Too bad I don't have a clue who I am."

"You may not see it, but I can. I see parts of you that are brand new and nothing like the girl I met in Chicago. Your laughter, the youthful playfulness that comes out every once in a while, those belong to *you*—*Elizabeth*." He's sure of his words. "Nina would have never run around this apartment, laughing and making me chase her the way you did the other night. As more time passes, more of who you are will unfold. But if you need to know who you are because you can't find it within you, then come to me and I'll tell you."

I nod, unable to speak around thick emotion. Staring into his eyes, I'm bewildered by the love he has for me. His patience and reassurance have started to form a solid ground for me. I trust him, but I still suppress so many insecurities, some of which I've yet to share with him. His intentions are good though; he only wants me to thrive and be happy. He'd never intentionally put me in a harmful or unsafe situation.

"So will you give her a call?"

For him, I'll try it his way.

He gives me her number, and when I call, she's thrilled at the mention of shopping and agrees to swing by to pick me up.

After I hang up with Davina, I walk into the office where Declan is. "I wanted to talk to you about something."

"Did you get ahold of her?"

"Yes. She's on her way to pick me up."

"What do you want to talk about?" he asks as he gets up from his desk and motions me over to join him on the leather couch that sits in the corner of the room next to the large windows.

"The penthouse in Chicago. I want to sell it," I tell him. "I'll never live there again. I wish I could erase all of its memories, but I can't, so let's just get rid of it."

"I'll take care it. All of it," he assures without any question.

"I need to go back though. There are a few things I need that were gifts from Pike."

"Okay. I'll put a call into Sotheby's to see what needs to be done to get it on the market," he says, taking all the pressure of having to deal with this off my back. "We can go straight there when we land to get it over with so it won't be weighing on you."

"Are you sure? I mean, you don't have to come with me."

"That place is filled with awful memories for me as well. Memories I too wish I could erase, but I'm not having you go there alone to face it all by yourself."

I sling my arms around him, so thankful because he's right—I know how painful it's going to be to walk through those doors again. It's the tainted sanctuary of ghosts from the past few years. It's Bennett, it's purple roses, it's all the disgusting moments I gave that piece of shit my body, it's where I saw the monster in my brother's eyes for the first time, it's where my baby died, and it's where Declan's spirit forever changed when he murdered Bennett in cold-blooded rage. It's the coffin that holds so many skeletons. I'd burn it to ashes if I could.

"It's one chapter of our past we can close. Just look at it that way." Once again, he is doing what he can to eliminate the pain we both feel about that place, the place he dreaded to send me back to after our time together, thinking Bennett was violently beating me.

So many lies.

So much bloodshed.

But without it, I never would have found Declan. So I'll bear its torture that singes my heart.

THE DAY IS just warm enough to go without a coat. I tilt my head back, looking up to the brilliant blue sky. The sun's rays heat my face while I breathe the crisp air deep into my lungs, and I swear I feel its particles cleansing me.

"Beautiful day, isn't it?" Davina asks as we stand in the middle of Piccadilly Circus.

Declan was right, I needed out of the confines of One Hyde Place. I needed sunshine and fresh air. I needed to feel this breeze whipping through my hair, to see that even though life seems to pause, it doesn't ever truly stop.

The streets are a cascade of people walking in every direction. Davina takes a phone call and I walk up the steps of the Shaftesbury fountain. A swell of freedom erupts when I reach the top step. I've seen grand landmarks in the States, but only with Bennett or because of him. Although he gave me all the freedom I wanted, I wasn't truly free. I was living in *his* life as *his* wife.

But here I stand.

No longer having to pretend.

No longer a prisoner to my own game.

And even though Declan keeps me safely under his thumb, I've never felt more boundless. So much so that if I lifted my arms right now, I bet I could fly.

"It'll only get better from this point."

I scan the throngs of people, searching, and then I spot him.

I gasp.

He isn't thirty-two years old. He's the twelve-year-old boy from our childhood. He stands beneath the colorful lights of the billboards, staring at me. Acutely aware of Davina's presence at the bottom of the fountain, I slip on my sunglasses to shield my heart's ache that puddles in my eyes. Davina's buried in her phone at the moment. I want to run to him, but everyone would think I was crazy.

My heart jumps to life. I'm giving him this, something we were both deprived of as kids, and because I've kept him alive, I can now give him all the joys that come my way. We can share them together.

He looks up at the bright lights, his boyish eyes filled with wonderment, and I smile. Turning to look at me, elation plastered on his face, he waves to me from a distance. In return I give the little boy who did everything he could to save me from the devil in the basement a subtle wave back.

"Sorry about that," Davina says, drawing my attention away from my brother as she shoves her phone down into her purse.

I smile, hiding my grief behind the dark lenses.

"You ready?"

"Yes," I respond, walking down the steps and taking one last look over to Pike, but he's gone. I tell myself he'll come back, because he always does.

Davina and I walk together to Bond Street where she assures me there is amazing shopping, and she's spot on. It's all the designers that still hang in my closet back at The Legacy. Familiar friends greet me as I pass them: Chanel, Jimmy Choo, Hermés. They're all here, reminding me of how I used them to deceive others.

"Here we are," she says, opening the door to Fenwick.

I walk inside the high-end luxury department store that Davina insists has a nice selection of less expensive designers as well. I told her I didn't need anything fancy, just your typical, everyday wear.

I remove my sunglasses and begin to scan the racks and pull items I'm in need of. Davina wanders off to shop a few racks over. I fill my arms with jeans, slacks, casual tops, and soft cashmere sweaters before a sales associate takes them to start a fitting room for me.

We keep the chatter among us light as we try on clothes. She talks to me about one client of hers that's a widow of an aristocrat who she swears is draining the family inheritance on a remodel.

"Her children are going to be bloody mad when they find out she's pissed all the money away," she says.

"How much money do you suspect?" I ask, tossing another top onto the yes pile.

"Around two hundred and fifty thousand pounds!" she exclaims. "The old woman has lost her mind."

Once we're dressed, we make our purchases and head to the second floor where Davina was able to get reservations on short notice at Bond & Brook. The restaurant is glamorous, gleaming in stark whites and silvers. We're seated at a table next to the windows that look down on the street filled with people who are anxious to spend money.

"I could only get us in for the afternoon tea seating, I hope that's okay with you."

"Of course."

Our waiter promptly sets our table with hot tea and Pommery Rosé champagne along with small bites, consisting of crab tartlets, butter pear beignets, and celery-cucumber sorbet.

"This looks amazing," I say. "Thank you for doing this."

"Of course. I'm just happy to see Declan sharing his life with someone. I was starting to worry he'd forever be alone." She gives a whisper of a laugh, but I know she means the words she speaks. "It must have been love at first sight then?"

"Why do you say that?"

"He said the two of you met at the opening of Lotus. That was the beginning of December, wasn't it?"

"Yes," I answer and then take a sip of tea.

"It's April, and he's already moved you in."

"I guess you're right." I'm a bit surprised, but hide it. It feels like so much more time has passed since the night I met him. "I can't believe it's only been four months."

"And I can't believe he's kept you a secret from me," she quips with a smile before biting into one of the tartlets. "Well, I know you're not working here in London, but what was it that you did when you lived abroad?"

"Um . . ." Declan told me to just answer the questions as Elizabeth, but I can't do that. I dab my mouth with my napkin, stalling time, but it moves forward regardless. "I did a little bit of . . ." I think back to how I met Bennett and continue, "I worked in catering for a short period."

I'm not sure if she picks up on my hesitation, but she goes on, saying, "That's so funny. I worked in that realm after university. I was a bartender for a catering company in Edinburgh."

"Really?"

"My parents aren't like most. They paid my way through my studies, but once I graduated, they cut the credit cards, and I was on my own. It took me a while to find work, so in the mean time, I bartended," she explains.

"Did you go to school with Declan?"

"No. Declan was an impeccable student. Me, not so much. I attended the University of Dundee."

"Where's that?"

"Just north of Saint Andrews where Declan went to school. Less than an hour's drive, actually," she tells me. "And what about you? Where did you go to University?"

"Where did I go?" I can't possibly tell her the truth, so I cover my ass and lie. "Kansas State." It's the university I told Declan Nina attended, but I immediately kick myself for lying when Declan made it clear not to, and when I continue, I stumble over my words, knowing I need to right the lie. "Well, I mean . . ." *Fuck!*

"Is everything okay?"

She sees right through me. When she stands, I wonder if somehow she knows I'm a fake. She comes to sit right next to me.

"Let me apologize," she starts, and I don't respond. I just let her continue. "I don't mean to pry. I can see I've made you uncomfortable."

"No," I say, attempting to cover myself. "I'm just a little on the private side."

"I can understand that. It's just, well, after Lillian's death, Declan changed a lot. He isolated himself from nearly all the family. The two of us managed to keep close though, and we've remained that way," she reveals. "I love him dearly, and when I spoke to him after our dinner the other night, he told me that you were an extension of him. So, I can't help but love you as well because of that."

Her words are heartfelt and take me aback. I can see no other motivations on her part aside from genuinely wanting to get to know me. Declan was right when he told me she was a good person, because that's the very impression she's giving me right now.

"I never went to college," I admit to her, needing to erase the lie. "I'm sorry I lied. I guess I was just embarrassed." Airing my truths is not what I'm used to. I'm a liar, a manipulator, an imposter. Or I *was*. But I've always been running from something, a runaway at the age of fourteen. Always dodging the law in one way or another. But today, right now, I'm going to choose to take a step forward as Elizabeth. If Davina believes as Declan does, that I'm an extension of him, she won't judge. "I was a foster kid. I didn't come from money, so college was never an option for me."

She smiles and places her hand on top of mine in a gesture that is both comforting and foreign. "Thank you for trusting me with that."

I nod, and after she gives my hand a light squeeze, she moves back to her seat across from me. She takes a sip of her champagne, smiles, and then adds in jest, "We should order more champagne . . . Declan's treat." She winks and pulls out one of his credit cards and laughs. "He slipped it to me when I picked you up in case you refused to use the other card he gave you."

I shake my head. "That wretch!"

"Well, that wretch is going to pick up our tab."

Conversation is less stressful now that the brick of worry and secrecy has been lifted off my shoulders. She asks about our trip back to the States, and I tell her all about Chicago. I'm not about to tell her my whole life story by any means, but for now, I'm enjoying the light conversation with someone other than Declan or Lachlan. Those two know so much of my darkness, but with Davina, I feel a little . . . de novo—and even a little normal.

fifteen

I stuff the manifest along with my notepad and contact list into a manila envelope and zip it up in my suitcase. Last night was another long night of letter scrambling. I know Declan thinks it's nonsense, and maybe it is, but I refuse to sit idle and wait. I'll always find a way to keep moving, because I have to, because I need to find him.

"Do you know where your duffle bag is? I need it for my workout clothes and trainers," Declan asks.

"It's on the top shelf on my side of the closet."

I sit on the bed and wait for him to finish packing. He walks out of the closet with the bag, and I admire him in his fitted button-down that's tucked nicely into his charcoal slacks. Always so polished and refined, even when he's dressed down in jeans and a cotton shirt.

"You want to wipe the drool off your chin and help me?" he heckles when he peers up at me and catches me gawking.

"You're so full of yourself," I shoot back when I hop off the bed to go grab his shoes.

When I return and set the shoes on the bed beside the bag, I watch him pull out a picture frame. He holds it with both of his hands, and I remember it being the picture I found of him in Isla's bedroom at The Water Lily.

"I forgot this was in here," he says.

"You've seen it before?"

"When you were missing, I went through all your belongings, and I came across this," he tells me. His eyes remain on the photo of himself as a little boy, and then he looks to me, asking, "Where did you get this?"

"At the bed and breakfast where I was staying. I found it in the owner's bedroom." I pause for a moment, and when he doesn't speak, I ask, "It's you, isn't it? I mean, your name's written on the back."

"Yes. It's me."

I look at him in confusion and he reflects it back to me.

"Do you know her? Isla?"

"No. Did you ask her about this when you found it?"

"She wasn't there. I found it when you were in London, and I had gone back to pack up the rest of my things. It was the day Richard kidnapped me."

"This photo was taken at my parents' home. This was the pond that was on the property. It would fill with lotus blooms, and my mum would spend hours out there."

"Maybe she was friends with your mother," I suggest.

"She never said anything. I saw her each time I went over there to visit you. If she knew me, why wouldn't she say something?"

"Do you want to call her?"

He hands the picture over to me, saying, "We don't have time. We need to get to the plane. I'll deal with it when we get back."

"Are you sure? You seemed bothered by this."

"I'm not bothered," he states and then throws his clothes and shoes into the bag before zipping it up. "You're probably right. She must've been friends with my mum."

He picks up the bag along with mine, and without another word, he walks out of the room, leaving me alone. Finding that photo has stirred up something inside him. His eyes exposed too much to me, more than he intended. Perhaps it was just the sheer memory of his mom, so I'll respect his request to avoid it until after our trip.

We secure the apartment before leaving to drive to Biggin Hill Airport, where the pilot is already waiting for us. Aside from him, we are the only others on the plane.

"How long have you had this thing?" I ask as I settle into my seat that's next to the window.

"This is more than just a *thing*. It's a G450 Gulfstream jet," he boasts, and I chuckle at him with a shake of my head.

"I see I've offended your toy," I go on to pester.

He takes the seat right next to me instead of across from me.

"Buckle up, because this *toy* is about to takeoff," he says with a sexy smirk and then reaches over to fasten my seatbelt for me, yanking on the strap to tighten it.

The plane is extravagant with its white leather seats and espresso wood finishes that add a masculine contrast. Double seats on the left and single seats on the right with a beverage station in the back next to a decent sized lavatory. There's a flat screen television above the small eating table towards the front of the aircraft next to the cockpit.

"Well, for what it's worth," I say as he fastens his seatbelt, "I like your toy."

"As long as my baby's happy."

The pilot looks over his shoulder from his seat in the cockpit, saying, "We've been cleared for takeoff, sir. Are you ready?"

"We're ready, William."

"Would you like privacy for the flight?"

"Yes."

I look to him, perplexed with a grin, and question, "You didn't want privacy last time?"

"That's because Lachlan was with us."

His flirtations spark the tinder inside me, but he simply winks and takes my hand in his, threading his fingers with mine as the aircraft begins to move.

"Prepare for takeoff," the pilot's voice announces over the speaker.

I grip Declan's hand tighter when the plane speeds up.

"You nervous?"

I look out the window as we lift off and ascend into the sky.

"Elizabeth?"

I roll my head over to him and nod, my fingers fixed around his. He tucks a lock of hair behind my ear, and I close my eyes as I lean into his touch.

"Talk to me."

I blink my eyes open. "It feels weird going back. Everyone there knows me as Nina. I can't be anything but *her* in that city."

"I know," he says, voice drowning in compassion.

"Does that bother you? Because it bothers me."

"It's part of who we are."

"But does it bother you?" I ask again.

Shrugging his shoulders, he admits, "Somewhat. But we're in this together. I'll do what I can to make this trip short and uneventful."

My stomach is in knots, wishing one of my many endless wishes to extinguish memories that are unvanquishable. I want to break out of the cobwebs I've spun that now cling to me like sand to a pearl. I'm no pearl though, more like the goop that embodies the pearl within the oyster. And I have to wonder, if beneath my protective shell, if you dug deep enough through the slime, would there be a morsel of purity?

I remember one of my conversations with Isla—she told me we're all threaded with holy fibers.

Perhaps.

"Come here," Declan says after a span of time.

He raises the armrest between us as I unfasten my seatbelt and then pulls me onto his lap. With my arms around his neck and his around my waist, I rest my head against his.

"We're going to be fine," he whispers deeply.

I nod. His hand slips under my top and trails up my spine, sending a rush of tingles across my skin. With eyes open, we watch each other intently. My hands find their way into his hair, and I grip fistfuls of it as his hand moves to trail across my stomach.

"Tell me what you want," he speaks in a husky breath.

He runs a hand over my breast and pulls the lace of my bra down underneath my top.

"You. Raw and base. Touch me as if I'm unbreakable."

He pinches my nipple hard between his fingers.

I yelp, and my body flinches at the sudden pain that shoots through the nerve endings that maze beneath my skin. "Yes," I breathe.

Black swallows green as lasciviousness fills the air around us, and he clamps down on my nipple again, twisting so hard I have to hold my breath as my fingers claw his shoulders.

"Like that?" he asks, releasing me from his fingers.

"Mmm hmm," I respond behind closed lips as my breast throbs to ebb the pain he's inflicted.

He smiles, but it's filled with imperious satisfaction.

"Good girl."

He slides me off his lap, stands me up, and then joins me. Slowly, he takes the hem of my top and pulls it over my head before removing my bra, my nipples hard from his assault. He removes the rest of my clothes until I'm standing there completely naked and exposed while he remains clothed in his slacks and button-down.

"Turn around, spread your legs, and bend over," he instructs, and I obey his word.

I turn, part my feet wide, and bend over, gripping my hands on to the armrests to steady myself. He then takes one end of the seatbelt and knots it around my left wrist and then does the same to my right with the other end of the seatbelt. He retreats back behind me, and I can feel his eyes on me, but he doesn't touch me. I close my eyes and wait, and after what feels like a few minutes, I hear him shift. Opening my eyes, I look between my legs to see he's on his knees, and then I close them again, startling when he finally touches me.

His fingers dig into my hips, and I feel his hot breath on my pussy seconds before his warm tongue glides along my seam.

And then, he dips it between my folds and finds my clit. I whimper when he presses the pad of his tongue against it in a back and forth motion. My breathing picks up and my eyes pop open when my knees begin to buckle. There's so much pressure and so much friction, quickly driving me to an orgasm. He's unrelenting, and then abruptly pulls away, leaving my core needy and begging.

He then strikes my ass cheek hard with his hand, creating a loud *smack*. I immediately feel the abused skin radiate in blazing heat. But before the tingles kick in, he brings his hand down in another ruthless blow.

"Ow!"

Cold air meets the pucker of my ass when he spreads me open. Sweat coats my neck, and my arms begin trembling. His mouth is back on my pussy, lapping his tongue, eating me out like a wild animal. He runs his mouth from my clit all the way back to my asshole. He ravishes me, tasting all of me, and the sensation throws me over, blurring my vision as I mewl in pure ecstasy. He devours me entirely—front to back—back to front, touching me in ways I've never experienced before. He fucks both my openings with his tongue, and it takes all my strength to keep myself standing.

Dragging his mouth to my ass cheek, he sinks his teeth into me, biting me like a barbarian before spanking me once again with a fierce hand.

"On your knees," he demands.

When I lower myself to the floor, he grabs on to me and flips my body around to face him, twisting my arms painfully—one crossed over the other. I scream out, but the pain from the transition dissolves. My ass throbs beneath me as I sit on the battered flesh.

He begins unbuttoning his shirt and stripping down. I admire his body as he stands naked in front of me. Taut muscles wrap around his broad shoulders and rope down his arms. His chest is defined in hard slabs that etch their way down to the deep V that leads to his thick cock. Aside from the bullet wound on his chest, his skin is smooth, but on him, the flaw is flawless; every part of his body is transcendental.

He lowers himself to his knees between my legs and lifts my hips to him, resting my bottom on top of his thighs as my feet are planted flat on either side of him. The head of his cock pushes against me, and he teases me when he drags it up and down between the lips of my pussy, wetting himself with my arousal.

"Tell me who owns you," he says as he holds himself in his hand and tugs my opening with the tip of his cock.

"You do."

"I want more."

"Then take it," I breathe, my whole body screaming in hysteria for him—for all of him. "You have me entirely. I love you, so take it all because it's already yours."

"Fucking Christ, I love you," he growls as he buries himself balls deep inside me.

My tits bounce as he fucks me with powerful thrusts while he holds my hips up. Throbbing flesh and burning arms cease to exist as I allow myself to get lost in this man I've fallen so in love with. I writhe against him every time he enters me, yearning for more. He reaches up and squeezes my one breast roughly before releasing his hand and slapping it. The piercing infliction on such tender skin battles against rhapsodic pleasure, and I cry out in pure carnal heat when he slaps my breast again before leaning down to lick and suck the supple swell of my chest.

The tether of the seatbelts cuts into my wrists as Declan dominates me, doing as he pleases with my body, because he can, because I give him that right.

He slows his pace when he pulls back from kissing me, asking, "Do you trust me?"

"I trust you."

He then takes both of his hands and places them around my frail neck.

"Do you trust me now?"

I nod.

"Give me the words."

"I trust you."

"Don't panic," he says firmly, and when he does, a shudder of fear blazes through me.

His eyes pin to mine, and I feel his fingers clamp down as his hands grow in strength, closing around my throat. He starts to pick up the pace, pumping his cock in and out of me. My hands fist into tight balls as his grip around my neck becomes more intense.

The pressure builds and builds as his hands constrict around me.

I gasp for air when he collapses my trachea.

He's choking me!

His arms strain even more, cutting off my airway completely as he stares into my tear-flooded, wide eyes.

My body lurches as I frantically gurgle, desperate for air.

I panic.

Oh, my God! I can't breathe!!

"This is trust," he grunts as he fucks me wildly, pounding into me. He's brutal. "Don't be scared."

My vision blurs, and I yank ferociously against the seatbelts. My hands and feet begin to prickle, and the sensation creeps through my arms and legs, taking me hostage. Chills wrack my body.

There's no more air.

Everything goes black.

And then . . .

Everything around me explodes in a blazing eruption of every force of nature imaginable when his hands let go of me. Bursts of shattering light impair my vision, blinding me from everything around me as my body contracts viciously, splintering every bone in my body. I spasm in a debilitating orgasm unlike anything that could possibly exist on Earth. I cum violently hard, crying out in an inferno of wild passion. Pleasure rolls in tidal waves through every muscle, every tendon, every cell. It crashes down on me over and over and over, refusing to let go.

I hear Declan moaning deeply in the far distance, I feel his body heat wrap around me. Warmth soaks into my skin, and it feels like medicine when it spreads through my bloodstream. It calms, bringing me back down. I focus on its comfort as my eyes begin to focus. My whole body goes limp, and when I can clearly see Declan, I'm consumed by an overwhelming need for closeness.

"Untie me," I cry out urgently. "Now, Declan. Untie me."

My voice trembles and cracks, and he moves quickly to free me, and with each arm he releases, I wrap it tightly around him. He holds on to me as I straddle his lap, and bury my face into the side of his neck. Our bodies are clammy and we cling to each other.

"I've got you, darling," he whispers again and again. "You're okay; I've got you."

And I know he does. I didn't think it was possible to grow more intimately with Declan, to be even closer to him. But what he just did . . . I swear to God I felt him inside every molecule I'm made of. I've never felt more exposed, more vulnerable, more naked than I do right now in this very moment.

He has me at my weakest.

I finally lift my head and look at him, our bodies still connected, and kiss him, tasting every part of me on his tongue like the savage animal I am.

"Don't ever leave me." I begin to weep. "Promise me you won't ever leave me."

"I'll never leave you," he affirms. "You're the color of my blood."

sixteen

By the time we landed and arrived at Lotus last night, I was completely depleted. As soon as we crawled into bed, I fell asleep. We took our time waking up and getting around this morning, but now that we're cleaned up and have had a bite to eat, we're on our way to The Legacy.

Up until this moment, I've been okay. But as Declan drives the familiar streets of the city, I feel sick to my stomach. We pull into the parking garage and park the car next to Bennett's SUV. Declan steps out of the car, but I'm frozen as I stare at the vehicle Baldwin used to drive me around in.

"Let's get this over with," Declan says when he opens my door. He reaches over me and unclicks the seatbelt. "Come on."

I take his hand and hold tightly to him as we make our way into the building and up to the top floor. When the elevator opens and we enter the penthouse, it all comes flooding back. Every smell, every conversation, every sexual encounter I experienced with the enemy.

I look to Declan—he's grinding his teeth. His only memory of this place is when he broke in and shot Bennett, killing him instantly.

"The bedroom is over here," I mutter, knocking him out of his trance.

He roams around while I go into the closet. I climb up on a stepstool to reach the box on the top shelf. When I pull it down, I rip off the tape and see a pile of clothes I used to hide what lies beneath. I dig down and grab the notebook Pike used to always sketch in. Page after page is filled with art created by his own hands. Some are of random strangers, some are visions from his dreams, but most are of me. I reach down and pull out a few other items I snuck in when I moved in here with Bennett. I had to have pieces of Pike with me always.

I dump out the clothes and put all of Pike's possessions back into the box. I try not to think too much. Being in this space is hard enough. When I walk back out into the bedroom I shared with Bennett, Declan is standing in front of the large armoire. As I walk over to him, I see he's holding the framed picture of Bennett and me on our wedding day, and my heart sinks painfully into the deep well of sorrow.

"It wasn't real," I say, keeping my voice soft because he looks like he's about to blow. "I hated that man. I still do."

He doesn't speak, his knuckles are tense and white as his fingers grip the metal frame. I reach out slowly and touch his shoulder.

"Please don't look at that."

"You look so happy," he says, his words dripping acid onto my heart.

"I was happy because I was one step closer to destroying

him. That's what's behind my smile," I tell him. "Not love."

"You let him touch you."

"Don't do this."

"He's touched every part of you."

"No."

He sends the photo flying across the room and the frame crashes into a lamp, sending them both falling to the floor, shattering the light bulb.

"Declan, please," I call out. "If you think I gave him what I give you, you're wrong!"

"This is what I hate about you," he seethes as he glares his animosity at me.

It's a painful reminder that he still harbors these feelings for me. He hides it well, but I can't pretend that a part of him doesn't still hate me.

"I look at the fucking bed and all I can see is your naked body fucking him!"

"It wasn't real."

He grabs my arms and slings me around, shoving me against the wall, and spits his venomous words at me. "It was real! What you did was real, so stop lying to yourself!"

He shields his pain in anger, and it tears me apart. I can take his temper, but I can't handle knowing how much he's hurting. That part cuts me deeply.

Capillaries burst beneath my skin under his strenuous grip on my arms that will surely bruise. He jerks me forward and then pushes me back, letting go of me before turning around. His hand rakes angrily through his hair as he storms out of the room and slams the door behind him, leaving me alone in evil's lair.

I don't go after him right away. I allow him time to cool off as I sit by the window and look down over Millennium Park.

"Are you okay?"

I look up to Pike who stands next to me as he leans against the window, and I nod, because I'm scared if I talk, Declan might hear.

"It's only natural for him to feel this way, you know?"

"I know," I faintly whisper.

"Deep down he's hurting. You have to help him carry the weight of that pain." Pike leans down and kisses the top of my head. *"Go talk to him."*

I stand and give my brother a hug, thankful that he's always here with me.

"I love you," I murmur in his ear.

"I love you too."

Picking up the box, I walk over to the door and open it gently. I step out of the room and see Declan sitting on the couch in the living room. His elbows are propped on his knees and he's resting his forehead on his fisted hands, staring at the floor. I set the box down on the coffee table and sit next to it, facing him.

My hands close around his fists, and he looks up at me with shame in his eyes, saying, "I'm sorry I lost it on you."

"No." I refuse his apology with a shake of my head. "You have every right to get your anger out. I'm the one who owes all the apologies, not you."

"I thought those feelings were fading because we've grown so much closer these past couple weeks, but seeing that photo . . ."

"You could hate me forever, and it would be okay. I'll love you regardless."

He unclenches his hands and places them along my jaw

while I still hold on to his wrists. I can see his emotions torment-ing him when he confesses, "I don't want to hate you."

"It's okay. I'm inherently yours."

I jump when the phone rings loudly, putting an end to our conversation. I rush over to answer it and tell Manuel to send up the agent from Sotheby's.

When I hang up, Declan walks to me and wraps himself around me. I hug him and listen to his heart, hoping I've reas-sured him enough to take the guilt of his feelings away from him. By the time the knock on the door comes, we're both calm and in a better place since the outburst.

"Good morning," the agent greets, shaking both mine and Declan's hands. "I'm Ray; it's nice to meet you."

"Thank you for coming on such short notice," Declan says. "We're just pressed for time and need to get the ball rolling on this property."

"Of course. If you don't mind, can I take a look around?"

"Please."

Declan waits in the living room while I show Ray around the penthouse as he takes notes and asks a few questions here and there. We then regroup as we sit down at the dining table.

"How many units was this originally?" Ray asks.

"It was four units before it was renovated into one."

After a few more questions, he pulls the amenities sheet out and begins punching numbers on his calculator.

"First, can I ask you what number you had in mind?"

"I didn't have one in mind. I don't even know what my hus-band bought it for," I respond, nearly wincing at the word *hus-band*, and it must be gnawing at Declan as well.

"When I combine everything together," Ray begins, "I think

a good starting point is looking close to ten point nine million for this unit."

I don't care what this place sells for; I just want to dump it. We won't be keeping the money anyway. "Sounds good. When can we have it listed?"

"That honestly depends on you. As soon as you're ready, I can send the photographer over to take pictures. Once that's taken care of, we can have this property live on our site within twenty-four hours."

"Great."

"We need to make a few arrangements first," Declan adds.

"Of course. Take care of what you need and call me when you're ready to move forward."

We stand, shake hands, and I walk Ray to the door, thanking him for his time.

"What arrangements?" I question after I close the door.

"We need to hire a packing service to clear everything out of here."

"What are we going to do with all of it?"

"What about his parents? Can you give them a call and let them know you're selling the apartment and see if they'd like us to have everything moved to a storage unit?"

"I suppose," I respond, dread sinking in.

"It has to be done."

"I know," I sigh. "What about you?

"What do you mean?"

"They're going to insist on seeing me. I mean, for all intents and purposes, I'm the daughter-in-law, and God only knows what they're thinking about me after I high-tailed it out of the country immediately after Bennett's funeral. If I meet them, you can't come with me."

"You're not going to see them." His edict isn't one I want to argue with. "Go ahead and call them."

I go to the kitchen and power up Bennett's old phone so I can get his mother's number. Before making the call, I take a deep breath.

"Put it on speakerphone," Declan instructs.

After a few rings, the call's connected.

"Hello?"

"Carol, it's me, Nina."

"Nina!" she exclaims. "My goodness, we've all been so worried about you. Are you okay, dear?"

"Yes, I'm fine."

"Where on Earth have you been?"

"Just traveling," I tell her. "I'm sorry I ran off so quickly without saying anything, I just had to get away."

"Where are you now?"

"Back in Chicago, actually, but only for a short while."

"Can I come see you?"

I look to Declan, and he's shaking his head.

"Um, I don't think that's a good idea, Carol."

"Nina, you're still a part of our family," she says, her voice teetering on tears.

"I know, but it's just easier this way. But listen, I wanted to talk to you about something."

"Yes. What is it?"

"I'm putting the penthouse on the market."

"You're selling it?" The quiver of her voice turns to shock.

"It's too much, and I'm not even here to use the space anyways. I can't live here anymore, it's too painful. Everything here reminds me of *him*," I tell her feigning my sadness as a widow.

"I understand, it's just hard to see something of his go."

"I've packed up a few things to remember him by," I lie. "But everything else, the furniture, his clothes . . . I was wondering if you could help me out."

"Whatever you need," she says. "How can I help?"

"Would it be okay if I had everything boxed up and sent to a storage unit?"

"Are you sure you don't want any of it?"

"I'm sure. I can't look at any of it anymore, it hurts too much," I say with a voice overflowing in sadness. "I have to force myself to move on."

"Move on?" she weeps.

"I'm sorry, but I have to . . . for me."

"Please let me come see you, dear. Let me say goodbye to you properly and not over the phone."

"I'm sorry, Carol. I just can't. I'll text you with the details of the storage unit once I can get everything arranged," I say quickly and then hang up before anything else can be said.

I'm scared to look at Declan, scared to see his reaction to all my deceit. I keep my eyes down when I walk out of the kitchen and into the living room. I pick up my box and head over to the door where he meets me.

"Look at me," he says, and when I do, I respond thickly, "I hate all of them."

"I know you do, but you can breathe now. It's over with and you don't ever have to be a part of those people again."

"I'm ready to go," I tell him as he takes the box from my arms and we leave, locking the door on all the haunting memories that remain in that apartment.

seventeen

I ONCE SAW A poster that read *Art is an Attempt to Bring Order Out of Chaos*. I don't remember where I saw it, but for some reason, I've always remembered it. Maybe that's why my brother turned to sketching. Our lives were beyond chaotic. He didn't start drawing until he was in his early twenties.

We used to ride the buses. It wasn't because we needed to go somewhere; we rode them to *feel* like we were going somewhere. I'd sit next to him and watch as he sketched random passengers. He was talented. We both knew his talents would never get us out of the slums, but he didn't do it because he had expectations; he did it to escape.

While Declan is with the columnist from *Forbes*, I flip through Pike's sketchpad. I ghost my fingers over his lines, over his shadows, over every inch of paper that his hand would've touched. He drew me more beautiful than what reflects in the mirror. Every picture is amazing, and I wish people could've seen him the way I did. He was so much more than a drug dealer covered in tattoos that parents would shield their children from when they'd see him walking down the sidewalk.

He was a savior.

My savior.

The sound of the door unlocking catches my attention, and I'm happy to see Declan.

"Sorry that took so long," he announces when he walks in and shrugs off his suit jacket.

He loosens his tie that's tucked into the navy vest of the tailored three-piece suit he wore for the photos. Walking over to me, he leans over the couch I'm curled up on and kisses me.

"What's that?"

"Pike's sketchpad."

He takes a seat next to me, asking, "May I?" as he holds his hand out.

I pass him the pad and watch as he looks through a couple of drawings.

"These aren't bad," he notes before turning to the next page that happens to be a sketch of me sleeping on a ratty couch we found at the Goodwill.

He stops and scans the image for a while before saying, "He loved you, didn't he?" When I don't respond, he looks at me and adds, "He's drawn every detail perfectly down to the faint scar you have right under your left eyebrow." He then traces the scar on my skin with his finger. "How did you get it?"

"I was thrown down a flight of stairs and busted my face up."

"Your foster dad?"

"He was mad at me for . . ." I stop as shame builds.

"For what?" he presses, and when I still don't respond, he

says, "I don't want you to hold anything back from me."

I've already told him all the filth from my past, so I don't know why this wave of embarrassment has come over me, but I push through it and answer him. "I'd been tied up and locked in the closet for a few days. I had been sick earlier that day and wound up not only defecating on myself but also throwing up. When he let me out, he was furious. He started kicking me in my ribs and then threw me down the basement stairs."

He tosses the sketchpad onto the coffee table and pulls me into his arms quickly. I don't cry, but that doesn't mean the memories don't inflict pain. Declan coddles me like one would a child, and I let him, because it feels good to be nurtured by him. His embrace is hard under his flexed muscles, but I find a way to melt into him anyway. I know he's upset with what I just told him because I can feel the tension in his body, so I keep quiet to allow him to calm himself down, and he eventually does.

"I never got to see where Pike was buried," I say after a good amount of time has passed.

"Why not?"

"I was scared. I was afraid to link myself to him and get busted for my con," I explain. "When Bennett and Pike died, and when I thought you were dead too, I laid low. But since we've been back, I can't stop thinking about where he is."

"Are you sure you want to do this?"

"Yes. He didn't deserve to die like he did and to be left all alone," I tell him through the heavy knot of sadness in my throat. "Do you think you can find out where he was buried?"

He reaches into his vest to pull out his cell, and without wasting a minute, asks, "Where did this happen?"

"He was living in Justice. It's the same county as here."

"What's his full name?"

"Pike Donley," I tell him.

He looks up the number to Cook County and is redirected to the coroner's office. He stands to walk over to grab a piece of paper and a pen as I hear him ask, "Who claimed the body?" He continues to take notes and ask questions as my gut twists and tangles while I listen to one side of this conversation.

Patience escapes me, and I walk over to where he's standing so I can read the notes he's taken. Matt's name is written on the paper. Declan ends the call and tucks his phone away.

"Why did you write down Matt's name?"

"He's the one that claimed the body. Who is he?"

"Um . . . just one of Pike's friends."

"You know him?"

"Yeah, he was Pike's buddy since we were kids," I tell him while still concealing the fact that it wasn't too long ago he was calling me to bail him out of debt.

"Well, since no next of kin claimed the body within the allotted time, Matt was able to do so before cremation. He paid the state fee for an indigent burial."

"What?" I blurt out, upset. "So what does that mean?"

"Nothing. Just that the state was in charge of the burial, that's all."

"Where is he?" My words increase in anxiety as the need to see his gravesite amplifies.

"Mount Olivet here in Chicago."

"I have to go."

"Elizabeth, you're upset. Why don't we take a little time and—"

"No!" I bellow.

143

"I think you should just—"

"Declan," I say, cutting his words off, refusing to wait any longer to see where my brother's buried. "If this were your mom, and I told you to 'Take some time,' would you be able to do that?"

He doesn't answer me.

"I didn't think so," I tell him and he sees my point when he says, "I'll call the valet to pull the car around."

I throw my jacket on before we head down to the lobby where Declan's Mercedes roadster is already waiting for us out front. I watch as the light drizzle from outside collects on the windshield and then gets wiped away with the wipers, and suddenly, the urgency I was feeling back at Lotus has dissipated. Pike is dead, and I'm not going to the cemetery to say goodbye because he's still with me. But it's a sinking feeling, maybe a part of me is still in denial, but it's the thought of seeing his name on a burial plot that I fear.

Declan begins to speed when we merge onto I-90 E, and I look over to him, asking somberly, "Can you slow down?"

He draws his foot back off the accelerator, slowing the car. "Is everything okay?"

I look out of my window, raindrops skewing my view, and admit, "I'm scared."

He takes my hand, but I keep my head turned away from him.

"We don't have to do this right now if you're not ready."

"Is anybody ever ready?" The question is heavy between us as I turn to face him.

He holds my hand tighter and doesn't respond.

"He needs flowers," I tell him. "Can we stop and get him some flowers?"

"Of course, darling."

I pull out my phone and find a florist not too far from the interstate, and when we arrive, my request is simple. "I need all the pink daisies you have in stock."

"Daisies?" Declan questions when the sales clerk goes to the back cooler.

"They're my favorite."

"I remember," he says with a subtle smile and then kisses the top of my head, resting his lips there for a moment while we wait for the lady to reappear.

"Any shade of pink?" the woman hollers from the back.

"Yes. Mix them," I shout back to her. "All of them."

I wait with Declan's arm wrapped around me, tucking me against his side, and when the clerk reemerges from the back, my eyes widen.

"Christ, that's a lot of flowers," Declan notes in surprise.

"One hundred and sixty-three stems," she tells us. "You wiped me out of inventory."

I watch as she wraps the daisies in huge sheets of brown paper and ties them up with several cords of natural raffia. "It's perfect. Thank you."

Declan pays and takes the flowers in his arms. Popping the trunk, he lays the bouquet down and we both laugh a little when they fill the trunk entirely.

We continue our drive, hitting light patches of traffic, and finally arrive at the gates of Mount Olivet. He parks the car at the funeral home that's right through the entrance.

"I'm going to go grab a map. I'll be right back."

An eerie chill creeps along my arms and it only takes a minute for Declan to reappear with a map in hand.

"Where is he?"

"Block two," he murmurs as he pulls out of the parking space and drives through the cemetery. I look at the gray headstones as we pass them, and before I know it, he's pulling the car along the edge of the grass.

"This is it," he says, turning the car off.

I look out the window and choke up, knowing that somewhere among all these gravestones is my brother. And he's all alone. I battle between not wanting to get out of this car and jumping out of this car to run to him. I'm so scared to see the evidence of what I've done.

Tears spill down my cheeks effortlessly, and Declan reaches his arm over to console me.

"This is all my fault," I strain out on a hoarse voice filled with anguish.

I turn to face Declan, and he doesn't say a word. I know what he's thinking; it's the same thing I'm thinking. No one can argue that this is very much my fault, and Declan isn't a man who will lie to comfort. We both know my part in all of this, and it makes it so much worse when there's no truth out there that can take away any amount of my responsibility.

"Do you want me to come with you?" he asks, and I nod because I know I can't do this alone.

We get out of the car, and he grabs the flowers from the trunk, placing them in my arms. With his arm wrapped around my shoulder, he leads the way. We walk around, looking at the names on the grave markers as my tears drip into the mass of daisies.

We wander for what feels like hours, but is probably only a minute before Declan stops.

"Elizabeth."

I look up at him and he tilts his head over to a flat stone, and when I see it, I gasp in horror. "Oh, my God."

And there it is.

His beautiful name engraved in stone, marking his death.

I step in front of it, my body shuddering in tormenting pain. Every dagger I've ever thrown coming right back to stab me in my chest, and Declan has to step behind me with both of his hands gripping my shoulders.

"How could I have done this?" I cry and then fall to my knees and out of Declan's hands as I clutch the flowers to my chest. "He was my best friend, Declan."

"I know," his tender voice consoles as he now sits behind me.

I lay the flowers on the grass beside me and lean forward on my knees, bracing my hands on top of his name. "I'm so sorry, Pike. I should've just killed myself." My words lose themselves within my agonizing sobs and falter when I can't focus on anything aside from the debilitating guilt and remorse. "It should've been me! It should've been me!" I wail repeatedly.

Declan reaches around my waist and pulls me away, off my knees and onto my bottom, and I fall back into him. I grab ahold of his arms crossing over my chest, and dig my nails into them as I sob, wishing I would've shot myself that day.

"He didn't deserve to die."

"Shh," Declan breathes in my ear. "I know, baby. I know."

"It should've been me," I keep saying as Declan continues to hush and console me.

His hold on me is merciless as I allow every emotion to swallow me up, and when it finally relents and spits me out, I'm utterly spent. The dipping sun measures the hours we've been here. My body aches as I move to sit up on my own, and when I turn back to look at Declan, I notice his bloodshot eyes. He's been crying with me.

"I'm sorry," I say, my throat dry and scratchy.

"Don't be. You needed to get that out. You hold so much inside of you."

"I'm a horrible person."

"You're not," he tells me. "You made horrible choices, but you're not a horrible person."

"I don't believe you."

"Maybe not today, but one day you will. I'm going to make you believe me."

He stands and reaches down to me, helping me up. When I'm steady on my feet, I turn and scoot the flowers to rest over where Pike lies. I take a moment, drained of all my tears, not to say goodbye, but to pay respect to the most selfless person I've ever known.

eighteen

T<small>IME FREEZES, AND</small> yet, the sun rises and the sun sets, only to rise once again.

I woke yesterday but was unable to get out of bed. Too much guilt. Too much sorrow in a world filled with regrets. So, I hid under the covers and slept, and woke, and slept. Declan checked on me throughout the day, allowing me to wallow in the misery of my wrongdoings. He ordered food from the kitchen, but I couldn't eat. I couldn't risk feeding the pain for fear it would devour me fully.

Emptiness is my companion as I stand here and stare out the window up into the blue sky. It's been two days since I faced Pike's resting place, and although I haven't seen him or heard his voice, I've felt his arms around me ever since.

"You're up," Declan says when he walks into the room, dressed down in dark denim and a plain cotton T-shirt. "How are you feeling?"

"Numb."

He walks over to me, saying, "I'm going to make you feel something today," before kissing me. "Get dressed."

"What are we doing?"

"Whatever we want." He smirks and then shuts the door behind him.

After I shower and pull my hair together, I match his leisurely attire and opt for jeans and a fitted top. When I walk out into the living room, he stands with my jacket already in his hands.

"You're up to no good," I tease.

"You look stunning."

"Yeah," I quip. "You're definitely up to no good."

Once we reach the lobby, he leads me out to the busy streets of The Loop and hails a cab.

"A cab? Where's your car?"

"We're lying low today. Trust me," he says when he opens the door for me. I scoot across the back seat and Declan tells the cabbie, "Navy Pier."

"Navy Pier?"

"You ever been?"

"Oddly, no. You?" I ask.

"No."

"So why are we going?"

"Why not?"

His spontaneity makes me smile, and I make the mindful choice to hand myself over to him today. Because, after all, he's the reason I keep going.

We're among all the tourists when we hop out of the cab. Two people who blend in with all the others. We walk hand in hand into a souvenir shop and look at all the trinkets, and Declan thinks he's cute when he buys me a cheesy Chicago shirt that reads *It's better in the bleachers* across the front.

"Wasted money."

He takes the shirt and slips it over my head, saying, "Then you better wear it and not let it go to waste."

He pulls it down, and when I push my arms out of the sleeves, he takes a step back and smiles.

"Are you happy now?"

He laughs, "You look cute."

With a roll of my eyes, I join in with a light chuckle. He's blithe and lighthearted, and it's refreshing to see this side of him. We've had so many days filled with dark clouds and suffocating emotions, but to see that rays of light can break through those clouds gives me hope for us.

We walk along the water enjoying the spring breeze. He buys me a funnel cake when I tell him I've never tasted one and then licks the powdered sugar off my lips after I inhale the fried treat. When I'm thoroughly buzzed with sweet carbs, he takes me up to the Ferris wheel.

"Come on."

"No way, Declan. That is way too high."

"What are you saying? Tough-as-nails Elizabeth is scared of heights?"

"Umm . . . yeah," I admit with my head craned back, looking up at the enormous wheel.

"It's a *Ferris wheel!*" he exclaims.

"Yes. I know this," I say, and with my arm up towards it, I exasperate, "and it's a deathtrap!"

He shakes his head, laughing, "It's the mildest ride here."

"Don't care. You're not getting me on that thing."

He releases a heavy sigh and succumbs. "All right. No Ferris wheel." Taking my hand, he says, "I've got something better in mind."

We make our way over to a small fishing vendor pavilion on the north dock. With bait and rods in hand, we find a spot to cast our lines.

"Give me your rod and I'll hook the bait for you."

"I'm capable of hooking it myself," I say with a confident air.

"Go for it, darling."

His eyes watch as I dunk my hand into the bait bucket, pull out a shiner, and pierce the hook through it.

Looking up at him holding his rod, I tease, "You need me to help you?"

"I'm impressed."

"I came from the streets, Declan. Baiting a hook is nothing," I tell him with a smirk and then cast my line into the water.

"So, I take it you've fished before."

I watch him cast his line out and respond, "No, not really. Only once with my dad. He would hold the rod for me, and when we would get a bite, he'd let me reel it in. What about you?"

"All the time. When I was living here, I'd take my boat out during my down time, which wasn't often, but I'd get away when I could and toss out a line or two."

"I got something!" I practically squeal when something tugs on my line. I laugh with childish excitement, and then a little fish surfaces.

"It's a perch." He takes the small fish and pulls the hook out, all the while smiling at me.

"I'm winning," I brag, and when he tosses the fish back into the water, he says, "I wasn't aware this was a competition."

"Well, now you are. And you're losing."

I grab another shiner from the bucket and cast my line.

"Tell me a story," I request. "Something good."

"My darling wants a story," he says to himself and then takes a moment, squinting against the sunlight reflecting off the water. "I did my undergrad at the University of Edinburgh and was living at my fraternity house. We used to throw a lot of parties. I was never much of a drinker, but it was the end of exam week, and I'd been under a lot of stress. The girl I was seeing at the time was at the party that night, and I had gotten piss drunk. She told me she was going to call it a night and crash in my room since she had been drinking too. She was nowhere near as drunk as I was, but still drunk enough that she knew better than to drive."

He pauses when his rod dips. Another small perch.

"One to one. It's a tie," he says with a grin, and then continues when he grabs another shiner. "Anyway, I stayed up for a few more hours before stumbling upstairs to my room. I was so wasted, and all I can remember is stripping off my clothes while everything around me was spinning. I pulled the sheets back and slipped in behind what I assumed was my girlfriend."

"It wasn't?"

"Each room housed three guys."

I start laughing and it isn't long before he joins me.

"I spent the whole night in my underpants snuggling with my roommate . . . Bean."

"Bean?"

"Uh, yeah, he had a bit of a flatulence issue."

I burst out laughing.

"Once I realized I wasn't cuddling my girlfriend, it was too late. A few of my frat brothers were standing in the doorway, snapping photos of the supposed indiscretion."

"What did your girlfriend say?"

"Ah, well, she was upset I got drunk and ignored her all night, and that was the end of her."

"You're an ass," I snicker, to which he replies, "So I've been told."

I startle and clutch my fishing rod when it's nearly yanked out of my hands. Grabbing ahold of the reel, I struggle to crank it.

"I need help," I call, and Declan sets his rod down, moves behind me, and grips the rod.

"You've got something big," he says when he puts his hand over mine and helps me reel in the line just like my dad used to.

I let him take control and move my hand with his. The fish fights us for a bit, and when it approaches the water's surface, I see how substantial it is.

"What is that?" I ask excitedly.

He pulls it up, announcing, "It's a big fucking bass." He kneels, pinning the fish down with his foot, and removes the hook. "You want to keep it? We could have the chef in the kitchen prepare it for dinner tonight."

Looking at the fish flopping around, I tell him, "No. Let him live."

"You sure?"

"I'm sure."

Declan drops the bass into the water, looks over the pier's edge, and watches him as he swims down, disappearing into the lake.

I bait my hook and return to our conversation, saying, "A part of me always wanted to do the whole college thing."

"You still could."

With shame, I confess to him, "I never even graduated high school, Declan."

He looks at me and there's a hint of surprise in his eyes. "How far did you get?"

"I never finished the ninth grade. When Pike turned eighteen, I ran away with him, so school was out of the question because I'd get busted by the state. I was always a good student though, made excellent grades. I loved reading and learning, so I had Pike buy me all the materials to get my GED even though it would never be official. Since I was still underage and in the system, I couldn't use my real name for anything."

"And when you were of age?"

"By then, it didn't matter. I knew we'd never have the means for me to ever go to college, so what was the point of going back to get my GED?" I say. "I did what I could though. I'd pick classes that interested me out of the local college class catalog and Pike would buy me the textbooks from a used bookstore. I'd read them, and in a pathetic way, it made me feel like I was making something of myself."

"You were."

"All I did was make a *mess* of myself."

"That too," he responds in light jest. "But you're bright and well-spoken. No one would ever suspect you only made it to the ninth grade. You're an incredible woman who's fighting hard to make things right."

"Things will never be right."

"Maybe the past won't, but right here, in this moment, this is where it all changes," he says. "You can do anything you want to do."

His confidence in me is powerful, making me feel like there's a future to look forward to. That the choices I make won't be for naught. And maybe he's right—maybe it's the here and now that I need to focus on to move forward. I've always been running, and now, for the first time, I no longer have to. I can stand here, in one place, and know that with Declan by my side, I'll be okay.

So with a little bit of optimism, I tell him, "I want to finish high school."

He smiles, pride in his eyes, and says, "We can get all the details on what needs to be done tomorrow. But tonight, I'm taking you out."

"A date?"

"It'll be a first for us."

After catching too many perch to count, we decide I win based on the bass alone. Being able to be out with Declan, free from lies and games in this city where we used to hide, feels great. This is where we fell in love, but that life was always tainted, and now . . . now we can create something new.

With the goofy shirt Declan bought me crumpled on the bathroom floor, I finish the last of my makeup after a long shower. Walking into the bedroom, I can see Declan out in the living room sipping Scotch. He looks good as he waits on me, dressed in his usual look—a sleek designer suit, tailored to perfection.

I pick out a flattering navy shift dress that I purchased on my shopping trip with Davina. After I slip it on, I step into a pair of nude heels and join Declan. We then make our way down to the lobby where his roadster is waiting out front.

We drive through the night to Cité, an upscale restaurant that's perched atop Lake Point Tower. We're seated next to the windows, which provide stunning views of the lake and city, and Declan takes the chair right next to me instead of across the table.

He was right—this is a first for us. We've never been on a date, and then it hits me that *I've* never been on a date. Not a real one, not with a man I love. The thought causes me to smile and Declan takes notice.

"What's that grin all about?"

"Nothing," I tell him, feeling a bit juvenile.

"That's not nothing behind those blue eyes of yours. Spill it."

"You're pushy, you know that?"

"I'm aware. And I'm waiting."

"Fine," I exhaust. "I was just sitting here, thinking . . . It's really silly."

"Humor me."

"Aside from fallacies . . . this is my first date."

"Ever?" he says in curiosity.

"Ever."

He slips his hand under the table and places it on my thigh, giving me a gentle squeeze. We order wine and he insists on the Siberian caviar service, promising I'll love it—and I do.

"You're quite divergent, you know that?" I say, setting my wine glass down.

"Why's that?"

"I remember you taking me to breakfast at that diner when I first met you. Stale coffee and pancakes."

"The Over Easy Café does not have stale coffee," he immediately defends, and I laugh, bantering, "Whatever you say. But, now, you have me here, drinking a bottle of wine that's so expensive, it's obscene."

"You don't like it?"

"I never said that; it's just a contrast from the 'not stale' coffee and the hot dog you ate from the street vendor today."

"So what would you prefer?" He leans closer to me and slips his hand back on my thigh.

"I like your contradictions," I admit as he runs his hand under the hem of my dress. My body tenses and I shift my eyes around the room, wondering if anyone knows what's happening under the table linens.

"You nervous?"

Giving him my attention, I ask, "You like making me nervous?"

"Yes."

"Why?" My voice trembles when his fingers hit the lace of my panties and then he nudges against my thigh for me to uncross my legs—and I do.

"Because I like testing you," he confesses, shifting my panties over. "To see how far you'll let me push you."

"When have I ever stopped you?"

"Never," he whispers on a husky voice at the same time he shoves one of his fingers inside my pussy.

I gasp.

He smiles.

Pride and domination color his eyes in heated black.

"You want me to stop?"

"No," I breathe, and he drags his finger out of me and rolls my clit in slow circles.

"Tell me why you yield like this to me."

"Because I love you."

He thrusts his finger back inside of me. "Say it again."

My breath catches, stammering unevenly as I resist the urge to grind down on his hand, nearly whimpering the words, "I love you."

He abruptly pulls out of me, leaving me yearning, and shifts my panties back over to cover me. My chest rises and falls noticeably as I watch him bring his hand up to his mouth and suck my arousal off his finger.

Unsatisfied and aching, I make it through dinner, and when the bill is paid, I'm quick to leave. Declan's cocky smirk should irritate me, but it only makes me want to fuck him more. He takes my hand, and once we're on the elevator, he further tests me by refusing to touch me. My body is on high-alert, sensitive to every element, begging to be touched—but he doesn't engage me.

"Asshole," I mutter under my breath, and he smiles.

The elevator doors open and as soon as we exit the building, my steps halt the moment I see her.

She stops in her steps as soon as she sees me, her eyes narrowing into daggers. It's a look I've never seen her wear, but it's wasted on me.

"You're back," she states.

"It's nice to see you too, Jacqueline," I condescend.

"Jacqueline?" Declan questions to himself, but we all hear.

"You," she accuses, looking at Declan. "You son of a bitch!"

"You're sorely mistaken," I butt in. "Your husband—"

"Is dead! Because of you two," she accuses. Her loud voice grabs the attention of a couple passersby, but they keep moving. She then looks down at my hand linked with Declan's. "And how fast you move on, Nina."

"You've got a lot of nerve. This coming from the woman who not only fucked my husband but was stupid enough to get pregnant. So, don't you dare stand there like you're a goddamn ice princess," I lash out while Declan allows me to handle her on my own.

Tears rise and then fall down her cheeks when she explodes, "You killed my husband! I have nothing because you took it away from me!"

"I didn't take shit from you. I freed you from that asshole. He fucking raped me and tortured me! And look at you," I belittle. "Standing there like *you're* the victim when you should be thanking me for ridding the world of that piece of shit."

Beyond what he did to me, my blood boils when I think of what Richard did to Declan's mother and the part he played in my father's life.

"How dare you tarnish his name with your lies. He'd never—"

"You can't be that ignorant. Surely you know by now the man he was, yet you're so weak that you're still defending him."

"What am I supposed to do? My life is over! My name doesn't mean anything anymore. And because of you, I'm left with nothing. Everything I ever had has been seized. I've been ostracized by everyone and I'm buried in debt."

"And yet you blame me," I say. "I guess you got what you deserved for marrying that asshole and screwing around with a married man. It seems all you have is the hope that your bastard son doesn't grow up to hate you, since he now carries all the wealth." My smile grows. "Must suck to know all that money is within reach, and yet Bennett forbade you from touching it because he hated you."

"You bitch!"

"You're done here," Declan barks, stepping between us. "That man you married was a cold-blooded killer. Accept it or not, I don't really give a fuck, but don't place blame where it doesn't belong."

Not allowing another second to pass, he leads me to his car, leaving her crying, alone, on the sidewalk. Declan closes my door, and I look at her through the window, hating her for the mere fact that she loved and supported such an evil man. A man who left me stripped naked for days while he degraded and humiliated me, beat me, and sodomized me. A man who took so much from both my life and Declan's.

Declan speeds off, and I refuse to let the memories of what Richard did to me come to life.

"Are you okay?"

"I don't want to talk about it," I snap.

I can't talk because all I can do right now is focus on forcing those memories back into the deep cave of my soul. Pinching my eyes closed, battling against myself, I hear the ringing in my head, and it feels like an axe to my skull.

I clamp my hands over my ears, and I don't even notice Declan pulling the car over. He reaches out to me and touches my arm, and when I open my eyes, I see Richard's smug face instead of Declan's. My body coils back, lurching away from him, and I scream, "Don't fucking touch me!"

"Elizabeth, it's okay," he insists, unbuckling my seatbelt and banding his arms around me as I fight against the high-pitched ringing in my head.

I release a wretched scream, my voice bleeding, "Make it

stop!"

"Open your eyes and look at me," he demands on a hardened voice. He grabs hold of my head and forces me to focus on him. "Breathe. I need you to breathe with me."

Everything around me and within me is a demented chaos of sounds, voices, visions. A hurricane spinning with inconceivable force, but his eyes remain still and steady. He's the one unwavering element in this maelstrom, and it takes all the effort in me to focus on him—on his words.

"That's it, darling. Just breathe," he encourages when I feel my lungs inflate.

My eyes never waver, and soon everything dulls into a low hum that I'm eventually able to silence. He's managed to chase away the demons I couldn't fight off on my own.

And it's here, in the ink of night, on a deserted side street, that I must face the fact that I undoubtedly need Declan.

nineteen

After my run-in with Jacqueline, all I want to do is sleep. The stress of my panic attack should've knocked me out, but I've been tossing and turning ever since my head hit the pillow.

When my cell phone lights up, I grab it from the nightstand. The screen reads: *UNKNOWN*, and I know it's Matt calling. I decline the call and turn the phone off. My mind races in a million different directions, stirring up even more memories. Unwilling to lie here in bed any longer, I grab the manifest and my notepad and go to the office to direct all my attention to this list.

I've made it halfway through the names, scrambling the letters around and around and around, not knowing what I'm looking for, but hoping I find something. I get through three more names.

Parker Moore

Dorrance Riley

Quentin Malles

All are dead ends, and before the sun starts to rise, I sneak back into bed without Declan noticing.

I manage to get a couple hours of sleep, and when I wake, Declan has already had breakfast delivered. The smell of his coffee and fresh baked croissants fill the air, and before I'm fully awake, he pours me a cup of steaming water and hands me a tea bag.

"Thanks."

While we sit in bed, Declan reads the newspaper and I watch as bister ribbons through the translucent water in my tea cup. Sleep still fogs my head as I continue to dunk the tea bag up and down until the water turns to a delicate amber, infused with aromatic herbs that help wake me up.

"He's in the paper," Declan murmurs.

"Who?"

He hands the *Chicago Tribune* to me, and there he is—Callum. He stands in his prison-issued orange jumpsuit with the headline "Player in Gun Trafficking Ring Indicted."

I look to Declan as he takes a sip of his coffee, and he says, "You know it's only a matter of time until we're getting wrapped up in this."

"What do you mean?"

"Our involvement. You were married to Bennett, ran in the same circle as Richard, and spent time with my father. That, along with the kidnapping and murder, we'll both be forced to testify," he tells me before tossing the sheets off him and getting out of bed in haste. "This is the last thing I need, that man tarnishing my name," he bites.

He's pissed about the attention this will draw to him and his company.

"Declan," I call out in a panic, my heart beginning to race

when it suddenly hits me. "What about me?"

He turns to look at me, becoming aware when he sees the anxiety in my eyes.

"They'll dig into my history and Nina only goes back so far. They'll know I'm a fraud," I blurt out in a pitchy voice. "I'll be charged with identity theft and embezzlement, along with any other crime they can pin on me."

"Fuck," he grits under his breath.

I guess it was inevitable that my con would eventually catch up with me. My mind goes into overdrive, thinking about how I could possibly finagle my way out of this, how I could possibly explain this away, but I can't hone in on anything.

"What do we do?"

"I'll put a call in to my attorney," he tells me. "I don't want you to worry; we have time. It could take up to a year for this to even go to trial."

"What about you?"

"What about me?"

I slip out of bed and walk over to him. "It's you that tells me that I shouldn't hide from the things that hurt me."

"He doesn't hurt me," he immediately defends, but I call his bluff, saying, "He didn't even try to stop the murder of your mom. He stepped aside and just let it happen. So don't tell me that doesn't hurt you, Declan. I know it does." I reach out to him and place my hand over his heart. "You and I share the same soft spot, the same wound—the death of a parent."

He covers my hand with his, and it's full of tension, squeezing me much too hard.

He's in pain.

(DECLAN)

Her bones are fragile in my grip as I fight against the agony that marks my soul in wounds that refuse to heal.

And she's right.

My mum has always been the weak link in my armor. She's the softest part of my heart and anything that comes close to touching it pains me. But that pain is tainted by the fury I hold for my dad now that I know the part he played.

I look down into Elizabeth's eyes and see the sorrow in them. She's called me on my shit, so there's only one option unless I want her to see me as a hypocrite.

"Let's go to New York then."

"You're going to see him?" she asks in surprise.

"Yes. And then I'm done with him."

I leave Elizabeth to drink her tea while I make the call to arrange the flight, and I'm told that we can make it out later tonight. When I return to the bedroom, I see her with that damn notepad. She thinks she's being sneaky and that I don't notice when she leaves my bed at night, but I do. The moment I lose the heat of her body, I wake up. I've chosen not to say anything and to give her the time she feels she needs.

Truth be told, Lachlan and I are hitting roadblock after roadblock. This man clearly doesn't want to be found, but one way or another, I *will* find him—for her.

She sets the notepad and pencil on the bedside table when she sees me.

"The plane will be ready at seven."

I SIT AND WAIT, looking around the white cinderblock room filled with the city's disgraced and their loved ones. Guards stand and watch the interactions, making sure the rules that were explained in detail are being abided by.

The metal door in the corner of the room opens, and this time it's my father who walks through. Donned in orange, he's escorted into the room, and the guard that's with him removes the shackles as my father's eyes find mine.

He's expressionless.

Once freed from the chains, he makes his way across the room. He looks hard, unshaven, and thinned out.

"Son," he remarks evenly when he approaches the table.

Animosity sparks as I look at this man who sits across from me. Memories of all the disdain he's spit my way throughout my life, only to evade his own wrongdoings, ignites rage inside me.

"How did you find out?"

"You haven't heard?" I respond and he shakes his head. "Your boss?"

"My boss?"

"Keep playing dumb with me," I taunt. "I know everything. I just want to hear you tell the truth for once in your life."

"Stop with the riddles, kid, and just tell me what you *think* you know."

My hands fist; it's a futile attempt to control my fury, and I glare at him. "I know about Mum. I know she died because of you."

"I loved that woman—"

His words—his flagrant lie—set me off, and I punch the table, losing control. "You fucking bastard!"

"Hey!" one guard yells, calling me into check.

"She died because of you," I seethe, lowering my voice. "Because of your greed, she had to pay the consequences."

"You don't know shit, kid."

"Admit it," I say.

He shrugs his shoulders as if he's clueless and guiltless, and I can't stand to look at his smug face any longer, so I speed this up. "You knew Richard was going to kill her. That's why you left the country, because you didn't want to be there when it happened. You were running from the guilt, weren't you?"

"How do you know about Richard?"

"You know he's dead, right?" I ask and he nods. "I killed him." His eyes widen when I tell him this, and I smile proudly. "Don't worry, Dad. Cops already know I did it."

He doesn't respond to what I've just admitted to him. He simply stares at me, dumbfounded.

"Because of him, I know everything you've been hiding from me. *Everything.*"

He takes a hard swallow and hangs his head, succumbing to the truth because he has no other choice at this point. He can't bullshit me any longer.

"I know it all, Dad," I whisper harshly, digging the knife into him even deeper, and when he finally gets the balls to lift his head to look me in the eye, he says, "Then you know what I'm facing."

"It's all over the news."

His demeaning voice shifts to that of neediness. "I need your help, son."

"Admit it first. Admit that you were the one responsible for

Mum dying."

"I need your help," he deflects, talking quickly in a hushed tone. "Camilla is my only line to the outside, aside from my lawyer, but I haven't talked to her in a week. I need your help to get in touch with Lachlan."

"Why?"

"I can't tell you why, but I *need* to talk to him."

"About Camilla?"

"Camilla? Why would I talk to him about her?" he questions in utter confusion. "What do you know?"

"Only that your girlfriend has conflicting fidelities."

"I'm getting the feeling he does too," he murmurs, jaw clenched in anger.

"What's that supposed to mean?"

"Ask him."

"I'm asking *you*," I say as my irritation grows in sync with suspicions that I'm missing some important details about Lachlan.

"I needed to keep an eye on you when you left Chicago," he says cryptically. "Tell me, because I need to know, who's Elizabeth Archer and what the fuck is she doing at The Water Lily?"

That fucking bastard. I will kill Lachlan when I get back to London, because it's now apparent that whatever involvement he told me he has with my father is a lie. The only way my dad could get that information would be from him. But it's his mention of The Water Lily that has me curious when I think of the photo that Elizabeth found there.

"I'll tell you what you want to know," I say. "But first, tell me what I should know about The Water Lily."

He looks at me suspiciously, saying nothing.

"Why is there a picture of me there?" I ask, giving him a bit of information to try to spur him into an answer.

"Because," he sighs, leaning forward.

"Tell me the truth."

He looks at me for a moment before revealing, "The woman who runs it . . ."

"Isla."

"Yes," he says. "She's your grandmother."

"What?"

"Isla is your mother's mum."

"That doesn't make sense," I mutter. "Why was she never around?"

"Because she never approved of me dating her daughter. It was years of ups and downs, and when I married your mum, that's what finally severed them—the fact that your mother chose me."

"And even when Mum died, you never told me."

"What was there to tell?"

I stand, unable to continue this conversation or look at this man who has filled my life with countless lies.

"Son . . ."

"Stop avoiding and just tell me."

He remains seated, staring up at me. For a beat, I don't think he's going to answer, and my anger burns. Then, he opens his mouth to speak. "Yes, I knew your mother would die, and I did nothing to stop it."

And that's the dagger that spears into what Elizabeth calls "the softest part of me." Blood from the wound that was created the day I watched her die pours out, drowning me, numbing me, debilitating me.

My hands shake when I brace them on the edge of the table and tell him, "You'll never see me again."

"Declan—"

"You're going to die in this shithole all alone, you mother-fucker."

I don't look back at him when I walk to the guard who stands at the exit, and I swear I leave a trail of blood in my wake from the wound he ripped wide open. When the guard pulls his keys to unlock the door, I hear my father call out, "Declan, come on. Come back," and then commotion before a guard yells, "Sit down, McKinnon!"

"Declan!"

More commotion.

"Get the fuck off me!"

"Get your ass on the ground, inmate!"

"Declan!"

"ANOTHER," I TELL the bartender in the lounge of the hotel, and he pours me a shot of whiskey.

I can't go back to the room just yet, I'm much too volatile. I've spent my whole life trying to measure up to my father's standards and prove to him that I'm man enough to persevere on my own in this world. And for what? It was all a lie. A lie that claimed my mother's life and mine. I lost a huge part of myself when she died and was left with scars that no man should ever have to bear.

The moment she died, I was blamed. It was me that wasn't man enough to save her, and my father spent his whole life making sure I knew I was the pussy he saw me for. He destroyed everything and has left me in this nightmare of realized deceit.

"How did it go?" Elizabeth asks when I eventually walk through the door of the hotel room.

I'm nothing but knotted up rage and anger and agony that alcohol can't even cure. I'm broken bones and bleeding wounds, empty and missing my mum like never before. My cold stone exterior masks the pansy I feel like. It shields the insecure man in me that wants to fall to his knees and have his girl hold on to him as he cries for all the years he's hidden behind strict control. And at the same time, I want to lash out, punch my fists through the walls, and spew the venom in my veins for all that son of a bitch has done to my life.

"Are you okay?" I hear her say through the static of vehemence rushing under my skin. "Declan?"

I bore my eyes into her, silently pleading to use her to expel my wrath onto. My hands fist, and I feel the vibrations in my flexed muscles when it all becomes too much to hold in.

Her hands touch my clenched jaw and she runs them down my trembling arms, all the while looking up at me so lovingly when I'm pouring out pure fury. She's a goddamn godsend when she perceives my reticence and gives me the permission I'm needing so badly.

"Touch me."

"I'll hurt you."

"It's okay," she says so fucking sweetly. "Give me your pain so you don't have to feel it."

I kiss her with binding brutality, and she allows it. I'm a wolf, devouring her, clawing her, ripping her clothes off in a storm of violence. She stumbles back as I force my body against hers, pushing her to the ground. I stand above her naked body and breathe in broken pants.

She's so small, milky white flesh, and ruby red-hair, and she must be crazy to submit to me right now, but she does, saying, "Don't hold back."

I strip, and she watches, inviting the beast to come out and play. I'm already rock hard, and when she sits up and wraps her delicate hand around my dick, it pulses and leaps in her grip. I slap her arm away. She lies back, and I reach down and flip her over. Kneeling above her, I grab a handful of her hair, yank it back, and strike her ass with my hand. She cries out, eliciting a heady arousal of power in me.

Reaching for my pants, I rip the belt out from the loops and fasten it tightly around her arms, above the elbows. She squirms and emits little ragged gasps, and I raise my hand, letting it drop in a sharp slap across her ass again. It immediately welts as the blood rushes to the surface, making my dick even more thick and hot with need.

She doesn't resist when I reach under her waist and jerk her ass up in the air and shove her knees under her so she's propped up like a fucking beauty. Tangling my hands into her hair, I shove the side of her face into the floor, and when I run the tip of my cock through her slick warmth, I realize she's ready for me, dripping wet.

I slam my dick inside of her with raging force, and without any restraint, I fuck her licentiously hard. I grab ahold of the belt to use for leverage, and with each pounding thrust, I drive her body into the floor.

My skin is covered in a sheen of sweat as I thrust my hips sharply, barraged by a million sensations all at once, blurring the edges of pain and pleasure. Elizabeth's yelps are muffled by the floor as I grunt freely into the air.

I pull out and shove her over onto her back, watching her wince against the pain of lying on top of her arms, but I see her hidden mirth. She then lances her nails into my heart, making me love her even more when her lips lift in a faint smile and she spreads her legs wider for me, inviting me to take more.

I can't *not* be one with her.

I hold my dick and slide into her swollen, ripe pussy. I still myself, and her needy body begins to clench around my shaft. Drawing back, I growl as I fuck her frantically and the room fills with a requiem of moans, gasps, and grunts. Elizabeth bows her lithe body up to mine in an attempt to fuck me back.

She's a fucking paradigm.

My cock begins to swell in her, building in a vigor of ecstasy at the same time I sense Elizabeth's body tensing up, faltering in rhythm. She stares up at me, and I reach underneath her and find her hand. I hold it tightly in mine, needing her to know that she's safe to allow herself to fall apart with me, that we're in this together in our most vulnerable states. Her eyes swim out of focus, and she draws in a tight breath before releasing an intoxicating moan, carnal and raw. Her pussy clamps in spasms around my dick; I buck into her, exploding, shooting my cum deep inside her, groaning in sync with her pleasure. Her hand squeezes mine as we ride out our orgasms together. She writhes under my body, drawing as much pleasure as she can from me, and I love how greedy she gets with me in these moments.

When we're sweaty, sated, and completely out of breath, I roll us onto our sides and unbuckle the belt, and like all the times before, she clings her arms around my neck. My cock twitches as I keep it buried in her and band my arms around her body as she holds on to me.

I'm sure she's unaware that I need her embrace more than she needs mine in this moment. She soothes me in a way no one has been able to, taking the toxins out of my bones and replacing them with her love. She fills me entirely, handing herself over so willingly for me to take whatever it is that I need, and she does it so perfectly.

I pull my head back to look at her, and she nuzzles her forehead against mine, keeping her eyes closed. When I lean in and kiss her, open and deep, I gather her completely in my arms. She becomes desperate, and I meet her urgency to be closer. I bruise her, crashing my lips with hers, and we bleed. Like cannibals, we feed off each other, sharing the blood from our hearts, uniting us even more.

twenty
(ELIZABETH)

Declan sits in quiet despair as we fly back to Chicago. I knew better than to push him to talk when he returned to the hotel last night. I could see the torment in his eyes, so I kept my mouth shut and handed myself over to him so he could use me for comfort. We spent the whole night on the floor together, naked and wrapped in each other's arms.

He's been quiet all morning, and I've followed suit, returning the silence. I don't know what was said between him and Cal or how it ended, but I doubt it ended well. When I look over to him as he sits next to me, I find him staring at me intently. I want to ask him if he's okay, but I don't. Instead, I simply give him a subtle smile and squeeze his hand that's holding mine. He kisses the top of my head, and I close my eyes, using his shoulder for a pillow for the remainder of the flight.

DECLAN HAS BEEN down in his office on the ground floor of Lotus since we returned from New York while I've stayed up in the penthouse. He's yet to speak to me, and I've been busying myself with the passenger manifest.

Michael Ross

William Baxter

Clint Noor

Ben Wexler

I've spent a couple hours on those names and have come up empty. Deciding to give myself a break, I call down to the kitchen and order some food and then mindlessly flip through a few magazines. Minutes dissolve into hours, and when the sun begins its descent, I sit on the edge of the bed and watch.

When the sun kisses the horizon, the bed dips beside me. We sit together in silence until the day shifts into night.

"She's my grandmother."

His slack voice cuts through the darkness, and when I turn my head to look at him, his eyes are focused on the sky.

"Who?" I gently ask.

"Isla," he reveals. "She's my mum's mother."

"He told you that?"

Declan nods. "I've had a piece of my mum here all along and he never told me."

There's longing in his voice, a feeling I'm no stranger to.

"I'll never speak to that man again," he tells me when he finally looks my way.

His eyes are flooded in pain, and it kills me to see him like this when he's always so pulled together. And in a rare moment, he stands in front of me before lowering to his knees, and then grips my hips and lays his head on my lap.

My undeniably strong Declan, slayed to the core.

Leaning over, I shield his body with mine.

I CAN'T SLEEP. DECLAN went to bed hours ago, but all I can do is toss and turn. My mind keeps drifting back to the past, and memories of my dad play in my head. Looking over at Declan, he looks so peaceful. I watch him as he sleeps, but it's impossible to ignore my stomach when it growls at me. Slipping out of bed, I pad across the room and shut the door quietly behind me. I head over to the kitchen and pull out a slice of cheesecake that room service delivered earlier. Grabbing my notepad and the list of passengers, I take a seat on the couch in the living room and begin working on the next name.

Asher Corre

Looking at the name, I pick up a strawberry garnish from the plate and eat it, and another memory of my dad finds me again.

"Happy birthday, princess."

"Daddy," I groan as I roll over in bed, rubbing the sleep dust out of my eyes with my hands.

"Wake up, sleepyhead."

I open my eyes to see my daddy sitting on the edge of my bed with a great big bundle of pink balloons and a smile on his face.

"Am I five today?"

"You are. You're getting so big, baby."

"Then you can't call me 'baby' if I'm so big."

"I'll call you 'baby' even when you're my age," he says. *"Come on, get out of bed."*

I groan again, still sleepy, and he sets the weight that's tied to the bottom of the balloons on the floor and then reaches his hands out in an over-sized gesture. I immediately squeal and throw the covers over my head.

"The tickle monster is gonna get you," he teases in a playful monster voice, and I start laughing before he even gets me.

When his fingers get ahold of me I squeal and squirm with loud giggles.

"Daddy, stop!"

"Say the magic word," he says in a sing-song voice as he continues to tickle me.

"Abracadabra . . . Please . . . Hocus pocus . . ." I ramble off, saying everything I can think of, and then he stops. My belly hurts from all the laughing, and I have to catch my breath.

"Are you getting up?"

"Yes, Daddy."

"Breakfast in ten minutes, princess. Get ready and don't forget to brush your teeth," he tells me as he stands and walks to my bedroom door. "Oh, wait. I forgot something."

I get out of bed as he walks back to me. He lifts me up, and I wrap my arms and legs around him like a monkey when he starts kissing my neck. The prickles from his beard tickle me, and I laugh.

"I love you, Daddy."

"I love you too, birthday girl," he says before setting me back on my feet. "Now get dressed."

Because it's my birthday, I decide to wear as many colors as I can find in my dresser, and when I'm ready and my teeth are brushed, I run out into the kitchen.

"Pancakes!"

"And whipped cream," he adds.

I take a seat at the table in front of a ginormous stack of pancakes, but before he puts the whipped cream on them, he says, "Open up."

He holds the can over my head, so I lean back, open my mouth, and he squirts my mouth full of whipped cream.

"When does my party start?"

"Your friends will be here at noon, so I need to get started on your birthday cake as soon as we're finished with breakfast."

"You're making the strawberry cake, right?"

"Of course. It's your favorite, isn't it?"

"Yes! Strawberries are my super duper favorite!" I exclaim.

I begin eating my pancake tower, but it doesn't take long for my belly to get full. I play with my dolls in the living room while Daddy cleans up, and when he's done, he calls me back into the kitchen.

"Did you want to help me with the cake?"

"Yes!" I say excitedly and then drag one of the chairs from the table over to the counter and climb up.

He pulls out all the ingredients from the pantry and fridge and helps me fill measuring cups that I dump into a big bowl. Once the cake batter is made, he lets me lick the spoon and bowl as he puts the pan into the oven.

While it's baking we play a couple games of Go Fish and watch Saturday morning cartoons. The timer goes off and we return to the kitchen.

"Is it time for the strawberry slime?" I ask.

"Yep!"

As Daddy prepares the strawberry gelatin, he lets me stab the holes in the cake with a toothpick. When the gelatin starts to thicken a little, I help him pour it over the cake. He puts it into the fridge to set before we go outside to play in the back yard.

"Will you push me high?" I ask when I run over to the swing set.

"You don't want to do it on your own?"

"Not today."

He pushes me, and when I call out, "Higher!" he says, "What if I push you into the clouds?"

"That's silly, Daddy. That can't happen."

We spend a good amount of time playing outside, and when we're done and the cake is ready, he lets me frost it with strawberry icing.

"You're the best thing that's ever happened to me, you know that?" he tells me as I smear on the icing.

"Am I your favorite?"

"My super duper favorite, but I need you to make me a promise," he says. "I need you to promise me that you'll stop growing up so fast."

"How do I stop growing?"

"Well," he says with animation. "I guess I'll have to stop feeding you."

I giggle, "You can't do that! What if I get hungry?"

"What are we going to do then?"

"I don't wanna be little forever though. I wanna be great big, just like you."

"Just like me?"

"Yep! Just like you because you're my favorite thing in the whole wide world," I tell him and then lean over to kiss his nose.

"You're my favorite too, princess pie," he tells me and then gives me a kiss on my nose as well. "So I guess I won't starve you. Here," he says, taking the rubber spatula out of my hand. "I always get the first lick."

I laugh when he licks some of the pink frosting.

He hands it back to me, saying, "Enjoy," and I begin licking the strawberry icing.

I take another bite of the strawberry as my heart aches at the memory of the last birthday I had with him, and get back to the next name on the list.

ASHER CORRE

I stare at the letters and begin scrambling them.

SHORE RARE C

HERO CRASER

I take a bite of cheesecake and continue. I know this is non-sense. I'm not even sure what I'm trying to decode, but it makes me feel better than doing nothing.

I continue to stare at the letters.

"My little princess pie," he says again as I lick the frosting. "My little Elizabeth Archer."

_ S _ _ _ _ O _ RE

A H E R C R

"Oh, my God," I murmur and then unscramble the letters.

ARCHER

My pulse picks up as I stare at the letters that spell my last name—his last name. I then look at the remaining letters.

S O R E

Tears prick my eyes and my hands tremble.

I take another lick of the sweet frosting, and he ruffles my hair with his hand, continuing his doting, saying, "My little Elizabeth Rose Archer."

R O S E

ASHER CORRE

ROSE ARCHER

"Oh, my God!" I blurt out as I lurch off the couch, covering my mouth with my two hands. My heart beats rapidly as I stare down in shock at the notepad where my middle and last name look up at me. This can't be a coincidence.

It's him!

And suddenly, I can hear his voice so clearly.

"My little Elizabeth Rose Archer."

"Declan!" I holler, grabbing the notepad and running across the penthouse.

I sling the bedroom door open, waking him up when it

slams against the door jamb.

"Declan, it's him! It's him!"

He leaps out of bed, still half asleep. "What's going on?"

"It's my dad!" I cry out. "Look!"

I show him the notepad, and he takes it from my hand.

"What am I looking at?" he questions at the paper that's filled with so many names, and I point to ASHER CORRE.

"That's him! The letters in that name spell ROSE ARCHER."

"Who's Rose?"

I look up at him, tears streaming down my cheeks, and I can barely breathe when I tell him, "Me."

He stares at me, confusion etching his face, and I claim without a shred of doubt, "My name is Elizabeth Rose Archer, and that man is my dad."

twenty-one

"There's a listing for an A. CORRE in Washington," Declan tells me from behind his laptop. "Gig Harbor, Washington. There's no more information."

"In Washington? Is that him?"

"Only one way to find out," he says. "I had the plane scheduled to take us back to London, so I'll have to wait until morning to call and get it rescheduled."

Adrenaline intoxicates me, putting my body on high alert. My heart pounds, begging me to strap on my shoes and run across the country to get to my dad because waiting seems like an impossible feat. I pace the room, and when that dulls, I pack my bags, and when that's done, I get on Declan's computer and search every social media site and people-finder database to see if anything pops up.

Nothing, aside from what Declan had found. City and state. That's it.

The night drags on, testing every ounce of patience in me.

Seconds feel like hours and hours feel like years, and after an eternity, the sun rises. Declan is beyond demanding when he calls to reschedule the plane, and I feel sorry for the poor sap that's on the other end of the line. He barks his orders, and when he hangs up, tells me, "Grab the bags."

"We're leaving now?"

"Yes."

We move at lightning speed as we get all our belongings together, but it's still not fast enough for my growing anxiety. Thank God for his private jet, because the flight takes less than four hours. Once we're settled into our hotel suite in Tacoma, I ask, "Now what?"

"Now we need to find a way to get his address."

"How far is Gig Harbor from here?"

"Twenty minutes or so. Not far," he tells me.

I sit and think, and it doesn't take but a couple minutes for the idea to pop into my head.

"Can you look up the utility companies in that town?" I ask Declan who is already on his laptop.

I walk over and stand behind him while he looks up the information for me. He pulls up the number, and I quickly punch it into my cell phone and send the call.

"City of Gig Harbor," a lady answers.

"Yes, I'm calling on behalf of my brother, Asher Corre. He's been in an accident and is currently in the hospital and unresponsive. We don't know when he's going to pull out of his current state, so I wanted to make sure that his bill is up to date," I lie, and when I look to Declan, he gives me a smirk at my quick thinking.

"What was the name again?"

"Asher Corre."

I hear her typing at her keyboard before saying, "Yes. Our records show that there is currently a zero balance."

"Oh, good," I respond. "In the meantime, would it be possible to have a paper copy of his bill mailed to the house. I know he pays online, but since I don't have access to his passwords, I want to make sure that I can pay via snail mail."

"Of course. Yes. We can definitely have the bill mailed out to you."

"Great. And just to make certain, can you tell me the address you have on file?"

"I'm showing 19203 Fairview Lane with a zip code of 98332."

"That's correct. Thank you so much for your help."

I hang up, and Declan asks, "Did you get it?"

"That was too easy, and that woman was too trusting," I respond and then hand him the paper with the address.

He punches it into his computer. "There it is."

"Let's go!" I blurt with excitement, anxious to see if it's really him.

"Hold on," he says. "We can't just go showing up on his doorstep. He's hiding from something or someone, so we need to be careful for his sake and also yours."

He's right. I need to slow down for a second and think this through.

"I think we should get in the car and drive by. Check the place out. We need to verify that this is indeed your father first."

"Okay." I'll agree to just about anything at this point.

We're back in the car and driving to the address we were given, and soon enough, we're pulling into a nice suburban neighborhood with large, New England-style coastal houses lining the streets. Children are outside riding bikes and playing, and people are walking their dogs. Everyone looks happy, enjoying the last hours of the afternoon before the sun sets.

Declan slows the car when he turns onto Fairview but doesn't stop as we pass the house.

"It's this one. The two-story colonial," he says.

I look out the windshield at the beautiful house, and my stomach knots when I think about that being my father's home.

"I say we give it a couple hours, let it get darker, and then we come back. Maybe we can catch him coming home from work."

Anxiety mixed with every other emotion swarms in the pit of my gut. How can this possibly be happening when I've spent my whole life mourning his death? And now there's a possibility that I might see him tonight, that he could be alive. It's too much for me to understand and digest.

"Elizabeth?"

My throat restricts like a vice around the sadness inside, and I simply look at him and nod my approval to his plan.

We kill time and head to a local coffee joint. Declan makes a few business calls while I sip a hot tea and read some local Gazette magazine with all the town's happenings. We drove around for a bit before stopping here, and it seems like a quaint place to live. There isn't much, and everything is really spread out, but the neighborhoods are nice.

"We should get going," Declan says, and I quickly order another tea to go.

Very few words have been spoken today; my emotions are much too high to talk, and Declan hasn't pushed for conversation, which I appreciate. I need the silence right now.

Hopping back into the inconspicuous four-door car that

Declan rented, we head back over to the house. This time, when we enter the neighborhood, the sidewalks are empty and the streetlights are on. Windows are lit while the families that live inside are probably eating their dinners, and when we pull up to what we think is my dad's home, a few rooms are lit up as well.

We park along the curb on the opposite side of the street, and I stare into the windows, hoping to see something.

"Someone is in there," I whisper.

"I don't see any movement, but I agree. Too many lights are on for nobody to be home."

No cars are in the driveway, but that doesn't mean there aren't any in the garage.

"What do we do?"

"We wait," Declan responds. "See if anyone comes out or if anyone comes home."

So that's what we do.

We sit.

We wait.

My mind doesn't though. It keeps spinning thoughts around, plucking at my heartstrings. They swirl in a kaleidoscope of what-ifs. So many that I can't keep them inside, so I ask Declan, "What if he's married?" My voice trembles in despair. "I mean, this is too big a house for just one person, right?"

Declan looks at me and takes my hand, his face mottled in sorrow, and after a span of silence, he responds, "It's possible."

I look at the clock; it's past eight. We've been sitting out here for hours when bright headlights beam our way.

"Elizabeth," Declan murmurs urgently when the SUV pulls into the driveway.

I hold my breath as my heart pounds rapidly against my

chest, the sound filling my ears. Leaning forward, I see the driver's side door open, and when a man steps out, his back is to me. He reaches into the car and pulls out a briefcase at the same time the front door swings open and a young girl comes running out. And when that man turns around, I choke back an audible gasp, gripping Declan's hand tightly.

"That's him," he voices with a look of pure astonishment, but I'm in a state of shock when I see my daddy pull this child into his arms and hug her.

"Dad, why are you so late?" I hear her muffled voice from outside the car ask him, and tears force their way down my cheeks like knives.

"I'm sorry, princess. I got tied up with a client," he says, and I remember his voice like it was just this morning when I heard it last.

But it was *me* that was his princess.

Everything plays in slow motion, and when I look at his face from across the street, there isn't an ounce of uncertainty he's my dad. It's that same face, the same eyes, the same smile that visits me in my dreams. Except now he's older with a head of silver hair. The last I saw him he was in his thirties, and now he's nearing sixty.

But that smile . . .

The smile he gives that girl—his daughter—that was *mine*. It was always mine, and now it's *hers*.

I swore to myself that if I ever found him, I'd run to him, grab him, and never let him go. But when I see a woman and a boy walking out of the house, it's another slap in my face—he's no longer mine to run to. He's *theirs*.

It becomes too much.

I can't believe life would do this to me.

I want to die.

"Drive," I cry, my voice shaky and unrecognizable.

But Declan doesn't start the car.

"Elizabeth . . ."

"Get me out of here," I plead.

He releases my hand and starts the car, and as soon as he begins driving, I split wide open and sob—loud and ugly.

"Oh, my God, Declan. He has a daughter. He has a whole family!"

He reaches over to me and pulls my hand into his lap as all the years of longing burn up in roaring flames. I was disposed of by my dad; I don't exist in his life.

How could he do this?

How could he replace me?

Not only did my mother not want me, but I never thought my dad would feel the same way.

"I thought he loved me," I cry, and the tears feel like hot splashes of acid as they coat my cheeks and drip from my chin. The pain overwhelms like a cleaver to my heart, and everything I thought I knew feels like pure deception. I feel worthless and unloved by the man I've killed for.

I never gave up on life because of *him*.

I kept going because of *him*.

It was all for naught though. He's moved on when twenty-three years later I'm still living for him, dreaming of him, longing for him.

To feel like a nobody to the person who's your everybody is a jagged spike that skewers through the scar tissue of every one of life's blows that mark a permanent wound on my soul.

Suddenly this car is suffocating.

It's too small.

My skin is too tight.

The air is too thick.

I can't breathe.

"Pull over!" I demand, and he does instantly.

Ripping off my seatbelt, I leap out of the car and run.

I don't know where I'm going.

But I run as fast as I can.

I run hard, feet pounding the grass under my feet as I zip across a random field.

"Elizabeth!" Declan's voice echoes behind me, but I don't slow.

My legs begin to burn, my lungs are on fire, but I keep going.

I can hear Declan's feet racing behind me, and I push harder, screaming out my pain. I force it out of my lungs and into the night. The air whips through my hair, and the tears on my face chill against the wind.

"Elizabeth!" he calls again before his hand clutches my arm, sending me tumbling to the ground.

With my hands pressed against Earth's foundation, I tilt my head up to the heavens I can no longer believe in and scream. I scream so hard it hurts, ripping through my vocal cords, searing them, slicing them.

Declan wraps his whole body around mine, every one of his muscles flexing, cocooning me in a steel vice grip. And when my screams strain into an unbearable bleeding agony, I melt and crumple into Declan's warm body.

And I cry.

I cry like I did when I was five years old and watched my

daddy as he was being handcuffed and taken from me.

I cry because that's what you do when the person you love most in this world doesn't love you back.

Declan strokes my hair, petting me while he presses his lips to my ear, whispering gently, "Shh, baby."

I allow my mind to focus on his touch, on his smell, and on the sound of his voice. He rocks me in a slow sway, comforting me, and I grip my hands to his back, fisting his shirt with my fingers. And through my cries, I ask, "Why did he do this to me?"

"I don't know, darling," he responds. "But we'll find out. I'll get you answers."

"I don't understand why he never came for me. He's been alive this whole time—my whole life—and he never came for me."

"Maybe it's not what you think," he says, and I look into his eyes and weep, "How could you not come back for your child?"

He doesn't say anything else, he's probably scared he'll dig the knife in deeper. Instead, he stands and scoops me up in his arms, cradling me against his chest. As he walks us back to the car, I rest my head in the crook of his neck and let the tears fall.

He puts me into the car, buckles me in, and not another word is spoken. When we arrive back at our hotel room, he takes over. I'm dead inside, so he bathes me, brushes my teeth, and puts me to bed—all in silence—all while I cling to him.

Because without him, I don't exist—and I need to exist.

I'M WALKING ALONG a busy city street. I'm not sure what city I'm in, but it's filled with noisy cars and too many people to count. I don't know where I'm going, but I go. I follow the crowds. Maybe they know where they're headed.

We all stop at an intersection and wait for the crosswalk sign to light up. Leaning against a large flowerbed that hugs the perimeter of a tall building, I look down to see pink daisies. I grab one of the stems, pluck it from the soil, and watch as a little caterpillar emerges.

I smile when I see my friend.

"There you are, Elizabeth," he greets in his British accent.

"Carnegie!"

I lower my hand for him to crawl onto and then lift him up to my face.

"I've missed you," I tell him.

"It's been much too long."

I stumble on my feet when a bicyclist nearly sideswipes me. Looking back to my hand, Carnegie is no longer there. I scramble, skittering my eyes along the sidewalk, turning in circles.

"Carnegie?" I call out, but he's nowhere to be found.

I'm jostled again, this time by a man as he rushes past me.

"Hey!" I shout, and when the man turns to apologize, I see his face. "Dad?"

"Sorry, miss," my father says as if he doesn't recognize me.

"Dad! It's me!"

He turns, no longer acknowledging me, and I chase after him.

"Dad, wait! It's me!"

He's only walking, but somehow the gap between us widens, and I'm losing him. I whip around a corner and nearly lose my footing. When I right myself, I catch my reflection in the mirrored glass of a building.

I'm five years old and still wearing my glittery princess dress from our last tea party. Turning back in the direction my father was heading, I run while continuing to call out to him. I weave through the crowds of people, dodging elbows, and pushing my way through.

"Daddy!"

I finally catch up to him when he's stuck at a crosswalk.

"Dad," I say when I walk up to him.

He looks down at me with an aged face and silver hair. "Little girl, are you lost?"

"No, Daddy. It's me, your daughter."

He shakes his head. "No, little girl." He then points his finger to a blonde-haired child across the street waving at him. "That's my daughter over there."

I wake with a start.

The room is black.

My heavy breaths are the only sounds I hear.

I roll over, my body numb.

Declan is sound asleep, and when I slide out of bed to get a drink of water, I see that it's five in the morning. I'm rattled by my dream as I sip from a bottle of water while I sit in the living room. I stare out the window at the full moon, and it feels strange to know that only twenty minutes away, the same moon hangs above my dad. Although I doubt I ever cross his mind like he crosses mine.

I think about the girl in my dream—the same girl I saw him call *princess* last night in his driveway. She was young, maybe eight or so. And the more I think about her, the more my hands tingle in acerbic bitterness. Vile thoughts run rampant, thoughts of kidnapping her, thoughts of killing her.

My legs shake erratically, bouncing up and down at a rapid pace. I can't sit still. They're out there—he's out there—and I'm stuck in this hotel room. Thoughts about his new family fester.

I peer at Declan through the bedroom door, and he's still fast asleep. Gently, I close the door after slipping on a pair of pants and a top. Grabbing the keys to the car, I quietly sneak out of the room. He's going to be pissed when he wakes up to find that I'm gone, but if I told him what I'm about to do, he'd refuse. And I can't just sit in that room and drive myself crazy.

Once I'm in the car, I drive back to Gig Harbor and park along the street a few houses down from my dad's. His SUV is no longer in the driveway where he parked it last night. I'm not even sure what I'm doing here.

Time passes, the sun makes her appearance, and eventually the garage door opens. A car begins to back out and then stops halfway down the driveway. I sink down, worried I'll be seen, but keep watching. The driver's side window rolls down and the woman I saw last night hangs her head out and hollers, "Come on, kids!"

A few beats later the blonde girl and the brown-haired boy

run out from the garage with backpacks hanging from their shoulders. They hop in the back seat, and when the car starts driving away, I sit up and follow. When we turn out of the neighborhood, I make sure to follow with one car between us.

Hate rises in my soul for these people that my father's chosen over me. Good or bad, I don't give a shit—I want to hurt them. I want to take them away from him, then maybe he'll be so lonely that he'll finally want me.

My knuckles are white as my hands choke the steering wheel so hard it just might snap. The car pulls off into a strip shopping center, and I follow, parking several spots down from them. The kids hop out of the car, cash in their hands, and run into a smoothie shop while the woman stays in the vehicle.

Without much thought, and honestly, just not caring, I get out of my car. I walk past the woman and see she's paying no attention as she's chatting away on her phone. She's blonde as well and appears many years younger than my dad, and I wish I had a brick to throw through her windshield to smash her pretty little face.

The bell above the door jingles when I step inside the smoothie shop. The two kids are watching the blenders mix up their drinks.

"What can I get for you this morning?" the guy behind the register asks in a much too peppy tone for it being so early in the morning.

I pick a random drink from the menu on the wall and shove him some cash.

"Hailey," one of the employees calls out, and the girl runs to grab her drink.

Her name's Hailey. *How fucking precious.*

When I see her walking to the door, I fake clumsiness and bump into her, sending her smoothie to splatter all over the floor.

"Oh, I am so sorry. I wasn't paying any attention at all."

"It's okay," she says. "Accidents happen."

I grab a wad of napkins, and with her help, we do our best to clean up the sticky mess

"Let me get you another drink. What flavor did you have?" I offer.

"You don't have to do that. I can get more money from my mom."

"I insist."

She tells me her drink and I place the order.

I reach out my hand and introduce myself. "I'm Erin, by the way."

She shakes my hand enthusiastically, and giggles, saying, "My name is Hailey."

"I'm going back out to the car," her brother announces as he takes his smoothie with him to the exit. "Hurry up; I don't want to be late to school."

"And that," Hailey says, "Is my annoying older brother, Steve."

Steve. My dad passed his name down to that little fucker.

"You look like you're all ready for school. What grade are you in?" I ask while we wait for her drink.

"Fifth grade."

"Wow. Big girl on campus. So how old does that make you?"

"Eleven."

Her perfect voice, her perfect hair, her perfect clothes all make me want to ball my fist up and slam it through her perfect smile.

"Hailey," the employee calls out, and I fight the overwhelming urge to grab her and run.

"I gotta go. Thanks for the smoothie, Erin." She's so polite it irritates me to the point I want to claw my own skin from my bones.

She practically skips out the door, leaving me to watch their car as it pulls out and drives away.

I snap around when there's a tap on my shoulder.

"I'm sorry, I didn't mean to startle you," the employee says as he holds out a cup. "I called your name, but I guess you didn't hear me."

Without a word, I turn away from him and walk out the door as he stands there like an asshole, still holding my drink.

I hate everyone in this shit town.

Sitting in my car, I can't bring myself to drive just yet. She's eleven years old and has the life I was supposed to have. I was supposed to be the bubbly and polite girl who wore the pretty clothes and grabbed a smoothie before heading off to school. I was supposed to be her. Instead, when I was eleven, I was tied up to a garment rod and locked away in a closet for days on end. I was in the darkness with no food or water, left to piss and shit on myself. And when I wasn't in the closet, I was down in that dank basement being molested, raped, sodomized, pissed on, beaten, and whipped. I wasn't skipping out the goddamn door with my Raspberry Paradise smoothie. Her biggest struggle in life is having an annoying older brother.

I should've grabbed her when I had the chance.

Anger does nothing but ferment in my bones. It aches and pricks from the inside out, and I ball my hands, pounding them against the steering wheel as I growl between my clenched teeth.

When I look up, I see an elderly lady staring at me in horror as she walks on by.

She has no idea that she's staring at a monster.

Smoothing my hair back off my forehead, I straighten myself and start the car. It's edging on eight o'clock, and I need to get back to the hotel.

I stand outside of our room and prepare myself for the wrath of Declan before opening the door.

"Where the fuck have you been?" he seethes as soon as I walk in. "Tell me it's not what I'm thinking. Tell me you didn't go back to that house."

Keeping my cool so I don't rile him up any more than he already is, I admit, "I went back to the house."

"Jesus Christ! What were you thinking?" he snaps, grabbing my arms and shaking me.

"I don't know, but I had to go. I knew you wouldn't allow it, so I snuck out."

He shoves me over to the couch and pushes me down, releasing my arms. I watch as he paces the room a couple times before walking back over to me. He takes a seat on the coffee table and faces me. His jaw is locked, a tell to his immense anger. I knew how much my sneaking away would affect him. Declan has to hold all the power for him to feel safe, and I stole that from him this morning.

"It's not what you think." I attempt to mollify him.

"Tell me, since you seem to know everything about me. Tell me what it is I'm thinking." He throws his derisive words in my face.

"I had to see them. I had to know more."

"*Them?*" he questions, growing more irritated. "You mean

his kids?"

I nod.

"Christ, Elizabeth," he barks, standing and walking away from me.

"Stop yelling at me!" I snap, getting off the couch and stepping up to him. "You're pissed, I get it! But the expectation you have for me to just sit and be patient is something I can't do."

"You *can't* or you *won't*?"

"I'm not apologizing, if that's what you're after."

I watch him grind his teeth as he glares down at me, and I turn this around on him, saying, "Why don't you tell *me* something . . . If this were reversed, and it were your mother in this situation, tell me you'd be okay just hanging back. Tell me you wouldn't act on every single one of your instincts."

His eyes pierce mine, and I push him even more.

"Tell me you could restrain yourself and stay away."

We meet each other's opposition, neither one of us backing down.

"He's my dad, so don't you dare yell at me and belittle me for acting on my desperation, because you'd do the same thing."

I turn to walk away from him, and when I do, he finally speaks.

"You won't defy me again. Do you understand?"

I look back at him and respond, "Then I need you to bend and trust me. I snuck away because I knew you'd refuse to allow me to go. All I'm asking is for you to at least try to see things my way every once in a while."

"Come here," he orders, and I obey, walking back over to him. He takes my face in his hands, telling me, "I'll try and bend for you."

"Thank you," I respond with an appeased smile.

"You will be punished, so I wouldn't be smiling if I were you," he threatens, and I don't contest.

Declan needs this to feel in control, and I want to give him that because it's what secures him. He depends on it. He can't function without it.

"I want you on the ground on all fours with your pants pulled down to your knees."

He lashes his voice out in anger, and I turn my back to him, positioning myself as instructed. It might be debasing for most, but I understand his need for this. It's how his life has molded him to be, and I'm the perfect one to give him this outlet that he's been deprived of in the past. I'm sure the women he's been with previously have valued their bodies in a way I don't. And because I love him so much, I have no problem handing myself over to him in this way.

I hear him move around the room, and then he kneels down in front of me to tie my wrists together with one of his ties.

"Tell me why I'm punishing you."

I crane my neck to look at him, and answer, "Because I snuck off and took the control away from you."

"Do you know what that did to me?"

"Yes."

He then stands and moves behind me.

"Keep your eyes on the floor," he commands, and I hear something rattling before being set on the ground. "Spread your knees."

I do, and I'm instantly greeted by the piercing pain of an ice cube being shoved into my pussy. And then another and another and another and another.

I cry out in blistering pain and then he begins to spank my ass with a force so great I have to tense my whole body up to keep myself from falling over. The ice feels like I'm being sliced with razors from the inside, and I know I should be focusing on the pain that's radiating from my ass because it's so minimal compared to what's happening inside my pussy.

With each welting blow he delivers, I scream out as the ice begins to melt and the water spills out of me and runs down my thighs.

"Tell me you're my property," he grits, and I instantly respond, "I'm your property."

THWACK!

"Tell me who owns you."

"You own me."

THWACK!

"Tell me you love me."

"I love you, Declan."

THWACK!

"On your elbows," he barks, and the moment I lower myself, his mouth is on my pussy, sucking out the melted ice from inside me.

His hot tongue is an erotic contrast to the freezing shards, and I let go of a heady moan while he buries his face between my legs. My mind rushes in waves of mania at the infliction of a multitude of sensations that I didn't even notice that he's now fucking me with his cock.

I close my eyes when the whole world blurs, and all that matters is this moment—having our two bodies blended as one—and it's only together that we're whole.

twenty-three

THE ICE BUCKET and tie still remain on the floor from earlier. Declan has refused to let me clean myself up, so I sit and wait for him to finish his shower. I decide to log onto the laptop and search to see if Hailey has any social media accounts. When no hits come up, I move on to search her brother, Steve, which brings me to a link for a Steve Corre in Gig Harbor, Washington.

Clicking the link, I pull up his page. His profile picture is of him and a few of his buddies. I start clicking on different tabs on his page, but there's no real information aside from his birthday, which lets me know he's thirteen years old.

It's not until I open one of his photo albums that the vile hate from earlier resurfaces. I scroll through picture after picture of family photos, my dad being in most of them. Photos of family vacations, birthday parties, holidays fill the albums—all the things I never got a chance to experience.

Once I was in Posen with Pike, I never got a birthday party, and most holidays I'd find myself locked in the closet so Carl and

Bobbie wouldn't have to deal with me. Pike would always manage to steal or use his drug money to buy me something small, but aside from those private gift exchanges in my bedroom, we never celebrated anything.

I despise these kids for the life my dad has given them, the life I never had. I look at their smiles, and I want to slit their throats. And then there's my dad. Enlarging a photo with him in it, I zoom in on his face. His eyes are still the same, even though the crinkles in the corners from when he smiles have deepened. He no longer has the scruff of a beard, exchanging it for a clean-shaven face. When I close my eyes, I can see the younger him in vivid color. I can hear his laughter. I can smell his cologne.

God, I miss him so much.

Opening my eyes, I'm greeted by this stranger who wears the same face. I don't know this man—Asher Corre. My heart double beats in love and anger. I love my dad, the man who danced with me, sang to me, and laughed with me. But I hate this man on the computer screen. I hate him for wearing the mask of my father, because he's nothing like my dad. My dad loved me beyond love, and *this* man, I don't even exist in his world. I'm nothing but an evaporated memory.

"What are you looking at?" Declan questions when he walks into the room, fresh from the shower dressed in navy slacks, a fitted light blue button-down, and the same black belt he used to restrain me a few days ago.

"Looking at family portraits," I respond, and he tilts his head in curiosity.

When he sits next to me, I can smell the cardamom from his shampoo. Even in the midst of everything going on around us and our quarrel this morning, I feel the need to be close to him.

He is already sliding the computer from my lap when he asks, "Where did you find these?"

"It's his son's social media page."

"His son? How did you even know how to find this?"

"Because I followed them. I got his name from his sister, Hailey."

"I need you to tell me what happened this morning."

"Can you control your anger?" I snark, to which he responds, "You're testing your limits today with that smart mouth of yours. Tell me what happened."

I go through everything that occurred, from following the car to what was said between Hailey and me.

"You shouldn't have ever approached that girl," he scolds. "She's just a kid."

"There are worse monsters out there than me, Declan. If I could handle my life at eleven, then surely she can handle a conversation in a smoothie shop."

"That girl is a part of your dad."

I look at him, angry that he would go there, and snap, "But I'm *all* of him."

"I'm on your side here."

"Then stop defending that family."

"I need you to see things rationally though," he says.

"Nothing about this whole situation is rational, Declan."

He backs off and turns his attention back to the computer, scrolling through the photos. When there's one I want to look at, I tell him to stop. It isn't until a few more photos pass that I realize the kid tags his location when he posts.

"Scroll slowly," I murmur to Declan when I lean in to get a closer look.

"What are you doing?"

"He tags his location in his pictures," I tell him, and we strike gold. "Stop. Click on that one."

Declan enlarges a photo of my dad and his son that has the comment: *Spending my day at work with Dad.*

"Enterprise Brokerage and Realty," Declan reads off.

Declan opens up another window and types the business name into the search bar, and up pops their website with my father's picture on the main page.

"He runs his own firm," he says. "We've got a point of contact now."

"Do we just call him?"

"No. We need to find a way to get him to come to us. But, listen, we have to be careful about this. Whatever he's hiding from is big. I mean, your case worker, a state employee, came to you and told you he died. The man even has a grave site, right?"

"Yes. In Illinois," I say. "I went to the cemetery. He has a gravestone and everything."

"So, this isn't some man who just skipped town. This is a man who needed to kill his identity."

"How do we do this?"

Declan takes a moment to think and then pulls out his phone. "I'll just schedule a meeting with him. There's nothing that links you and me that he would be able to find out about. We've never even been photographed together."

I nod, and when he dials, I tell him, "Put it on speakerphone," because I need to hear his voice.

With each ring, my pulse quickens, and then the line connects.

"Enterprise Brokerage and Realty, how can I help you?"

"Is Asher Corre available?" Declan asks, his accent seeming to catch the woman off guard.

"Oh . . . um, yes. Whom shall I say is calling?" she says, and I roll my eyes at Declan when her whole voice changes in reaction to his voice.

"You can tell him this is Declan McKinnon with McKinnon International Development."

"Just one moment."

I'm practically holding my breath while we wait, and then he picks up the call, his voice crystal clear.

"Asher Corre here."

I bring my hands to cover my mouth when I hear the voice I never thought I'd hear again.

"Good afternoon. This is Declan McKinnon, owner of McKinnon International Development. I have to apologize for the short notice, but I'm in town for a few days and was hoping to discuss a possible land purchase for commercial development."

"What line of commercial development are you in?"

"Hospitality on the high-end scale."

"So I see. I just pulled you up on my computer. McKinnon, is that of Scottish descent?" he asks Declan, and I can't believe he's actually having a conversation with my dad. Declan responds, and then my father continues, "I can start pulling some locations to email you?"

"Call me old-fashioned, but I hope you don't mind my preference to conduct business in person rather than over the phone. I want to establish that you're the right man to be working with. After all, if a purchase is made, you'll be receiving a substantial commission. I want to make sure it's going to someone with integrity."

"I couldn't agree with you more. I'll tell you what, how does your evening look tonight?"

"I have a few emails that need attending to, but other than that, I'm free."

"Would six o'clock work?"

"That works. I've had a tiring couple of days, so why don't we meet at The Pearl's Edge where I'm staying. I'm in the Presidential suite."

He doesn't even hesitate when he responds, "I'll see you at six, Mr. McKinnon."

I watch Declan end the call and set the phone down. "His voice . . ." I start and then lose my words.

"Are you okay?"

I can't speak for a while as I try to digest hearing my father on the phone. It doesn't even feel real, and to know that he'll be here in only a few hours is something I'm unable to process.

"Darling?"

"I never thought I'd hear that voice again. I believed it was gone forever, and now . . ."

"I know. You don't have to try to put it into words."

"I don't even know how to feel. One minute I'm relieved he's alive, and the next I'm so furious. But now, he's coming here, and I'm excited and terrified."

"There's no right way to feel. I think the most important thing is to allow yourself to feel it all," he says.

"I just need you to hold me right now," I tell him.

I curl up in his arms and close my eyes while he runs his hands up and down my back. I open myself up to his comfort and take all I can. It's a myriad of extremities in my heart and head, but somehow, Declan is powerful enough to temper the storm in me.

His warmth is able to relax me enough that eventually I drift off, and when I wake, he's still holding me. I look out the windows and see the sky rippled in waves of pinks and oranges.

"How are you feeling?" Declan asks softly.

My voice is sleepy when I respond, "That's a hard question to answer."

He leans down and kisses me. "Why don't you freshen up before he gets here?"

What does one wear when they meet their dead father for the first time after twenty-three years? After I shower, I dig through my suitcases that I never got around to unpacking yesterday and pull out a pair of black pants and a flowy green top. I busy myself, focusing on making sure I look nice for him; maybe it's me subconsciously distracting myself or maybe it's because I honestly want to look pretty for my dad.

I don't really know.

I dry my hair and fix it with free-flowing waves and then apply my usual light makeup and sweep a little gloss across my lips. I slip on a pair of black flats before giving myself a lookover in the mirror.

My stomach twists in nervousness. I have no idea what I'm going to say to him or how I'm going to react. I've dreamt endlessly about magically getting my dad back, and now that it's here and it's real, I'm suddenly terrified.

"You look perfect."

When I turn to Declan leaning against the threshold, I give him a tight smile. "Are you sure?" I ask, suddenly feeling self-conscious.

"I know you're nervous and worried, but try not to psych

yourself out."

"What if I can't do this?"

"And what if you can?" he counters. "Come here."

I walk into his arms and hold on to him.

"You're trembling," he notes. "Why don't I get you a drink to help with your nerves?"

I follow him into the living room and before we make it over to the wet bar, there's a knock on the door.

Stopping dead in my tracks, all the air is sucked out of my lungs, and I'm momentarily paralyzed. Declan looks back to me, and I'm in shock.

"That's him."

twenty-four

My whole body freezes, and I swear my heart skips a beat or two. I'm wide-eyed as Declan looks at me. I can't speak. My skin pricks in goose bumps

Declan places his hands on my cheeks and tells me with sure-fire intensity, "You can do this."

Nodding my head, I speak around the lump lodged in my throat. "Don't let go of me."

"I won't."

Hand in hand, we walk over to the door. Each step I take feels like a marathon's worth of strides. My heart tremors, pumping erratically beneath my bones.

Another knock.

I reach out my jittery hand, and a wave of nausea hits hard when I hold my breath and open the door.

It's him.

His eyes meet mine, and I can't speak. I can literally reach out and touch him, but I don't. I'm too scared he might disappear

211

if I make any sudden movements. He looks at me in confusion. His eyes give a little flick, and I wonder if there's maybe a hint of recognition.

"Dad."

My voice falters and his eyes widen in curiosity, but it's when that very look morphs into astonishment that I know he knows. In one fluid movement, he takes a step towards me and pulls me into his arms.

"Oh, my God," he breathes in disbelief, and I wrap my free arm around him as the tears start falling. "Elizabeth?"

"It's me, Dad," I tell him as my emotions swell to ungodly proportions.

His hold on me is the strongest I've felt in my whole life. And all of a sudden, my fears, my reservations, my hatred, it vanishes. Declan lets go of my other hand, and I cling it around my dad. His back quakes in my hold, and I hear the click of Declan closing the door as the two of us cry.

He cradles my head in his deft hand, the same way he did when I was a little girl, and chokes out, "My baby princess."

He draws back, bracing my head in his hands, and scans my face.

"My God, you're *so* beautiful," he says thickly.

His words mend wounds, and when my face crumples in sobs, I drop my head and he pulls me back against his chest. My body heaves as I release years and years of agony. I want to speak a thousand words, but I can't stop crying. I can't stop clinging. I simply can't let go.

"Let me look at you again," he says when he pulls back and dips his head down to my level.

He's blurry colors and lines, and when I blink, he comes

into clarity only to be dissolved all over again. Tears continue to flood and fall as he wipes my cheeks with his thumbs. My hands clutch to his sides, and I painfully weep. "I've missed you so much, Dad."

"Oh, sweetheart, I've missed you even more. The pain of losing you . . . I feel it every second of every day."

"Then why? Why didn't you ever come for me?"

"Oh, princess," he sighs, hanging his head. "I wanted to. So many times I wanted to."

"Then why didn't you?"

Something inside me shifts, and all the pain and anger begins to rise through the enormous joy I feel from being in his arms. It collides and battles, and when he looks up at me, I take a step back and snap, "You just left me!"

Declan takes my hand as my father stares at me, drowning in visible shame.

"Darling . . ."

"I needed you," I sling at him. "I've needed you since the day I lost you!"

"I'm so sorry, sweetheart. Why don't we sit down and talk?"

I turn to Declan, shaking my head, and he encourages, "Nothing you say will be wrong. I won't let you fall apart, okay?"

Leaning my head against his chest, he strokes my hair back and kisses my head before placing his hand on my back. "Let's go sit."

We walk over to the living room, and I take a seat next to my dad on the couch as Declan sits on the other side of me, extending his hand out to my dad, saying, "I'm Declan, by the way."

My father shakes his hand, responding, "Asher."

"That's *not* your name," I accuse, my voice still shuddering through consuming emotions as I look into his eyes. I try with everything I have to pull myself together, but I can't stop the deluge of new tears that fall.

Declan places his hand on my leg, and my dad holds my two hands in his. I watch as he takes in a deep breath before saying, "I'm not sure what to say or where to begin. I never thought I'd ever be sitting next to you, looking into your eyes, holding your hands, hearing your voice."

"You could've been. All these years, you could've had me. But instead, you left me to battle this world on my own."

"You have to believe me when I tell you that's the last thing I ever wanted to do."

"But you did it anyway."

He drops his head again, and I can see his eyes well up.

"I need you to tell me why," I insist. "I need to know why you abandoned me."

"I didn't abandon you, sweetheart."

He blinks and a couple tears skitter down his aged cheeks.

"You did!" I lash out, yanking my hands from his. "You're here! Alive! And living a fucking lie!" I suck in a ragged breath, stand up, and pace across the room before crying out, "You have a whole family! I saw them! A son and a fucking daughter!" Gripping my head with my hands, I stand and face him. "You just . . . you just replaced me as if I never existed. As if I never even mattered."

"No one could *ever* replace you," he asserts, standing up and walking over to me.

"I'm just a forgotten nobody."

"I've never forgotten you," he says as he starts to unbutton the top of his dress shirt. "You've always been with me."

As his collar and shirt begin to fall open, I see the ink of a tattoo, and when he exposes his chest, I stop breathing.

There, across the span of his chest, from shoulder to shoulder, is my name branded on his skin in large script.

"Even if I wanted to, I could never forget about you."

I reach out and run my fingers over the letters of my name. "When did you . . . ?"

"Shortly after I was sent to prison. I had my cellmate do it."

I press my hand to his chest and feel his heart beat into my palm.

"I don't understand. They told me you died in there."

He buttons his shirt back up, asking, "Will you let me explain?"

I nod and he holds my hand as we walk back over to the couch where Declan is still sitting. My father keeps my hand in his and Declan wraps his arm around my waist as I face my dad.

"They told you why I went to prison, right?"

"Gun trafficking."

He nods. "Seven years into my sentence, the feds came to meet with me. It seems that one of the guns was used to assassinate four government officials from the United States Gun Trafficking Task Force while they were in Argentina to bust one of their bigger drug cartels," he explains. "All the guns that went through me were inspected to ensure the serial numbers had been properly shaved off, but when you're working with the street runners, mistakes are bound to happen. Anyway, the feds offered me a plea deal. I hand over the names in exchange for an immediate release. I knew the risk, but I would've walked through a firing squad to get you back," he says fervently, and I strengthen my hold on his hand.

"So what happened?"

"Turns out, it was a ruse," he reveals. "Once I handed over the names, that was it, I was given two options: go immediately into witness protection, or go back to my cell. If I went back to my cell, I would've been dead in a matter of days; I was a nark and some of those guys I was in there with were in some way affiliated with the names I had just given the feds." He takes my other hand in his and looks at me intently. "They used you to get to me, princess. I knew from that moment that I'd never see you again, and it felt like I was being murdered anyway, because my life didn't exist without you in it."

"And your gravesite?"

"Since the threat level on my life was so great, the feds thought it best to stage my death. I begged them to let me take you into the program with me, but they refused. My hands were tied. A part of me thought it would be better for you that way though. I figured it would give you closure instead of me simply disappearing with no trace." He takes a moment to collect himself before saying, "And here you are. All grown up and so gorgeous."

I continue to shed heartache as memories from the day I was told he died fall from my eyes and down my face. I remember lying in bed with Pike. He held me for hours as I sobbed.

"They assured me you were in a good home and that you even had a foster brother."

Declan's hand suddenly constricts on my leg; he thinks I'm going to tell my dad about my suffering. A part of me wants to because it was a lie—I wasn't in a good home—and the resentment of what could've been festers in me. I want to tell him about the torture I endured so I can slap him in the face with it.

I'm furious that I was cheated from the good life he assumed I had.

But I'm not going to tell him—I can't. I have to lie, because telling him the truth would serve no purpose. The past is done, and it can't be changed, it would only hurt him to know, and in the end, I just want his love.

"They told me you were happy and thriving."

I muster up a smile. "Yes, I was happy."

"And your foster parents . . . they were good to you?"

"Mmm hmm," I respond and nod. "I was well taken care of."

The lie is a rusted spike through my veins; it's nearly debilitating to see the relief in his eyes.

"Are you all still close?"

"No. They actually died," I tell him. "And so did my brother." And the tears that puddle in my eyes from the mere mention of Pike are taken by my dad as sorrow for my whole foster family. They aren't—they're solely for Pike. What he doesn't know and will never know is that all three of them died because of me—by my hands.

"I'm so sorry. Do you have other family?"

"Only Declan," I tell him.

"Are you two married?"

"No," Declan answers. "We live together though."

"Close?"

"Declan's home is in Scotland, but we recently moved to London."

"Wow. That sounds amazing," he says with a sullen expression. "Can I ask how you found me?"

"I saw your face on the news," I tell him. "Someone Declan

and I know was able to get ahold of the passenger manifest. It took a while for me to discover that Asher Corre was you—was *me*."

"Rose Archer," he murmurs. "Like I said, you've always been with me."

My chin quivers, and I have to ask, "Those are your biological kids, aren't they?"

"Yes."

I look away from my dad. It hurts too much to think they are getting everything I was deprived of.

"I met Gillian shortly after I entered the program. I was so low from losing you, and she helped me stand back up."

"She knows about me?"

"I had to lie to her. She knows I had a daughter named Elizabeth, but I had to tell her that you . . ." His words stall, and I pick them up, positive of what they are and resume for him, "You told her I died, didn't you?"

He nods. "I would've never done so, but the tattoo . . . it's what I was instructed by the government to tell people if anyone were to ask."

"You love her?"

"I do."

"And you gave your son your name—your *real* name."

"I did."

"And your . . . your dau—" I stammer through mounting anguish. "Your daughter . . . you lo—"

"She didn't replace you," he insists.

"But you love her?"

"I do. But don't you dare think for a second that it's the same love I have for you. It isn't. I will *never* love anyone the way

I love you."

"You call her princess," I state. "I heard you call her princess."

"You heard me?"

"I was parked across the street from your house last night,"
I confess. "You were late getting home."

"Sweetheart—" he starts and then stops when I drop my
head and start crying.

He wraps his hand behind my head, and I lean against him
while Declan rests his reassuring hands on my shoulders. My father's lips press against the top of my head, the same way Declan
often does, and I squeeze my dad's hands.

How can I finally be with him and at the same time feel so
lost? Feel so excluded?

I want to scream out how unfair this is the way a child would,
but I hold it inside.

"You won't be able to tell them about me, will you?"

"No."

I look back up at him, and with a defeated shrug of my
shoulders, I ask, "So what now?"

He presses my hands to his chest, affirming, "You are my
daughter. Nothing will ever change that. You are the beat of my
heart. It's always been you."

Lifting up on my knees, I sling my arms around his neck and
latch on to him as he holds me close.

"I love you so much, Dad."

"I love you too, baby girl," he responds. "I love you too."

We embrace each other for as long as it takes for me to cry
out all the tears my body has to give, and he never loosens his
hold on me. He remains constant, never attempting to pull away

from me, all the while repeating how much he loves me, how much he's missed me, and how much he's dreamt about me.

And when nothing else remains except swollen eyes and stinging cheeks, I let go of his neck.

"Can I see you tomorrow?" he asks.

"I'm scared to let you go," I tell him. "What if you don't come back?"

"I'll come back. I put my life on that promise, okay?"

"Okay," I respond, but the fear remains. Terrified that this could possibly be the last time I see him, I grab him and kiss his cheek.

I know all too well how much life can change in an instant.

"I'll be here at nine a.m."

He stands and pulls me up with him, giving me another strong hug. This time, he kisses my forehead and then my cheek and then my forehead again.

"No more tears," he says as he walks to the door with me tucked under his arm.

"Promise me you're coming back."

He lifts my chin, saying, "I promise," and then plants a kiss on top of my head again.

"Declan," my dad acknowledges, "take care of her tonight, will you?"

"Every day of my life, sir."

My father hands me off to Declan, and I trade the warmth of my father for the warmth of my love. I can't stomach the thought of watching him walk out the door, so I bury my head against Declan's chest until I hear the click of the door closing.

twenty-five

When you make a wish on a star and it delivers, serving its purpose, then what happens? Does it die? Does it go on to serve someone else's wish? Maybe it rejoices, exploding into a million shimmering, dusting sparkles that flicker down through the stratosphere. It could be that those very particles are what create hope in this world. And maybe that's why I always carried a little piece of that star with me. As much as I wanted to give up on hope, as much as I thought the notion of it was a crock of shit, a miniscule piece of it always lingered in me.

It's a rainy morning as I move about, again full of jittery nerves, and get ready to see my dad—my wish upon a star. Declan has ordered up a tray of food, but I'm too wound up to eat. And I'd be lying if I said I wasn't also scared that he wouldn't show up. I'm all too familiar with Murphy's Law. That law has plagued my life continuously, so why wouldn't it do the same now? Nothing in this world is resistant to change. It can happen in a split second, with no warning at all.

But my mood shifts as soon as I hear the knock on the door.

I look over to Declan, and he wraps up the business call he's on.

This time, I don't feel like passing out. Instead, there's an air of effervescence when I open the door and see my dad standing there with a bouquet of pink daisies. I smile with a wisp of a laugh when he steps inside and closes the door.

"I hope you still like daisies," he says when he hands them to me, and I'm in his arms the next second, responding, "They're my favorite."

Neither of us rushes the embrace. We settle in it and allow ourselves to bask in the comfort we were both robbed of for over twenty years. I inhale, taking in his scent, which reminds me of the past. How is it that I can still remember the way he smelled all those years ago? But I do remember, and it's the same now as it was then. My eyes fall shut as I revel in the moment, a moment that most would fleet through. Yet, when someone has been so deprived, they understand the importance a single touch can hold.

"I couldn't sleep at all last night," he tells me, still holding me in his strong arms, allowing me to decide when to let go, but I'm not ready just yet.

"Me neither."

After another minute or so, I finally loosen my arms and pull back.

His eyes roam my face for a moment before he finally says, "I just can't get over how much you've grown and how much time has actually passed."

"Are you saying I look old?" I quip, making him laugh, and it's such a beautiful sound.

"Old? Are you kidding. Have you seen this gray mop on me?"

I smile big. "You wear silver well."

"Distinguished?"

"Very distinguished."

"Good morning, sir," Declan greets as he approaches us.

"Declan," he responds, shaking Declan's outstretched hand. "Please, call me Asher."

I flick my head to my dad, and he catches my shift immediately, apologizing, "I'm sorry. Habit after nearly fifteen years." He then looks to Declan again and corrects to appease me. "Call me Steve."

"I ordered up some breakfast," Declan says and leads my dad to the dining table that seats eight.

"This room is impressive," he notes as we take our seats next to each other.

I lay the daisies on the table in front of me, suddenly feeling nervous. My dad senses my unease right away, takes my hand in his, and smiles at me. "I'm nervous too."

"You are?"

"Yes," he says through an awkward laugh.

"Steve, would you like some coffee?"

"Sounds great, Declan. Thank you."

Declan pours a mug of coffee for my dad, a tea cup of hot water for me, and then takes a seat across the table from us.

I pluck a buttery croissant from the platter in front of us and then dunk a bag of tea into my cup. The silence between us is thick, and when I look up, my dad is staring at me over the rim of his mug, which makes me pause.

"What?"

With a grin on his face, he shakes his head and answers, "The last time I saw you, you were sipping make-believe tea, and now here you are, all grown up, drinking the real thing."

I smile through the heartbreaking memories of that day. "And I remember you licking imaginary frosting from your imaginary cupcake. You didn't even use a napkin."

"You remember that?"

I nod as the ache inflames. "I remember every detail from that day."

My eyes brim with tears, and I fight hard to keep them from falling.

"I'm so sorry that had to happen in front of you. It killed me to know that was your last image of me."

"You're here now." I need to steer away from what will ultimately break me if I think about it too much. "And oddly enough," I add with a smirk, "this kind of reminds me of that last tea party. I mean, I don't have a sparkly princess dress on, but I've got my pink daisies, tea, snacks, and you."

"True," he says. "But back then, I was your prince. And it seems that position is no longer available."

I turn to Declan who comically lifts his coffee cup in accomplished pride and exaggerated dignity, and I laugh.

"He's seems like a suitable replacement, right?" my dad jokes.

"He fits the role perfectly."

"Since that's the case, an interrogation is in order, don't you think?" my dad says.

"I'm up for the challenge, Steve."

I take a sip of my tea, thoroughly enjoying the fact that the three of us can make light of the situation at hand, and at the same time, knowing I can share this huge piece of my past with Declan.

"So, I did indeed look you up on the Internet. You're quite accomplished for being in your early thirties."

"I'm a hard worker."

"What took you from Scotland to Chicago?"

"My father had done a few developments in the States before I graduated with my master's degree. I had always been interested in the business, so I moved here and worked with him for a little while before going out on my own. I found a great location in Chicago and decided to go for it."

"Lotus, right?"

"That's right," Declan says.

"It's an exquisite hotel," I note to my dad.

"But now you're in London?"

Declan takes a sip of his coffee before answering. "Yes. The build won't begin for another year or so. I just bought the property and am currently working with the architects on the scope and concept for what I'm wanting out of the building."

"You enjoy what you do?"

"I love it. I'm a hands-on man and the job lends itself to fulfill that capability. It's also a great feeling to see the process from beginning to end."

"I can only imagine the pride you must feel to see your ideas come to life," he says before asking, "Tell me, how did the two of you meet?"

"I met him at the grand opening gala," I tell him.

Seeming satisfied after grilling Declan, he then turns to me. "What about you? What is it that you do? Did you go to college?"

I've already lied to him and allowed him to believe I had

a good childhood and lived in a loving foster home, which he naïvely took for truth, but I need him to believe it. I refuse to punish him with my reality, since he's not to blame for his absence in my life. We were both robbed from each other and lied to, but I keep the lies alive and tell him some half-truths.

"My foster parents died before I was old enough to attend college. I lived with my brother for most of my life because of the financial situation we both found ourselves in. I did take a few classes here and there, but ultimately never got the chance to seriously pursue anything that would lead to a career."

"Well, you must have done something right to be in the midst of people who were attending this gala. Doesn't seem like something anyone off the streets could just attend; the hotel seems quite exclusive and private," my dad says.

"I had a few friends in that circle," I lie—sort of.

"So, how long ago was that?"

"A little over four months," Declan responds.

"That's quick."

"Maybe for some," Declan tells him. "But look at her—I'd be a fool not to snatch her up."

"You make it sound almost like a hostage situation," I tease.

"It's love, darling," he says and then adds, feigning an evil grin, "It takes everyone hostage."

We continue to talk, and my dad and I do our best not to dwell on all that was stolen from us and enjoy that we have each other now. I suggest getting out and going for a walk, and he informs me that, even after all these years, he is still at risk and has random surveillance as a safeguard—a service provided by witness protection for those whom the government sees fit.

"Even after all these years?" I ask him.

"People in the circle I was working in don't take what I did lightly. Lives were lost after I gave the feds what they wanted. I turned my back on them, and now I'm marked in vendetta for life. Those affected will seek out their revenge until one of us is dead."

I don't doubt him, because I'm one of them. I will forever carry the torch of vengeance for those who wronged me and stole from me. Even though I have my father right here in flesh and bone, I'll still seek revenge from those who took him from me in the first place.

His phone rings, and when he pulls it from his pocket, he looks up at me with an apologetic expression. "I'm sorry. I have to take this."

At the same time, Declan also receives a call and excuses himself to the bedroom. My father walks to the other room when he accepts the call, but it isn't far enough to keep me from hearing parts of his conversation.

"I'm with a client . . . I won't be . . . I know . . . I love you too."

"Was that your wife?" I question with a tinge of disdain leaking through after he hangs up.

When he looks at me from across the room, he's visibly uncomfortable. "Umm . . . yes."

I stand and don't say anything. The light mood from earlier is now vexatious as real life intrudes on our clandestine gathering.

"I'm going to have to leave soon."

"Why?" My chest sizzles in irritation when jealousy rears its ugly head.

"Hailey has a recital today."

How fucking lovely.

"You've missed a million things in my life, you can't miss one of hers?"

His forehead creases in confliction, but my resentment spares no lenience.

"It isn't fair," I say thickly.

"I agree, but it's what we have to deal with."

"So . . ." I begin and then pause when Declan walks back into the room.

"Is everything okay?" he asks, sensing the tension, and my father responds, "I have to leave."

"It seems his other daughter has a recital that he can't miss," I tell Declan while keeping my eyes on my dad.

Declan places a supporting hand on the small of my back, and I continue what I was saying. "So, how does this all work then? I mean, if you can't tell them about me . . ."

"I don't really know, sweetheart."

"I mean, when I leave, I won't be able to call you unless you get yourself a burner phone, but then it's only a matter of time before your wife will accuse you of an affair, and then what happens? You'll resent me?" I sputter off, allowing my thoughts to get the better of me.

"We don't have to figure this all out today," Declan says, trying to reassure me, but I'm well aware how sensitive time is and blurt, "Come back with us."

"Princess . . ."

"When we leave, get on the plane with us. Declan owns the plane; no one would even know you were on it."

He moves towards me, saying gently, "I can't leave my family."

His words burn like acid, and I snap. "I'm your family!"

"You are," he says quickly. "But so are they, and I can't just disappear."

"Like you did with me?"

"It's not the same."

My body heats with rage and jealousy. I'm giving him a choice, and he's choosing wrong.

"They've had you!" I cry out. "They've had more years with you than I ever got!"

"Hey," Declan says softly, trying to get my attention, but I ignore him and lash out at my dad.

"So is this what I'm left with? Scraps? That's all I get of you, whatever time you can manage to sneak away from your precious little family?"

"Elizabeth," Declan says in another attempt to get my attention as my dad stands there speechless.

"You used to be mine," I tell my father on a quivering voice. "It was you and me, and we didn't have to share with anyone."

"And now we do." The sorrow in his eyes is reflected in his voice.

"But they get you first."

"I know it isn't fair. I want as much time as I can get with you, but I have three other people who love me and depend on me, and I can't walk away from them and cause even more people the pain I've caused you."

"Why not? It's okay for me to suffer but not them?"

"It's not okay for you to suffer. It was *never* okay, but I wasn't given a choice. No matter what I did, it was inevitable that you would suffer. It didn't matter if I went into the program and lived or if I went back to prison and died."

As I look at him, I can feel the neediness expand in my soul.

Its growth makes me feel like I have so much empty space that needs to be filled. I'm hollow and starved for the one thing I've been deprived of, and it's a horrible feeling I'm forced to withstand.

"Can I come back tonight? Around ten or so?"

I nod, because I'll start crying if I speak. I refuse to cry, but the blades of despair are slaughtering me from the inside.

"Declan?" My father turns from me, seeking permission from the man I love.

"Of course. Come as late as you need."

With his hands on my shoulders, he looks in my eyes with sincerity, saying, "I'm sorry."

And I nod again before he pulls me to him and hugs me. I take his embrace, and with a deep breath, I take in his scent once again, because the same fear remains that he just might not come back.

"I love you."

"I'm sorry," is my response.

"Look at me. You have nothing in this world to be sorry for. It's okay to be angry; I'm angry too. I'm pissed and bitter. I want to grab you and steal you away, do everything in my power to make up for all the time we lost. But do you understand why I can't?"

"I do."

I don't.

"I know it doesn't make it easier, and I'm so sorry. If I'd known that there was a chance in this lifetime that I'd be seeing you again, I would've waited alone so that nothing could stand in the way of me disappearing with you. I need you to believe that. Tell me you believe that."

Taking a hard swallow, I force the words out through all the pain that's suffocating me. "I believe you, Dad."

twenty-six

My DAD DID come back later last night just as he promised. He and Declan talked business and politics while drinking Scotch. I enjoyed watching the two of them together, debating and laughing as if they'd been friends for years. Dad wanted to know what life was like for us in Scotland and now in London, and although our time there has been plagued by so much darkness, Declan did well to veer around all that. When Dad asked about the house in Scotland, I told him all about my time at Brunswickhill: the history of the estate, all the amazing parts of the land surrounding it, the clinker grotto, the atrium, the library. I went on and on, because truthfully, I love the house so much; it's what most little girls dream a palace to be like.

The more we are around each other, the more comfortable we become. The ease of last night felt so natural and so promising. Having the two men that I love so much in the same room with me is amazing. I try not to focus on the nuts and bolts of how this is all going to work moving forward. Declan told me after my father left last night to just enjoy this time we're able to share in the here and now, and that we will figure out the details later. I accepted his suggestion to live in the moment.

My father returned a couple hours ago with another bouquet of pink daisies. We've been hanging out on the couch, watching an old James Bond movie that my dad claims is one of his favorites. Once the movie ends, we order up some lunch, and are now eating our food as we sit in the living room together.

"Declan, tell me, are your mother and father still living in Scotland?"

Now, it's my turn to give Declan a preemptive squeeze like he had when my father asked me about my childhood. I'm not sure what Declan will say, but I need to let him know that I'm here.

"No. My mother actually passed away when I was a teenager."

He doesn't say anything about his father, and when he turns away from my dad, I know he won't. Before my dad can ask another question, I turn my father's attention to me.

"Dad, I umm . . . I thought you should know that I had a friend of mine look into finding my mother."

He looks at me nervously. "You did?"

"Yes," I tell him and then add, "I know what she did."

"Sweetheart, I'm so sorry. I never wanted you to know about her because I didn't want you to think—"

"That she didn't love me?" I cut in. "Dad, she didn't love me. The thing is, her being sick and depressed when she sold me is one thing, but she's been a free woman for a very long time and still has yet to contact me."

"I don't want to make excuses for that woman and what she

did. It was a rough period in our lives—one I had to move on from—which is why when you were little and would ask me if you had a mom, I would always deflect. And since you were so young, it was easy to do."

I can talk about that woman without getting worked-up because I've closed myself off from that facet of my life even though it goes against Declan's word. He's made it clear that he no longer wants me to avoid that which hurts me. But my mother's truth about what she did to me when I was a baby is too painful for me to think about, and with everything else going on, Declan hasn't broached the subject of my mother since.

"Do you think you'll ever see her or talk to her?"

"No," I state firmly. "She's never been a part of my life and I don't see a need for it now."

"I don't want to tell you what to do in this situation, but I think staying away is the best choice. I'd be afraid she'd only hurt you."

"Have you spoken to her since all that?"

"No. As soon as I had you back in my arms, I was done with her and, aside from the day I had to testify at her trial, I never spoke to her or saw her again."

When there's nothing else to be said, we sit in a short span of silence before my dad attempts to lighten the mood. "Tell me something good. Something funny from your childhood."

He has no idea that there's nothing funny about my childhood, but Declan catches the conversation before it drops and says to my dad, "Better yet, why don't you tell me more about Elizabeth. What was she like as a little girl?"

Thank you, Declan.

My father's face instantly lights up with a smile as he reflects on the past. "She was a spitfire of a girl, but in the most endearing way possible."

"So I see that part of her hasn't swayed." Declan's voice is full of humor, but I keep my attention on my father as he goes on.

"She didn't have any women in her life, it was only me and a couple of my good friends that surrounded her," he says and then turns to look at me. "But, somehow, you were so soft and pink and everything a little girl should be."

He says this with a doting smile, which makes me smile as well.

He turns back to Declan and tells him, "I used to have a short beard, almost the same length as yours, and one thing she would always do was rub her tiny hands over it. She'd giggle and tell me she liked the way it felt as it crackled against her palms."

I look over to Declan when my dad says this because I do the exact same thing to Declan's beard every single day. And I do it because it's always reminded me of my dad, and it simply makes me feel good. Declan gazes into my eyes and gives me a hint of a smile when he puts those two puzzle pieces together.

"But as girly as she was, she still wanted to be my right-hand man," he continues with a chuckle. "I can remember when we moved into the Northbrook house . . ."

"We didn't always live there?"

"No. After everything with your mom, I decided it would be best that you and I had a fresh start together. I bought that house for us."

"I never knew that," I murmur.

"You were only three years old at the time, but you insisted on having a little tool belt of your own so you could help me hang the window treatments and artwork on the walls. I wound up tracking one down at a nearby toy store, and you wore it proudly as you followed me around the house."

I laugh when he tells me this, saying, "I don't remember that."

"Well, you were so young, but, yeah, you'd pull out your plastic hammer and tap it against the wall every time I would hammer in a nail." He stops for a moment and smiles at me before continuing, "There was one time when I had a couple buddies of mine over, Danny and Garrett. Do you remember them?"

I do my best to think back and vaguely recall, "You mean Uncle Danny?"

"You *do* remember," he says happily. "Danny was a good friend of mine and he insisted that since you didn't have any aunts or uncles, that you should call him Uncle Danny."

"I don't remember his face or anything, but I do remember an Uncle Danny," I tell him.

He turns to Declan and explains, "Danny and I had known each other since our twenties, and when it was just Elizabeth and me, he'd started to come around more often to spend time with her. But anyway," he says, shifting his attention back to the story. "I was in the attic, laying insulation because it was unfinished, and I wanted to turn it into a storage space. You were downstairs playing with Uncle Danny, and I had stumbled and my foot slipped off the rafter I was standing on and my one leg fell right through the floor." He starts laughing. "I hollered down to you two, and instead of Danny coming to help me, he took you out to the garage where my leg was hanging through the ceiling. He picked you up so you could reach me and encouraged you to take my shoe off and tickle my foot."

Declan and I join in my father's laughter as he tells this story I have no memory of.

"The more I laughed, the more you tickled, and the more I started to slip through. But I could hear you giggling, and you were having the time of your life."

"Well, it looks like your leg survived that ordeal," I tease.

"It did," he says and then faces Declan. "But if you really want to know what she was like as a child, she was perfect. She had the softest heart and always wanted to please people. If I told her to do something, she always did it and never fought me. She was kind and she was sensitive," he says and then looks at me, finishing, "and she was my every dream come true."

He goes on to tell a couple more funny stories, and when we finish our lunch and clean up, he turns to me and asks, "You feel like getting out of here?"

"I thought you couldn't . . ."

"Forget what I said. You want to go for a walk?"

"Um . . . yeah. That sounds great, Dad."

"It's a little cold outside, but why don't I take you over to Owen Beach?"

With a smile, I respond, "Okay. Let me go change my clothes, and I'll be ready." I give Declan a smile when I walk past him and into the bedroom. Closing the door, I rush into the closet like a kid about to go to her favorite candy store. I slip off my dress pants and pull on a pair of jeans before grabbing a hooded raincoat. I dig through Declan's clothes, looking for his jacket, and when I find it, I make a quick stop in front of the mirror to wrap my hair up in a bun on top of my head.

As I walk out of the bedroom, I notice the two of them standing off by the door talking in hushed tones with one another.

"What are you two talking about?" I announce as I approach, and when Declan turns to me, I hold his coat out and wait for his answer.

"You, of course."

I narrow my eyes at him in mock annoyance and then laugh when he kisses me.

"I don't have a whole lot of time before I have to leave, so why don't we take two cars for time's sake, and I'll just leave from the beach?"

"Not a problem, Steve. We'll just follow you there."

The drive is a short one, and pretty soon, we're driving among fresh blooming buds of spring. The sky may be dank and gray, but the pink cherry blossoms make the gloom beautiful. I press my hand on to the window, absorbing its bitter chill as Declan pulls into a parking spot that looks over the desolate beach.

My dad opens his door next to our car, and when he opens my door and takes my hand, Declan says, "I'll wait here."

I look over my shoulder. "You sure?"

"I need to make a few calls," he says. "Go share a walk with your dad."

Hand in hand we walk over the mounds of driftwood on the beach and down to the water's edge. The wind gusts, creating a mist of sea spray that mingles with the cloud's sprinkles that fall from the sky. I reach back with my free hand and pop the hood of my raincoat over my head as we stroll leisurely across the dense, water-puddled sand.

"Is this where you came when you left prison or have you lived other places?"

"Only here. I love it. The mountains, the water, the gray. I love the cold."

"I do too. Winter has always been my favorite for some reason. Maybe it's because it hides the truth of Earth's death under a blanket of false purity."

"False purity?"

"The white fluffy snow seems so innocent, but in actuality, it's the weapon that kills what lies beneath."

He looks down at me, asking with slight humor, "You always think this much?"

"Sometimes."

"I do too."

I stop and turn to face him, and the wind kicks against us when I ask, "What about?"

"You, mostly."

He drapes his arm around me, tucking me against his side as we look out over the water.

With his eyes cast out, he says, "I've always had a lost soul."

We don't look at each other as we speak, my arm now slung around his waist.

"Me too."

"Sometimes when I see a little girl with red hair, for a split second, I feel hopeful that it's you, but then I realize that you wouldn't be that little girl anymore."

"I used to sneak out of windows in the middle of the night when I went into foster care. You told me about Carnegie the last day we were together. I used to think that if I walked far enough to find a forest, you'd be there."

My tears blend with the mist that collects on my face and trickles down my cheeks as we speak.

He turns to me, his hands running down my arms, and his

eyes fill with years of inconsolable pain that I know too well.

"I am so sorry, princess. I have so many regrets in my life, but none bigger than losing you."

I see his tears too.

"I was careless."

"No, Dad."

"I was. I should've never gotten involved with the people I worked for."

I look into my father's reddened eyes as blades nick my heartstrings.

"I will never be able to make up for all my wrongs, for leaving you fatherless, for causing you so much heartache," he chokes out in shame.

"I don't blame you, Dad."

"You should."

"But I don't," I tell him, and he pulls me into his loving arms that I've craved since I was five years old. "All I ever wanted was this. You holding me. I've needed your arms so badly," I say, the words wrapping around my throat, making it hard to speak.

"I need you to listen to me," he says insistently, and I look up at him. "I need you to know how much I love you. I need you to know that without you, my heart is incapable of ever being complete. You . . . you are the very fibers of my being."

I rest my head against his chest and listen to his heartbeat as he continues, "I remember the day you were born. The nurse placed you in my arms, and I was forever changed. You softened my heart instantly, and I knew I would never be the same. I've never been so in love like I've been with you. I need you to never forget that."

"I won't."

"Let me look at you," he requests when he takes my face and cranes it up to him. He shakes his head, saying, "I just can't believe how beautiful you are. My baby, you're all grown up."

Reaching my hand up, I run it along his jaw where his beard used to be. "I can't believe I found you."

"You did. And I will forever be thankful for that. To see you, and to know you're okay."

He leans down, pushes the hood of my raincoat back, and kisses the top of my head. His back shudders against my hands in sadness as he continues to plant kisses in my hair.

"You and I," he eventually says. "We're unbreakable even when we've been broken."

"I've never let you die, even when I believed you were dead."

We stand here, together in the misty rain, and we're tear-stained souls who've finally united when the world has kept us apart for so long.

"I can't believe I have you back," I weep.

He wipes my face with his hands. "No more tears, okay?"

I nod and inhale deeply to soothe myself.

When he turns his head to look up where our cars are parked, he says, "That man up there . . . He's a good one."

I watch Declan, who's talking on the phone, and smile. "He's really good to me, Dad. I don't deserve him."

"You do. You deserve each other. I see how he looks at you, as if it's the last time he'll ever look at you." He moves to stand in front of my view of Declan. "That's the look of a man who's desperately in love," he says. "Even though I love you in a very different way, it's the same way I look at you."

His words comfort in ways I can't explain, and I smile up at him.

"There's that gorgeous light," he adulates, and then kisses my forehead. "I love your smile."

"I love you, Dad. So much."

"I love you too, princess."

When he looks at his watch, he groans. "I've gotta run."

He takes my hand and leads me back up to the car, and when he opens my door, he leans down and looks to Declan, giving him a nod. Declan returns the gesture without any words spoken.

"Thanks, Dad," I tell him. "I needed this."

"I did too, sweetheart."

He leans in and kisses my cheek, and I kiss his before he runs his hand down the length of my face.

"Drive safe, okay?"

"You too."

"I will never love anyone the way I love you," he tells me before he closes my door.

Declan then takes my hand and pulls it into his lap after we pull out of the parking lot and start heading back to the hotel. I reflect on the words my dad said to me, words I've been longing to hear, to know that I was never disposed of. To know that he's hurt for me like I've hurt for him dissolves all resentment. And he's right, even when we were apart, we were still together as one because neither of us let the other fade from our souls. No one can break us.

Walking through the door of our hotel room, a wave of unease hits me out of the blue.

We forgot to make plans to see each other again.

"Declan, did my dad say when he was coming back?"

He shrugs his jacket off and tosses it over a chair, saying,

"No."

I watch Declan as he moves aimlessly around the suite as worriment nags me.

"Declan?"

"Yeah," he calls out when he wanders into the bedroom, and I follow him.

"Something doesn't feel right."

"What do you mean?"

"He's never not said when he'd be coming back."

"Maybe he just forgot."

"No. This doesn't feel right to me."

He runs his hands down my arms and scoops my hands up in his. "Darling . . ."

"Declan, something is wrong here, and I don't trust it," I say as a surge of fear takes over me. My hands start shaking. "Can you drive me by his house?"

"Why?"

"I don't know, but my gut is telling me that something is happening here that I don't know about," I tell him in a tremoring voice, panging in terror.

"I don't think that's a good idea."

"Either you take me or I'll go on my own. You can't stop me and you know it."

"Elizabeth, no."

"Why are you fighting me on this?"

"I just don't think it's safe," he says, and I plead, "You promised me you would bend. I need you to bend."

He releases a deep breath. "Okay."

Declan grabs the keys, and I rush out the door.

He drives with a white-knuckled grip on the steering wheel.

"Why are you so tense?"

He doesn't speak, only reaches over to hold my hand, which does nothing for my anxiety. I stare at him as we pull into the neighborhood, and there's a look in his eyes I've never seen before. My stomach holds the weight of a thousand pounds, and I want to scream at the top of my lungs to drive faster!

The moment he pulls onto Fairview, I see the sign.

I never knew the twist of fate that day held for me. But when I look back, I should've known. It was too much. Too much freedom. The words were too strong. The feelings were too intense. The truth was all around me, but I was too consumed with my dream come true to realize the evil nemesis that couldn't just let me be. If I would've paid better attention, I would've said more to him. I would've made sure he knew every beat of my heart, the depths in which I've always loved him, and how utterly perfect I've always thought he was. He was selfish though, and I can't blame him. Because looking back, I know he wanted to see my smile, pure and true, for one last time. There's no way I could've given him that if I knew what was coming.

I sling open the door before Declan stops the car and run up to the now vacant house. In an utter panic, I yank on the front door, and when that doesn't budge, I peer into the windows. My heart snaps loose inside of my chest and falls into the depths of fiery hell. Once again, I'm faced with the stench of tragedy.

"Where is he?" I scream out as Declan walks up the circle drive. "Where is he?"

"Baby, please."

He reaches for me, but it isn't his touch I want so I slap his hand away, seething, "Don't fucking touch me!"

He reeks of guilt.

"Tell me where he is!"

He stares at me with pity. "He's gone."

"Where?"

"Let's get back in the car."

"NO!"

I can't move.

I can't breathe.

All I can do is stand here, a bleeding mess as every part of what makes me human blisters in monumental agony. They grow, filling with the acid of heartache only to pop and sear me from the inside out.

"You knew," I accuse bitterly, my hands fisting at my sides. "You knew, didn't you?"

"Yes."

"You unimaginable bastard!" I shriek, slapping him across his face, and he takes it. I slap him again, and then hammer my fists against his chest, causing him to stumble back.

He doesn't fight me as I yell at him through my tears, "How could you?"

Another searing slap.

"Are you done hitting me?"

"No!" I spit out as I ram my palm into his shoulder, and that's when he grabs ahold of my wrist.

"How could you not tell me?"

He jerks my wrist, forcing me into his arms, but I don't want his embrace—I want my dad.

I fight against his hold, but he dominates my strength and forces me back down the driveway and into the car. Shock riddles my system as I stare at the *For Sale* sign in the front yard.

Declan gets into the car and speaks in an even and controlled tone. "I am so sorry, baby."

The salt of my pain eats away at my flesh when I turn to face him. "I need answers."

"He got caught," he confesses.

"No, he didn't," I cry, unwilling to believe him.

"They allowed him to have this one last day with you while they emptied the house."

"No."

"He's gone."

"NO!"

And it was in that moment the world fell from its axis and tumbled into nothingness. I only existed in a realm of blank space. I don't know what happened next. I don't remember the drive back to the hotel. I don't remember going to bed. Nothing existed that night. I suppose the pain must've been so incredibly excruciating that I couldn't tolerate it and all my senses seized. Maybe it was something greater that was sparing me of having to carry that memory around with me for a lifetime. Whatever it was that saved me from the horror of that night—thank you.

twenty-seven

I sit in my car with my gun and watch Archer and his daughter on the beach. I'm far enough away from their cars, so they don't take notice of me, but my eyes never leave them.

I've been anxious ever since I got the phone call on their new whereabouts, and that anxiety is at an all-time high now that I'm here. When someone does you wrong, it doesn't simply disappear. It festers and marinates, growing like wildfire. I think of my brother who lost his freedom. He's been sitting in prison for over a decade. His wife lost her husband. His children lost their father. My parents lost their son. It's a ripple of destruction, and Archer will pay for all that he's destroyed. But this isn't my payback—it's my brother's.

As this little family reunion wraps up, I go ahead and pull my car out and wait down the street for Steve's car to pass. It doesn't take long for him to leave, and I cautiously trail behind him. Once we make it over to Gig Harbor, the traffic thins out. Winding through the heavily wooded backstreets, it's go time.

I hammer my foot on the accelerator, and swerve across the double-lines.

When my car evens up to his, I jerk the wheel and run him off the road into a ditch. In rapid-fire movements, I'm over to his car with my gun aimed on him.

"Open the fucking door."

He does, begging, "Take whatever you want, but pl—"

"No talking." I shove the muzzle to his forehead as he looks at me in horror. "This is vengeance for my brother. You ratted Carlos Montego out to the feds, and now he's spending the rest of his life behind bars." His eyes flinch when I mention my brother's name. "He told me to kill you, but I'm going to give you a choice," I tell him, fucking with him, because no matter what he says, he's dying. "I know your daughter is here and staying at The Pearl's Edge."

"No, please don't—"

"Choose. You die or she dies. You have five seconds."

I pull the slide back and chamber a round when he pleads urgently, "Kill me. Don't hurt my—"

BANG.

BANG.

I fire two shots into his head, and he falls lifelessly to the ground, maroon blood oozing out of him. Quickly holstering my gun, I look around, but there's still not a car in sight. I grab him under his arms and drag his body out into the woods. The adrenaline pumping through my veins helps me move at a velocious rate. Tossing this fucker behind a pile of brush, I run back to my car and high-tail it out of there with the thrill of vengeance roiling through me.

It's finished.

twenty-eight

RAIN FALLS AGAINST the window, its particles alone and bleak, waiting to be joined by other raindrops. And once mended, they fall, trickling their way down the glass. I lie in bed on my side and watch this endless pattern repeat itself again and again. I've been up for a while—I don't know how long, but long enough to notice the storm intensifying every few minutes or so.

The somber clouds hang like a veil—cloaked in the darkness of dysphoria. I know the sun is out there somewhere far, far away. She refuses to shine her light on me, but that's okay. I don't want it anyway. I'd rather drown in my misery than be ridiculed by resplendent radiance.

The weight of Declan's arm as he drapes it over my hip alerts me to his rousing. A part of me is angry that he knew and didn't tell me that yesterday would be the last time I saw my dad. But at the same time, I need him close and for there to be no animosity between us. He continues to prove to be the one man I can count on. He's all I have left—again.

I roll onto my back, snug up against him, and watch him watching me.

"I'm sorry," I rasp against the strain of my throat, an attestation of how much I probably screamed and cried last night.

"You slap hard." His lips tick in a subtle grin, and then he shifts, saying more seriously, "Don't you ever be sorry for how you feel. It's okay."

I don't say anything else, exchanging words for reticence. I close my eyes and seek solitude in the warmth of Declan's body. We remain in bed for most of the morning, drifting in and out of sleep, because sleep is much more appealing than having to face the truth. Reality can go fuck itself for all I care; I'd rather frolic among the fantasy of dreams.

Eventually, Declan decides it's time to wake. I remain under the sheets as he calls up for coffee and tea. He then goes into my toiletry bag and finds my prescription bottle. I take the pill he hands me, and again, cheek it. Once he's in the bathroom and I hear the faucet running, I drop the pill behind the headboard.

"He'll be furious if he ever finds out."

"He won't."

Pike stands and leans against the fog-covered window, looking out at the storm.

"Everything they told me about my dad was a lie, you know?" I whisper, keeping my voice low so Declan won't hear.

Pike walks over to me, kneels beside the bed, and holds my hand. *"I know."*

"He was everything I thought he would be after all these years."

"Are you hungry at all?" Declan asks when he walks back into the room, and suddenly Pike is gone.

I shake my head when I look at him from over my shoulder and then turn back to the window. Declan encourages me to get out of bed and freshen up, and like a machine, I do it—all the while numb.

Did last night really happen or was it a mirage?

When I slip back into bed and sit against the headboard, Declan hands me the teacup. I cradle it in my hands as the steam ribbons into the air, eventually evaporating in a metaphoric display.

Declan sits next to me with his coffee in hand. He takes a sip and then punctures the silence. "Talk to me."

I keep my eyes on my tea. "What's there to say?"

"Tell me how you're feeling?"

"I don't know how to feel right now," I respond despondently.

"Do you want to know how I feel?"

When I look at him, his face is marred in suffering.

"I feel like I failed you." His words weigh heavy in the air between us. "I promised you I'd never let you fall. And when your father pulled me aside and told me it was his last day with you, I knew the best thing for you would result in you falling in the worst way possible." He sets his coffee mug on the bedside table and then turns to me. "I was powerless to save you, and it kills me to know I couldn't protect you from this pain. I was put in the worst position last night, and I am so sorry."

Declan isn't a man who ever apologizes, so to hear the sincerity in it is a blatant reflection of his grief. I want to say something, tell him I understand, tell him it's okay, but it hurts too much to speak.

He leans over and opens the drawer to the bedside table, pulls out an envelope, and hands it to me. "Your dad gave this to me yesterday."

I hold it in my hands for a moment before breaking the seal and opening it. His written words cover the paper entirely, and agony conquers numbness and takes over.

"I don't know if I can do this, Declan."

"It might help," he suggests.

Taking a deep breath, I release it slowly before lowering my eyes to his words. Declan wraps his arms around my shoulders and holds me against him when I start reading the letter to myself.

My beautiful girl,

I know you must be hurting, because I'm dying inside. I wish I could be there to comfort you and wipe your tears, but I also know that you're in good hands with Declan. I don't want you to be upset with him. I told him not to tell you I'd be leaving. If I told you, I knew I'd never be able to leave you. I couldn't have our last day together with you in tears. I hope you can understand that.

The thing is, the government found out that you and I had made contact. They stepped in, and as much as I hate it, I have to agree with them. Your association with me puts you at an unbelievable risk, and if anything happened to you, I'd never be able to live with myself. You are too precious for me to put you in harm's way. Selfishly, I want you, but because of the mistakes I made in my past, this is how it has to be.

I don't know where I'm relocating or what my new identity will be, but I need you to let me go. Please don't try to find me. I don't say this because I don't love you. I'm saying it to save you. After you read this letter, I need you to destroy it because no one can ever know that I'm alive.

These past few days were a gift. It was never supposed to happen, but it did, and I will forever be thankful that I have a daughter that fought her way to find me. You are strong and beautiful and smart, and you are destined to do great things. Promise me, you won't let my mistakes stand in your way.

I don't want you to ever forget how much I love you. There hasn't been a single second that you haven't been in my heart. You are irreplaceable and unforgettable. I need you to believe that.

I'm going to take you to the beach tomorrow. I'm going to hold your hand. I'm going to make you smile. And whatever I wind up saying to you, I need you to hold on tightly to those words and carry them with you through your life.

You're my forever princess.

I love you,

Dad

I drop the paper that's covered in my tears and fall against Declan. He envelops me and I sob. There's nothing for me to say, so I let pain devour me. It strangulates and paralyzes, cutting fresh wounds in my soul, marking me with this pain for life.

I want to drown in it.

I want to escape from it.

I'm all over the place.

The vacancy inside of me is about to surpass my body's elasticity, and I grow desperate to fill the void I fear will be the death of me.

I cling to Declan, slinging my leg over his hip and pulling him against me as we slip down in the bed. Drawing my head back, I look through my tears at his blurred face.

"Breathe." His hushed voice lulls, and while he wipes the tears that continue to fall, I give myself the time I need to settle myself down.

The pounding of my heart transitions into neediness, I pull Declan's head to mine and kiss him. He lets me control it, and I keep it soft and move slow. My lips meld with his, and he brings my body in even closer.

I feel a few lingering tears as they slip out and fall down the sides of my face and into my hair.

He rolls on top of me, parting my lips with his tongue and dipping it into my mouth. With my hands getting lost in his hair, I pull him down on me, needing to feel his weight on top of me. We continue to kiss in this new way. There's no urgency or need for control. Declan drags his lips from mine and runs them down my neck before he breaks the kiss and looks down at me.

I gaze up at him, desperate for this closeness, and make my request.

"Show me how tender you can be."

I know I'm asking a lot. Declan isn't one who feels safe when he opens himself up to vulnerability, but I need this. For this moment, I need him to love me in this way—stripped down and free from the barriers he likes to keep on me.

I watch as his eyes soften, and when he gives me a nod, he drops his lips back down to mine. My hands roam freely, something he never allows because I'm always restrained. I slip them under his shirt and feel his abs flex from my touch. We undress each other slowly and soon our clothes are on the floor.

Flesh against flesh, his skin heats mine. He keeps his touches soft, taking my breasts in his hands. His breath ghosts over them and over my puckered nipples before taking one of them between his lips. He sucks lovingly and the sensation causes my back to bow off the bed and into him. My eyes fall shut, and with my hands running along the dips of his muscular arms, I release a breathy moan.

He moves to my other nipple, showing it the same affection before dragging his hot tongue down my stomach. When he reaches the curve of my pussy, he puts his hands on each thigh and spreads my legs.

"God, I love this part of you," he whispers in a husky voice.

I move my eyes down to him and watch as he stares at my pussy. I reach both of my hands down to him and he takes them in his, lacing his fingers through mine. And before he makes his move, he lifts his eyes and fixes them to mine. We watch each other as he holds my hands and dips his tongue into the slit of my pussy. He sends a sizzling current through my whole body.

He moves painfully slow.

I spread my legs wider as he laps and kisses and sucks. Every movement softer than the one before. He groans from deep inside his chest, and when his tongue slides inside of my body, I can't hold on. I mewl in pure ecstasy and grind myself over his face, clutching my fingers around his hands. I grow hotter as he sparks the live wire in my soul, the one that incessantly aches for him.

He moves his lips to my thighs, dropping whispery kisses over every inch of my skin as he lets go of my one hand and drags the wet arousal out from inside of me with his finger and uses it to rub my clit.

Our bodies move together and we're unrushed, unmasked, and completely exposed.

When he finds his way back up to me, I hold his face in mine and kiss him deeply, fusing my lips with his as I glide my tongue along his. He settles himself between my legs, his hard cock pressing against me.

"I want it real slow," I tell him.

"How slow, baby?"

"So slow I can feel you entering my soul."

He reaches down and holds himself in his hand.

Never has the sensation been more intense than in this very moment as he pushes inside me.

It's exquisite.

It's torturous.

It's effervescent bliss.

And when he's fully immersed in me, I'm saved. Free from my cankering misery, I hold on to Declan as he fucks me in slow agonizing strokes. His moans blend with mine, our bodies coalesced like never before. Our souls tethered into one.

He flips us over and I roll my hips over his cock. He sits up and kisses my neck, my tits, my mouth while I fist my hands in his hair and rock into him. When he leans his head back, I stare into his eye as I ride his cock.

"I love you." My words resting on broken pants.

He groans through rictus lips before reaching his hands around the backs of my shoulders and pushing me farther down on his cock. I can feel him throbbing inside of me and then he lifts me off him. Lying on my side with him behind me, he pulls my leg up and buries himself deep inside of me.

He slips his one arm under my head, and I hold his hand while he uses his other to turn my head to him. We kiss, and I reach down between my legs to feel his cock as he fucks me.

"Touch yourself."

Taking my wetness from his dick, I move to rub my clit in slow circles, and my hips buck when I do. He drapes my hair behind my shoulder and kisses the veins on my neck, sending my body into shivers. It doesn't take long before my pussy grows wetter and the onslaught of an orgasm begins to build inside of me.

Declan shifts to his back with me on top of him, my legs bent and feet planted on the bed, and he thrusts into me from behind. My back lies against his chest, and he's now massaging my clit alongside my fingers. Our hands grow wet as he continues sliding himself in and out of me.

"Oh, God, Declan."

"That's it, baby. I want to feel you all over me."

With my hand locked to his, I rock my hips down on him, unable to still myself and greedy for him to fill me with his cum.

"Fuck me," I tell him, and with our fingers mingled in my pussy, he pumps his hips up into me.

My eyes fall shut as my ass slides back and forth over the top of him. Nerves begin to fissure, limbs begin to tingle. He presses his fingers down on my clit, and I rupture. He pounds his thick cock into me, driving my orgasm out of me. I writhe against him, pulling every bit of pleasure he has to give, and then I feel him cum. He groans heavily, spurting his life source inside of my body, grabbing my pussy with his hand and grinding me roughly against him.

We ride each other, taking every piece from one another that we can. My head slips off the back of his shoulder, and he kisses me deeply, our tongues tasting and licking. When he rolls us back to our sides, he pulls himself out of me, cum dripping onto my thighs as I turn over to face him.

He plants his lips on my sweaty forehead.

"Thank you."

"I love you," he tells me. "If this is what you need, I'll give it to you as many times as you need it."

We stay in bed for most of the day, naked and wrapped in each other's arms. If I'm not sleeping, then I'm crying.

If I'm not crying, then we're kissing and touching.

And if we're not kissing and touching, then I'm sleeping.

The cycle laps as the hours pass. Eventually Declan takes a shower, leaving me alone with the rain that has yet to let up. With the blankets tucked around me, I feel at peace here in the hotel room with Declan and away from anything that could have the potential to hurt me.

A buzzing sound alerts me. I sit up and look around the room, unsure of what the noise is. Then, when I spot my purse on the floor next to the closet, it hits me. I slip out of the bed and dig my hand down past my wallet and grab my cell phone.

UNKNOWN reads across the screen.

I accept the call.

"Hello?"

"Hey, kitty."

twenty-nine

"I THOUGHT I told you not to call me." My voice is razor sharp, but I keep it low because Declan is in the shower.

"I wouldn't call you if I weren't desperate. I need your help, so it's time you got off your high horse and remember where you came from and the people that took care of you."

As I kneel by the wall next to the closet, I respond, "Took care of me?"

"Who helped Pike save you from your foster parents? Who drove the car? Who let you live with them?"

"Let's get one thing straight, you were Pike's friend, not mine."

"Are you going to help me or not?"

"Not. Like I said, you die and I have the guarantee that I can move forward without having to look over my shoulder."

"You're gonna die too," he says, his words catching me off guard.

"What are you talking about?"

259

"It was the only way to ensure I stay alive."

"What the hell are you talking about?" I grit as I stand.

"You think you're running this show? Think again. You might not value my life, but I'm not willing to lose it over an uptight cunt like you."

I try to keep my voice from quivering. "What did you do?"

"I gave them your name. Told them you had the money. So you have no choice but to help me. After all, your life is on the line too now."

The shock and fury that surge through my veins is rampant fuel, and I'm not even thinking about keeping a hushed tone when I spit my fury. "You motherfucker!"

He laughs, saying, "Next time don't fuck with me when I ask for help, kitty."

I start when the bathroom door busts open and Declan rushes out with only a towel slung around his waist.

"Are you okay?" His words shoot out quickly. "Who's on the phone?" He doesn't wait for me to respond when he takes it right out of my hand. "Who the fuck is this?" He pauses and then holds the phone out and clicks it onto speakerphone.

"Can she hear me?" Matt questions.

"She can hear you."

"They know you're in Washington."

As soon as he says those words, I reach over and end the call.

"What the fuck is going on, Elizabeth?" Declan ferociously demands.

I tell him about Matt, about his calling me when we were back in London, and about the loan shark. And then I tell him that Matt traded me in to save his life.

"There's a bounty on my head now."

Rage takes over Declan in a deadly way that scares the shit out of me. He stands in utter silence as he bores his eyes down on me, and when his nostrils flare angrily, he fumes in an even tone, "Why didn't you tell me about this sooner?"

"I thought I handled it. I thought it was under control."

"You thought wrong, goddammit! And now you have a hit out on you!" His voice ricochets off the walls, his neck blotching the color red in white-hot anger.

"I'll just pay them off, Declan,"

"You think that'll solve this Matt situation? The ease at which he was able to dispose of your life is not something to fuck with. And what happens when he finds himself in trouble down the road? You really trust him when he says he's going to leave you alone after this?"

Declan rips his hand through his wet hair and paces off across the room. I watch as frustration and fiery anger boil over, and I'm quick to make my resolve.

"I'll kill him," I say too fast and too eager.

Declan snaps his head over to me with a look of horror on his face. Maybe I should be worried about how he'll respond or how he'll think of me to know I can rid someone of their life so easily, but I'm not. Declan knows I have three kills under my belt. Hell, he has two himself. He knows the tar my black heart pumps. And when he speaks, I know we're one and the same—two monsters bound by one soul.

"No," he states. "I'll kill him."

"Declan, no. I can't let you do that. Matt's my problem."

He strides over to me in quick steps. "I won't let you kill anyone else, you hear me? I don't want your hands branded by any more blood. I'll take care of it."

"Declan—"

"I'm not arguing with you about this. My word is final," he states adamantly. "Pack your suitcase. They know where we are, so we're getting the fuck out of here."

"Are we going back to Chicago?"

"Yes. We're taking care of this issue now and then going back to London," he says. "But listen to me . . . Bennett's money . . . we're dumping it on the loan shark. Not only will we finally be rid of it, but it'll be enough to make these people forget you ever existed."

Taking a hard swallow, I know this is ultimately the best resolution for us. And now, once again, I'm plagued by my past, which is now forcing the man I love to take another life.

Declan's able to schedule the plane to go out today, and with the vicissitude we now face, there's no time for me to mourn the loss of my dad. We move with urgency, making sure our belongings are packed and ready to go before we head out.

We sit hand in hand during the plane ride.

"Declan, you don't have to do this."

"It's not up for discussion."

The plane lands and we drive straight back to Lotus. Every step Declan takes is purposeful, wasting not a second.

Tension is ghastly as I watch Declan take out the pistol he always travels with. He releases the cylinder and gives it a look before spinning it and locking it back in place.

"Declan?"

Laying it flat on the table in front of where I sit on the couch, he looks down at me. "You're going to call him from your phone."

"It's an unknown number he's calling from."

"There's an identification service I had Lachlan install on your phone. It traps the numbers from any restricted calls your phone receives."

I pull out my phone so Declan can show me where to retrieve the number, and with a few simple clicks, it pops up.

"What do I say?"

"You tell him you're here in Chicago and want to get this over with tonight."

It's after two a.m. and my heart rate picks up. "It's the middle of the night."

Disregarding my hesitation, he goes on to instruct me on everything I need to say.

"You got all that?"

Taking a deep breath, knowing what's about to go down, I steel myself for the inevitable as I dial Matt's number.

"Hello?" Matt says after two rings.

"It's me."

"How'd you get this number?"

"Everyone is traceable. Even you, asshole," I tell him, slinging his words back at him from when he first made contact with me. "I'm here in Chicago."

"You move fast."

"You want to live, don't you?"

"Yes."

"I'm here to save your life, so I need you to do this my way." I'm firm in my tone and a tad shocked when he keeps his mouth shut and listens. "I don't want any fuck-ups or you getting greedy on me. We're meeting tonight. You're to call the shark to meet us. I'll make the transfer from my phone and wait until we get the verification from the shark's account that the money has been successfully transferred."

"Come alone. The last thing I need is your boyfriend fucking shit up because he can't keep his cool."

"Don't worry. I'll be alone," I lie. "You have ten minutes to call me back to tell me the location of our meeting place."

I hang up before he can respond and look to Declan. He smiles. "Good girl."

He takes a seat next to me as we wait in the darkened room, the only light coming from the glow of a lamp on the entryway table. Declan drapes his arm around my shoulder, and when I turn my head to him, he peers at me through dilated eyes, exposing the devil inside. He's the creation of my monstrosity.

I touch his face, and he kisses me with venomous passion before ripping away from me when my cell vibrates against the wooden table.

"Yes?" I answer.

"Twenty minutes. Metra railroad yard. Meet under the Roosevelt overpass."

"How many are coming?"

"Just me and Marco, the shark."

"Twenty minutes."

I disconnect the call and tell Declan where we're meeting. He grabs his gun and then goes to the entry closet where the safe is. I can hear the beeps of the keypad as he enters the code, and when the steel door slams shut, he returns with another revolver.

"Just in case," he says when he hands me the gun.

It's heavy and cold in my hand, and when I release the cylinder, I see that every chamber is loaded.

"You know the plan?"

I nod.

"Tell me."

"I know the plan."

"You're not to draw your gun unless absolutely necessary, okay?"

Blood swims rapidly through my body, and when I slip the gun into the back waistband of my pants, I lower my top and shrug my coat on to conceal it.

"Ready?"

"Yes," I tell him and then walk into his arms for comfort and strength. He holds me, kisses the top of my head, and assures, "We stick to the plan and then it'll all be over and we can go back home, okay?"

"Let's get this over with."

Declan goes first, leaving me behind until I get his call. I wait anxiously as he goes to switch off the security cameras. After a few minutes of pacing the room, my phone rings.

"I'm in my office," he states.

I move quickly, making my way down to him, and we exit the building through the back corridors that lead into the parking garage. Before I know it, we're zipping through the streets of Chicago on our way to the river.

The drive is tense. No words are spoken at all. We both know our parts and what we have to do.

Turning into the train yard, Declan hits the lights. Everything goes black as we weave through lines of train cars. When we edge closer to the water, I spot Matt with a tall man, thick with bulky muscles.

"That's him," I whisper.

Declan stops the car and shuts it off. "You ready?"

Our eyes lock. "Yes."

The moment Declan opens his door, Matt draws his gun and fires. It's a botched shot, but sends me into instant defense mode. Without sparing a second, all guns are drawn in an outburst of chaos.

"What the fuck, Elizabeth?" Matt shouts, but my focus is on the automatic Marco has aimed at me while Declan claims Matt as his target.

So many words are being thrown around at the same time as sparks of fear ignite within me.

"On your fucking knees," Declan yells.

"Fuck you!" Matt throws back.

It's a frenzy all around me, but my only point of concentration is right in front of me—Marco and his gun.

"Elizabeth," Declan's voice calls from behind in worriment, to which I respond in a steady voice, "I'm okay."

"What the fuck is wrong with you?" The shark snaps at Matt, berating him as he keeps his gun pointed at me.

"Marco," I greet in a strong voice, needing him to see me as nothing other than a woman in complete control. He stands a good one foot taller than me and the moon reflects off his shiny bald head. He's intimidating as hell, but I refuse to let it show. "I'm not looking to bullshit around tonight. The fact that my pistol is on you is a mere result of your client firing his gun. Clearly he's as dumb as he looks because without us, you don't get your money and he's a dead man." With Marco's gun targeted on me, I instruct, "You need money from this ass wipe, and I intend on covering his part along with enough to make you forget this night ever happened. But I'm going to need you to holster your gun. You do that, and mine is down as well. But you need to get that little shit under control too."

"You're my kind of girl. Elizabeth, right?"

"It's whatever you want it to be; I'm not here to make friends."

"I like you," he says before taking his aim off of me and swinging his arm around to Matt.

"You're a fucking idiot!" he scolds and then pulls the trigger, sending a bullet straight into Matt's leg, collapsing him down to the ground in an instant. Marco doesn't bat an eye when he holsters his gun and turns back to me while Matt screams in agony.

I watch as Declan picks up Matt's gun before I look back to Marco and shove my pistol into the waist of my pants. "I give you my word that we have no intention of doing you any wrong. That man right there," I tell him, nodding my head to Declan. "He's not too happy that your client has put me in harm's way. So, let me tell you how this night is going to go. You give me the account number you want me to wire the money into. I suggest it be whatever offshore account you no doubt hold, because I intend on dumping a lot of fucking cash into it. Then we wait. When the money is transferred, my friend holding the gun is going to teach Matt a lesson. You're more than welcome to watch, but I'll leave that choice to you. Then I plan on going home and getting some sleep."

My orders are to the point.

"You're good," he compliments.

"I've dabbled in enough cons for one life."

"Elizabeth!" Matt's voice is terror-stricken. "What the fuck is going on here?"

"Shut the fuck up, dickfuck!" Declan shouts, and when I look at Matt over my shoulder, I tell him with a smile, "Who's the cunt now?"

"Please, man. Don't kill me!"

Declan steps closer and presses the muzzle of the gun against Matt's forehead. "I told you to shut the fuck up."

Matt continues to flap his pathetic mouth, begging Declan to spare his life, but I turn back to Marco. "Let's speed this up; I've had a long day."

"My phone is in my pocket," he tells me so I don't assume he's reaching for a weapon.

"I'll get it." I trust no one.

I pull it out and hand it to him before retrieving my own phone. I wait as he pulls up the bank account he wants to use for the transfer. He proceeds to provide all the information that I need to conduct the wire, and once the country code and numbers are all entered, we wait for the delivery. It takes about fifteen minutes for Marco's bank account to update and reflect the deposit.

"Fuck me." His face grows in satisfaction when he sees the amount of zeros in the transaction.

"Are we done here?"

His eyes meet mine, and he shoves his phone back into his pocket. "Done and forgotten."

"Marco, come on, man! Don't leave me here," Matt begs through the pain of his bloody leg.

"I'm not leaving. Not yet anyways." Marco backs up, and when I turn over my shoulder to look at him, he straightens out his coat and says, "Can't be getting my new coat dirty," with a wink.

When I focus back on Matt, his eyes spiral out of control as he continues to plead. "Come on! I swear to you, I'll leave you alone, Elizabeth. Don't shoot me."

"You threw my life away to keep yours, and now you're begging me to save you? You're unsaveable, Matt. You always have been."

"It's me, Elizabeth! Come on!" His body tremors in inexorable fear. It coats his face in a layer of sweat.

"The only thing I owe you before you die is a *thank you.*"

"What the fuck?"

"Thank you for handing me the match the night we burned Carl and Bobbi. It's the best gift you ever gave me."

"You fucked up the moment you put her life in danger." Declan's voice is guttural, his eyes merciless.

"Don't do this, man. Plea—"

BANG.

Matt's blood sprays across the side of my face and clothes as the crack of gunfire echoes through the night. His body collapses as dark blood pours out of the hole in his head. Clumps of his brain litter the gravel surrounding us. Declan stands above his unmoving body, aims the gun down, and ensures his death.

BANG.

BANG.

Behind the ringing in my ears, I hear Marco's distant voice, "That's gonna be a bitch to clean up," followed by stones crunching under his feet and the slam of his car door. The tires of his SUV roll over the rocks of the train yard, and then he's gone.

Declan remains fixed above Matt's dead body; he's a cold-blooded phoenix, no longer the man he once was when I met him in Chicago. He's the creation of my monstrosity, forever changed as a result of my demented soul. He fell in love with the devil when he fell in love with me.

When his eyes shift to me, I go to him, grab his blood-streaked face, and affirm, "I love you," before kissing him through the metallic taste of death.

thirty

"At least you got to see him. You always said you'd do anything to have him back for just one more second. You got that and more."

"It still hurts."

"I know."

Pike tightens his arms around me as I lay my head on his chest. He's been with me ever since Declan left earlier to pay Lachlan a visit. I haven't been able to get out of bed since we returned to London yesterday. Everything came to a standstill when we boarded the plane in Chicago. All of a sudden, there were no more distractions, and the weight of the past few days came crashing down on me.

I'm sad.

I miss my dad.

"He's alive though."

"Is that supposed to be a good thing?"

His fingers comb through my hair while I grip a wad of his white shirt that embodies the scent of his clove cigarettes. *"What do you mean?"*

"I mean, if his life is plagued with the agony he told me he carries with him every day, wouldn't death be better? This world forces people to endure incredible pain. It's like we're all a bunch of masochists because we continue to choose life over death."

"That's a morbid thought."

"But it's true, right?" I tilt my head back to look at his beautiful face—young and free from stress. "Do you feel anything now that you're . . ."

"Dead?" he says, picking up the word that hurts too much to say. *"I miss you, but it doesn't feel like it did when I was alive. It's hard to describe. Somehow, I'm always at peace even though I miss you."*

"Missing you is excruciating."

"I wish I could take it away from you, but you have so much to live for. You have a life with Declan. He's good to you. He protects you. There are no boundaries for him when it comes to protecting you—he'll do anything."

I move to sit up in bed, and when Pike does the same, we face each other. "Are you mad about what we did to Matt?"

"No. I agree with Declan; all bets were off the moment that fucker put your life on the line."

I gaze into his eyes and release a deep breath before telling him, "I don't know what I would ever do without you."

His hand comes to meet my face, and I notice his eyes morph into a laden expression. *"Do you think I took advantage of you?"*

"What?"

He drops his head for a beat before returning to me, and he finally voices for the first time what I've always known. *"I was in love with you my whole life."* His eyes glaze over, tear-filled, and he tells me, *"All I wanted was to make you happy. No matter what you asked of me, I gave it to you—even when I knew it was wrong."*

"You didn't take advantage of me, Pike." I take his hand from my cheek and hold it in my own. "It was me. I took advantage of *you*. I knew you were in love with me, and I used that to steal from you. I took your love, and I used it to comfort my pain. And I am *so sorry* I played with your emotions the way I did."

"Don't be sorry."

He takes me into his arms, and as we hold each other, I ask, "Do you still feel that way about me?"

"No."

"Does it hurt you to see me with Declan?"

Relaxing his grip, he pulls away and runs his hands down my arms. *"No."* He holds both of my hands and we sit face to face on the bed. *"I love you, I always will and nothing will ever change that. But something happened when I died. The way I loved you changed. I know Declan is good for you. He's able to love you and care for you in a way I wouldn't have ever been capable of. Seeing you two together settles me. I know you're going to be okay in this life because of him."*

"You and Declan are the best things that ever happened to me in this shitty life."

"And you are the best thing that ever happened to me when I was alive. And Declan is the best thing that's happened to me in my death, because he's giving you everything I wanted to but couldn't. You're the best part of me, you know?"

I look into the eyes of my savior, and although I wish I could turn back the hands of time and not have pulled that trigger, at least I know he's moved on to a better place. And now, in his death, he goes on to serve as my orenda in this vicious world. He claims that it's only Declan who provides my safety and comfort, but it's the both of them together that blend the elixir that just might be my saving grace.

(DECLAN)

I ʜᴀᴛᴇ ᴛʜᴀᴛ I had to leave Elizabeth back at the apartment, but I don't feel safe handling this situation with Lachlan around her. Between his calls to Camilla and the insinuations from my father that Lachlan is withholding information from me, trust is now riddled with uncertainty.

I'm a sparking fuse dangling over gasoline as I make my way to his hotel. Hot off the kill from the other day, I've been unable to quell the viperous animal inside me. It's spitting at me to fix my own unresolved issue—the way I handled Elizabeth's for her. But I will go to any length possible to ensure Elizabeth's safety. I failed to protect her from Matt putting a hit on her—I won't fail again.

With my pistol holstered under my suit jacket, I step off the elevator and make my way down to his room. After a couple swift knocks, the door opens, and I whip out my gun, barreling the muzzle into Lachlan's forehead. I use the force of the gun to push him into the room and then kick the door closed.

"What the hell?" His wide eyes are consumed with sheer horror and fear.

I back him up as he lifts his hands in surrender, and when he falls back into a chair, I hiss venomously, "I'm going to give you one more chance to tell me what the fuck you are doing talking to Camilla and my father before I put a bullet in your head. You've seen me do it before, so make no mistake, I *will* do it again."

"What I told you was the truth." His words tremble just as his hands do.

"And now I'm demanding the *whole* truth."

I bring my thumb up and engage the hammer, chambering a round, and he gives in to the fear like a whore's pussy.

"Jesus! Okay! Okay!"

"I'm not fucking around!"

"Shit, okay. Please, relax with the gun, man," he blurts out in a panic. "I'll tell you everything, just . . ."

"Start talking!" My bark is pure sulfur, and he's terrified as he squirms, slipping down into the chair. "Now!"

"I'm stealing from Cal," he jabbers out instantly.

"What the fuck are you talking about?"

"I'm . . . It's . . . The thing is—"

"Goddammit!"

"I can't fucking think with a gun to my head!" he hollers from his slouched position in the chair, and I draw the gun back, keeping it targeted on him. His eyes never stray from my weapon. I stand a few feet back and watch as he clumsily sits up.

"Start talking."

"Camilla called me when your father was arrested. When she realized the evidence was stacked against him, she knew she'd be left out to dry without a penny. She called me, told me her crazy scheme to embezzle his money. She had it all planned out. Told me to reach out to him. She figured he'd be desperate to have someone in his corner, and aside from the fallout we had when I found out about the two of them, I was, in fact, a man he had thoroughly trusted for years."

"Speed it up."

"I reached out to him with the help of Camilla, and before

I knew it, he was wanting me to keep an eye on you, which was when I started reporting to him about you," he confesses.

"You told him about Elizabeth?"

"Yes."

"Get to the part that's going to save your life and spare me the headache of cleaning up your murder," I threaten.

"Camilla convinced him to trust me to launder his hidden assets through your charity foundation. She vowed we'd split it fifty-fifty, but I had my own plans. I promise you I never filtered any of that money through any of your businesses."

"Where is it?"

"With a junket in Macau."

I disengage the hammer and lower my pistol, and Lachlan drops his hands and releases a heavy breath of relief.

"I never lied when I assured you have my loyalty. You and Elizabeth, but never your father, and if that's an issue with us then—"

"It's not an issue. He's done," I tell him and then take a moment to process the fact that this man has taken it upon himself to undermine my father and his girlfriend for financial gain in the name of revenge.

"This is why Camilla keeps calling. I had to keep her believing that we were on the mend and working together, but I just got word the other day that he's been indicted. It's only a matter of time before he confesses. He knows he's safer in prison than out. If he allows this to go to trial, it won't matter if he wins or loses—he's a dead man."

He's right. I know him admitting his guilt to forego a trial will be inevitable. A trial would mean witnesses and handing over names. It would be him turning his back on those only a man with a death wish would do. Which is why I refuse to allow Elizabeth to get worked up about her crimes being uncovered.

"I need you to go back. You said the money was with a junket?" I ask. "I'm not skilled in the world of embezzling, so I need you to tell me what's going on. No more bullshitting me."

"Working in the world of finance all my life, I've come to know a handful of shifty people. One of them was able to hire me a junket in China. For a twenty percent fee, he exchanges my cash for poker chips. With Macau being the casino capital of the world and Hong Kong having so many intermediaries that are willing to transfer funds to anywhere without asking too many questions, it was my safest option."

"What happens with the chips?"

"My junket gambles a little and then cashes them in along with other gamblers' legitimate chips. The casino accountant then books my money as paid-out winnings."

"Where does the money go?"

"The funds are wire-transferred in such a way that the money crosses multiple borders to frustrate detection."

"Explain," I demand needing to know exactly how he plans on transferring what I assume to be millions.

"For instance," he continues, "the money might end up in a US trust managed by a shell company in Grand Cayman, owned by another trust in Guernsey with an account in Luxembourg, managed by a Swiss or Singaporean or Caribbean banker who doesn't know who the owner is. It's a whirlwind, basically."

"Were you ever going to tell me?"

He leans forward, resting his elbows on his knees, and then looks up to me. "There's no way to answer that. If I say yes, you'll think I'm a liar. If I say no, you'll think I'm a liar for the mere fact I never told you. But, if you need confirmation of where my interests lie, then I'll give you the accounts. You see, the money was simply a bonus to Camilla landing on her ass, dirt poor and alone. The latter was the capstone."

Testing him, I click the barrel open and dump the bullets. I walk over to him, lay the gun on the desk, and tell him, "I want all the accounts."

"Now?"

"Now."

He gets up and steps to his laptop next to my unloaded pistol. I follow, and when he sits in the desk chair, I stand over his shoulder. I watch as he bypasses the Internet and accesses the deep web through Tor, which is an anonymity network that ensures nothing he does will be indexed.

In a few quick swipes of the keyboard, numbers and codes begin to filter in. "There you go," he says and then points to the screen, explaining, "This column lists the country codes, this one here lists account and routing numbers, and this column here is—"

"Close it down."

He looks at me in confusion but does as I instruct and proceeds to logoff. I'm satisfied that without the threat of force, he handed over all the information without an inkling of hesitation.

"I don't want his money. You can do whatever you want with it."

Lachlan closes the lid to his laptop, picks up the gun, takes one bullet from the floor, and slides it into one of the cylinders. He then gives it a spin before locking it into place.

"Here," he says in an even tone as he hands me the gun. "I'd take a bullet for Elizabeth. You on the other hand . . . I need to come down from you shoving that muzzle into my head, but I'd take a bullet for you as well. You want me to prove my loyalty to you?" He takes a couple steps back. "Pull the trigger."

A sane man would take his word for it, but the gesture isn't enough for me, not after everything that has compromised my life and Elizabeth's. She's much too precious to take anyone's word at face value. So I stretch my arm out in front of me, but with a slight adjustment, one that Lachlan won't be able to detect, I mark his right arm as my target.

He offered this test of integrity, and when I cock back the hammer, I slip my finger over the trigger, and follow through.

I squeeze and fire, but all that sounds is the *snick* from the chamber rounding.

Lachlan's face drops, stunned that I pulled the trigger and then relieved when he realizes his game of Russian roulette just played out in his favor. He falls back into the chair as I holster my gun. And now that I have the confirmation that the only reason he withheld information from me was to fuck over Camilla and my father, I turn and walk to the door.

"Stop by later this afternoon. Elizabeth would enjoy seeing you now that we're back," I say without turning around.

And then I leave.

thirty-one
(DECLAN)

Elizabeth is still in bed sleeping when I get home from a long day of meetings. It's been days of the same. She's heartbroken and trying to cope with losing her father for the second time in her life, so I haven't wanted to push her too much. I'm worried though. She's been living in shades of darkness since we returned from the States. It's more than the moping around that concerns me though. After my talk with Lachlan the other day, I came home and heard her voice coming from the bedroom. But she was in there alone. When I opened the door, I could tell she had been crying, so I decided not to question her.

I have to remind myself how fragile she still is. It wasn't that long ago when she completely broke down after she found out about her mother and had to be medicated. She's experienced only a handful of episodes since that night, but none that measure in magnitude.

Walking over to the edge of the bed, I watch her as she

sleeps peacefully. Her face is soft and her breathing is steady. I run the backs of my fingers along her cheek, feeling her smooth skin warm against mine. I can finally look at her without the past fueling my hate for her. No longer do I want to cause her pain and suffering. No longer do I want to punish her.

Seeing her with her father helped stitch the wounds she inflicted with her deceitful ways. For the first time, I saw through all the walls she's spent her whole life building and into the very core of who she is. Watching her with him, hearing their stories, and learning about who she was as a little girl suddenly made her transparent, and I could finally see the purity and softness that's shrouded beneath years that have hardened her.

I let her sleep while I go into the closet to hang up my suit jacket, and when I go into the bathroom to splash my face with cold water, I realize I forgot to grab a hand towel. Turning off the faucet, I walk into the toilet room and pull a towel from the linen cabinet. That's when I look down and notice something sitting in the bottom of the toilet bowl. I flick the light on to find it's a tiny blue pill, half-dissolved in the water.

I go to her sink top and pick up her prescription bottle to confirm it's the same pill.

She's been lying to me.

I have to wonder why she'd flush the pill instead of taking it because she *needs* to be taking them every day.

Going back in the bedroom, I sit on the edge of the bed where she's still sleeping. The dip of the mattress beneath me causes her to stir awake. Her eyes flutter open, and I handle her delicately. "You've been sleeping long?"

She looks at the clock on the bedside table and responds, "Not too long. How was your day?"

"Busy. What about yours?"

She sighs when she sits up and leans back again the head-board. "Same as the day before."

"Did you remember to take your pill today?"

"Yes," she answers with a curious look on her face. "Why?"

"You know how important it is that you take them every day, don't you?"

Annoyance paints her eyes. "Yes, Declan. I know. Why are you telling me this?"

"Because I want you taking care of yourself."

"I am."

"Then tell me why your pill is in the bottom of the toilet."

Her eyes tick, widening for a fleeting second, but I catch it.

"Do you want to explain to me why?"

Her throat constricts when she takes a hard swallow, and she shakes her head slowly. She's scared.

"How long have you been doing this?"

"I can take care of myself. I don't need you parenting me," she snaps.

I harden my voice, demanding, "How long?"

"I'm fine. I don't need them."

"How long, Elizabeth?"

She takes a deep breath, steadying herself to take me on when she admits, "Since I got them."

My teeth grit in an attempt to temper my anger, and when she notices my mood shift, she tries coaxing me. "Declan, I'm fine."

"You're not fine."

"I am."

"I heard you talking to someone the other night, but nobody was here," I say, calling her out.

"What are you talking about?"

I stand and pace back a few steps as my irritation grows. "You were in this room with the door closed. You were talking to someone. Who was it? And don't you dare feed me a lie."

Her eyes dart to the corner of the room, and when I look over to the window where she's focusing, the truth hits me.

Pike.

I turn back and take a few steps towards her. "What are you looking at?"

Her eyes, now rimming with tears, shift back to me.

"I need you to talk to me," I plead as I sit back down on the bed next to her. "Is it your brother? Are you seeing him again?"

(ELIZABETH)

"Don't lie to him."

I'm completely caught. He's going to run now that he knows I'm crazy and that I've been lying to him. Panic pangs through my body as Declan stares at me.

"Trust me, Elizabeth. Trust me enough to tell me."

He scoops my hands into his, and I can see the worry pouring out of him.

"Is that who you're looking at? Is he here?"

I close my eyes, scared of what his reaction will be, but I can't hide from the truth he now knows. My hands tremble in his when I finally nod my head yes.

"He's here?"

I nod again, and when I get the courage to open my eyes, I confess, "I need him."

"Baby," he breathes, cupping my cheek with his one hand. "You can't do this to yourself. It's not healthy, and I need you healthy."

"But . . . he's my brother."

"He's dead."

I blink and the tears fall. "I know that. But I still need him."

"Need me more."

His words expose an insecurity I wasn't aware of. I look into his eyes—really look—and I see what I've never seen before—self-doubt. The green in his eyes brightens in vibrancy, the effect of unshed tears that threaten to fall.

"I do need you," I tell him.

"It's not enough."

"Don't you dare choose me over him."

I turn back to Pike as Declan keeps his eyes on me.

"This has to end, Elizabeth. You have to start taking your pills. I need you well."

I don't look at him when he says this, instead I stay focused on Pike as my tears fall.

"He's right."

"No."

Pike walks over to me and crawls onto the bed, sitting on the other side of me, across from Declan.

"No!" I repeat fervently as I feel the fibers of my soul shredding apart.

"You can't keep hanging on to me like this."

"But I need you."

"I can't let you do this to yourself anymore," Declan says,

and when I look back to him, I cry, "But I need him."

"And I need *you*. You have to let him go," he insists. "You have to take your pills and get better."

I turn to Pike again, and when I do, Declan adds on a severed voice, "As much as you need him, I need you more."

"I don't want to lose you, Pike."

"It'll be okay."

"It's not okay. None of this is okay."

"It's time to let me go."

His request burns pieces of my heart into ash. I can feel it—scorching hot and blistering inside me, and I can't seem to cry hard enough to temper the flames. How do I let go when I don't know a day of survival without him?

"Don't leave me!" I sob frantically.

"Baby, this is killing me to see you like this," Declan says, breaking by my side.

"Say goodbye to me, Elizabeth."

My face crumples as the agony of losing my brother for good strangles my heart, paralyzing the ventricles. Tears force their way down my cheeks, cutting me like shards of ice.

"Don't leave me."

"You're the best sister anyone could ever have, and I was so lucky that you were mine."

"Don't you dare say your goodbyes, Pike."

"Look at Declan. Look at what we're doing to him."

I turn to my other side and see Declan's head in his one hand while his other is holding on to me, and he's crying.

Oh, my God, he's crying.

"Declan, please don't cr—"

"I need you," he beseeches desperately.

"We can't continue this."

I watch as tears fall down Declan's face, and it's a punch to my gut to see how much pain he's in. A man who never cracks is now crumbling before me—because of me. Every tear of his is a fissure in my breaking heart, cutting its way deeper into the delicate tissues.

I can't do this to him.

I love Pike. He's sacrificed himself again and again, my whole life, just to protect me, and no words exist to express how much he means to me. But now it's my turn to protect. And it's Declan that I need to take care of, because I need him strong so he can care for me in return.

As much as this kills me, I dig deep inside all my rotted wounds to grab on to the strength I need to say goodbye. "I never would've survived this world without you, Pike."

"But you did survive. And you're going to be okay without me."

"I love you."

"I need you to promise me that you'll listen to Declan, that you'll start taking your pills and get yourself healthy."

He's adamant, and I give him my word through the strain of my throat. "I promise."

I watch as his solid form ghosts into opacity, and I cry harder.

"I love you."

"Pike!"

Opacity transfuses into a cloudiness.

"I'm going to miss you."

"I'm gonna miss you too."

Cloudiness disappears into nothingness.

And when the lingering vapors of his scent fade away, I fall into Declan.

"He's gone," I wail amidst the trauma of freshly crenelated wounds that bleed inside me.

"I'm going to take care of you. I need you to believe in me."

"I do believe in you. It just hurts to let go of him."

"Look at me," he demands, and when I do, his face is streaked in tears shed. "I love you to the point it hurts, but I relish the pain of it because it reminds me that what we have runs so deep within me. And I swear to you, I will *never* stop loving you."

I wipe the trail of tears from his face.

"Tell me it hurts you to love me too."

Bracing my hands along his jaw to feel his stubble against my palms, I give him the purest part of me. "There's nobody in this world I could possibly hurt for more. Pike helped me survive, but it's you who helps me live. I was never able to do that until you."

And in the madness of heartache and profound love, Declan takes me as his, holding me, fucking me, healing me. Tears never stop falling from my swollen eyes as I open my heart and allow Declan the freedom to climb inside and take full ownership of all that I'm made of.

I no longer know where I end and he begins as we cement the amorphous lines between us.

We're serpents who feed off one another for sole survivorship.

We're everything love is meant to be.

thirty-two

Tears crystalize into salts, salts flake into dust, and dust gets swept away into the endless sky. And in the end we are left with a choice: swim or drown. The right choice is often the hardest. Drowning is so easy to do and takes no effort—you simply go weak and float deeper in the despair that consumes. But Pike wouldn't want that for me, and I need to fight for Declan.

So I took my love's hand and started to kick, trusting that together I would find my way to the surface. That was two weeks ago, and today I feel hopeful.

It was four days ago that I laughed for the first time since I said goodbye to my brother. A part of me thought I'd never laugh again, but I did, and oddly, it was Davina that pulled it out of me. Declan thought it would be good to have her over for dinner. He didn't tell her anything we had been dealing with, but she knew something was wrong when I walked into the living room a disheveled mess. One would think a guest would be somewhat reserved, but not Davina. She called me out, telling me I looked like shit. It wasn't just her crass honesty, it was the appalling look on her face and in her tone of voice, which she somehow managed to deliver in a caring way.

And I laughed.

That was all it took.

For a couple weeks Declan has postponed all his meetings and has given Lachlan time off. Declan and I need this time for us to be together and to mend. I feel myself healing little by little.

Declan has been showing me around the city. We've dined everywhere from The Tipperary to the Michelin-awarded Le Gavroche. I fed the ducks at St. James Park, and Declan couldn't hold in his laughter when two geese started chasing after me. The next day, we opted for Hyde Park where we were able to lay under the sun, wrapped in each other's arms. We kissed and talked for hours that afternoon. And then there was the London Eye. Despite my fear of heights and Ferris wheels, I threw caution to the wind and got on. Although I never got off the bench in the center of the glass capsule, Declan appreciated my effort.

We've been desperate for this time together, and now that we have it, we want more.

"If you could go anywhere in the world, where would you go?" Declan asks as we lie in bed, bodies naked and sticky with the smell of our sex in the air.

"Back to Brunswickhill."

"Of all places, you choose our home in Scotland?"

"I love it there."

Running his fingers lazily through my hair, he comments, "You love it that much?"

With my head tucked under his chin, I nod and then kiss his neck as I drape my leg over his hip. Declan grabs my ass and pulls me closer to him, forcing my pussy to grind against his hardening cock. Eager for him to fill me again, I reach down, take him in my hand, and guide him inside of me.

"Fuck me, baby," he growls in need, and when he rolls onto his back, I reach my hands behind me to grab his thighs. Opening my body up to him even more in this position, I fuck him as his hands touch every part of me—caressing, squeezing, pinching. He drives me wild, making me cum all over him, the whole time reaffirming my place in his world—in his heart.

"Let's go there," he says in a heavy breath as our hearts slow. "Where?"

"Your fairytale castle." He gives me a sexy smirk, and I release a soft laugh when excitement swells at the thought of going back to Scotland.

SOMETHING HAPPENS TO me physically as we drive through the gates of Brunswickhill. I can't fully explain it, but maybe this is what home feels like. It's just the two of us, hand in hand, and for the first time in a very long time, my heart doesn't feel so heavy.

When we get to the top of the winding drive, I hop out of the car, drop my head back, take in a deep breath, and smile.

"What are you doing?"

Declan wraps his arms around my waist, pulling me in close, and with my lips still painted in joy, I tell him, "It feels good to be back."

"This house is your home now."

"I've never had this before. I've never known home until right now—right here with you."

"It's a first for me too, darling, but I wouldn't want this with anyone but you."

His lips land on mine, taking me in a claiming kiss as my hands get lost in his hair. I taste his happiness when he dips his tongue inside my mouth and glides it along mine. This foreign feeling that swirls inside me takes me over and laughter slips out. He doesn't stop dropping kisses on me though, and it's only a matter of seconds when he begins to laugh too.

"What's so funny?" he mumbles against my mouth.

I pull back and look up at him. "I'm just happy."

Declan walks back to the Mercedes and pops open the hatchback to the SUV to grab our luggage, and as he does, I turn to look at the large, tiered fountain.

"Declan, look!" Amazed by the blooms, I walk over to the massive fountain and inhale the earthy scent.

"They've always bloomed in there," he tells me as I look in wonderment at all the lotus flowers.

White mixed with every hue of pink, each one flawless despite the murky water they rose from. They glow as they bask in the sunshine.

"They're so beautiful."

"Come here," he says. "I want to show you a part of the house you've never seen."

We walk inside the double doors, and he drops our luggage in the foyer, taking my hand and leading me up the stairs all the way to the third floor and into his office.

"What are you doing?" I question as he runs his hand along the wall.

When he stops moving, he casts his eyes to me and, with a smile, gives the wall a push.

"Are you kidding me?" I laugh in surprise when it's revealed that a portion of the wall is a hidden spring-loaded partition that opens up to a secret spiral staircase.

"Come on."

I follow him up the narrow stairs, and when we reach the top, there's another door that he opens. My eyes widen in amazement when I step out onto the rooftop, exposing a panoramic view of all of Galashiels. Declan reaches out for me, knowing my fear of heights, and walks me to the wall's edge.

"You see that river?" he asks as he points out.

"Yes."

"That's the River Tweed. It divides Galashiels from Abbottsford. And you see that castle-like estate down there?"

"Yes."

"That's Sir Walter Scott's home."

"The poet?"

"Yes."

"That's no home," I note as I look at the majestic estate that's nestled down below from where Declan's estate sits perched high on this hill. "That's a palace!"

He chuckles. "It's a museum now. There's also a quaint restaurant that's known for their shortcakes in there."

We walk the border of the rooftop, and I look down to the grounds below, admiring all the colorful blooms that are coming to life as the weather warms. The past couple months of spring have done wonders, exposing more pebbled creeks that stream down various hills. There are too many flowers to count, along with a few stone benches—some that rest under trees and some that are out in the open. From up here, I can see the grassy paths that lead from one garden nook to the next, to the next, and to the next. A part of me feels like I'm cheating myself of the wanderlust of exploring and getting lost in the maze down there.

My very own Wonderland.

"It's stunning, isn't it?"

"It's breathtaking," I say and then turn to face him, pressing my body against his with my arms wrapped around his waist. "I never thought anything like this could exist in this world."

"I feel the same when I look at you."

We stand here, on the rooftop of our own personal castle, and wrap ourselves around each other. Declan cradles my head to his chest as he plants kisses down on me. We hug; it's all we need to do in this moment of much-needed peace, and finally, I can breathe. The weight of the world's afflictions are becoming less and less suffocating as I continue to move along this path Declan is providing me. Of course a part of me still aches for my dad and for my brother, but that's a sadness I'll have to brave for the rest of my life. There's simply no cure for heartbreaks that surpass unfathomable agony. Some wounds run so deep that there's no possibility of healing. But here, with Declan, I'm hoping one day the pain will become more tolerable.

"I was thinking about something on the plane ride here," Declan says, breaking the silence between us. "We should go to The Water Lily."

I smile when I think about Isla. Staying with her when I was at my ultimate lowest, thinking Declan had died at the hands of Pike, was probably the best place I could've wound up. We had so many great conversations, and I realize now that I know so much about his grandmother when he's never really spoken to her.

"Isla has a beautiful heart," I tell him. "I miss her."

"Why do you think she never said anything to me? She has a

photo of me in her room and she knows who I am."

I see the little boy lost deep within his eyes as I look at him. "Maybe she was scared. Maybe she didn't know what to say."

"Maybe," he responds. "How about we pay her a visit tomorrow? Let's take the rest of the day for us." He leans down and kisses me before saying, "Take a walk with me."

We head back down the hidden staircase and then down to main floor of the house. Walking through the atrium, we make our way outside.

"Everything looks so different than it did when we left a couple months ago," I say as we stroll aimlessly through the flowers.

We make our way up a stone pathway that runs alongside the clinker grotto and then wander along another grassy path, weaving through trees and stepping over a narrow babbling brook. I look down at the house, and laugh to myself when I see the huge gaps that still remain in the now-flowering bushes that rim around the exterior wall.

"What's so funny?"

"I still can't believe you ripped out all the purple bushes," I tell him, and when he looks down to the house to see the gaps, he shrugs. "My darling hates purple," he says nonchalantly and continues to walk.

"Sit with me," he says when we find ourselves surrounded by bright yellow daffodils.

I settle myself between Declan's legs and back against his chest as he sits behind me. We both look out among the flowers as I sink into his hold.

"Tell me you're happy," he says, and I answer honestly, "I'm happy."

"You know, the first time I ever saw you, I knew I had to have you." I rest my head against him as I listen to him speak. "I'd never felt that intensely about anyone before. I can still remember how beautiful you looked that night in your navy silk dress and long red hair. I was beyond fascinated by you."

"And I remember you, not even wearing a bow tie to your own black tie affair," I tease.

"I know our start was fucked up, but I wouldn't change it. Because without it, we wouldn't have *this*."

"I'll never forgive myself though."

"I need you to know something." The seriousness in his tone makes me sit up and turn to face him. "I need you to know that I've forgiven you, and that hate I used to feel towards you . . . it's no longer there."

His words soothe, and when he begins to kaleidoscope, I blink him into clarity. But these tears don't hurt—they heal. He places his hands on my cheeks and kisses me again.

"You give yourself to me in a way no other woman could. And even if they could, I wouldn't want them to. I'm not perfect—you've even called me out on my flaws a few times, but you've never thrown them in my face with ridicule," he says with gratitude. "And when I tell you that I need you, I mean it. I can't battle this world without you by my side. You're the bravest woman I know."

"I'm not."

"You are. My God, the life you've been dealt, everything you've had to endure, and here you are, still fighting. Still trying."

"Because of you," I tell him. "Every breath is a choice, and I choose to keep taking them for you."

"I'm going to give you a long life filled with breaths then," he affirms before he takes my face in his hands and looks stead-fastly into my eyes. "I once told you that the truest part of a person is the ugliest."

"I remember that night."

"The ugliest parts of you are your darkest. And trust me when I tell you that I want to love all of your darkest parts." He reaches into his pocket, and my heart beats a beat I've never felt before as he pulls out a ring. "And I promise you that I will love all of your darkness if you promise to love mine too."

"Declan . . ."

"Marry me."

And that was the moment all my dreams came true. We sat there in the garden of daffodils as he held that ring, which embodied exactly what we were between his fingers—two people who harbored so much darkness. The cushion-cut diamond was brilliant and so very black with intricate facets, encircled with tiny, sparkling white diamonds that also adorned the delicately thin platinum band.

But it wasn't the ring, it was him. It was always him. The only one who was strong enough to love me for me. He took all my rot and all my scars and somehow made me feel like a true princess.

My whole life, I was waiting for someone to save me, and he did. I knew in that moment that I would never be unloved, I would never be abandoned, and I would never be left to fight the monsters alone.

"Yes!"

My eyes never leave his beautiful face as he slips the ring on to my finger, and once in place, I throw myself into his arms, knocking him back to the ground. And we kiss like no two people have ever kissed. I pour my soul into his mouth as his hands grip me tightly—we're so needy for closeness.

But that closeness is severed the moment I hear the *snick.*

I jump back and turn in an instant to find myself staring down the barrel of a pistol.

"You move, I shoot her," the man snarls to Declan. But I know Declan isn't armed right now.

We're helpless.

I'm frozen in place. I can't even feel my heart beating anymore.

"This is vengeance. Your father fucked with the wrong family the moment he handed my brother's name over to the feds sixteen years ago. But because I'm sadistic, I'm going to give you the choice. Either you die or your father dies. You have five seconds."

I turn to Declan, already knowing my choice as I mouth *I love you* through razor-sharp tears.

"Elizabeth, no!"

"Don't hurt my dad. Kill me."

"Eliz—"

BANG.

epilogue

I LOOK UP INTO the brilliant, rich blue sky. There isn't a cloud in sight as the sun shines down in rays of glittering warmth. I look around to find I'm surrounded by gigantic, lime-green canopies, but when I take a closer look, I realize they aren't canopies, but instead, blades of grass.

Carnegie?

My eyes dart down to reveal my bright pink accordion body.

I'm back.

"Hello?" I call out, wondering why I'm all alone, and when I hear a rustling in the distance, I call out again, "Carnegie? Is that you?"

"Elizabeth!" he hollers back, but his accent isn't right. "Elizabeth!"

No. It can't be.

"Declan?" I scoot around to see a blue caterpillar emerge from behind a blade of grass.

"Elizabeth," he exclaims in his unmistakable Scottish brogue as he inches over to me.

"What are you doing in my dream?"

"Dream?" His beady eyes drop in dread.

"What's wrong?"

"Darling . . ."

"What's going on?" I question in fear.

"You died."

Horror fires off inside me as I look at him. "Then . . . Then what are you doing here?"

"Don't panic."

"Oh, my God!"

"We're together, Elizabeth. That's all that matters."

"If I'm dead, then . . ."

"I am too," he tells me. "He shot me right after he shot you."

"NO!" I cry out, and he's right here next to me, comforting, "It's okay, darling. We're still together. Nothing can hurt us now."

"But you're . . . you're dead because of me!"

"No, baby. You made the right choice. That guy was there for revenge, and no matter what you said, he would've killed us anyway," he tells me. "But look around you. This place is incredible."

I stare at him in utter shock and ask, "How are you so calm?"

"We've both been here for a while, a few days or so, but you've been sleeping. I've had time to digest it all, but this place doesn't allow stress to last very long." He slinks his way closer, running his body along mine, and the moment I feel his touch, my heart settles peacefully.

"We're okay?"

He nods and then tells me, "We're not alone either."

299

"You mean Carnegie? Did you meet him?"

"I did, but there's someone else you're going to want to see."

"Who?"

"Your brother."

"Pike?" I perk up in astonishment. "He's here?"

"He's out with Carnegie right now gathering berries."

"You talked to him?"

"Yes, but don't worry. We've had a lot of time to reach an understanding with one another."

"He's not a bad guy," I immediately defend, and he stops me.

"I know that now. Come on. Let's go find them."

We maze around enormous flower stems and even more gigantic tree trunks as we scoot together, side by side. Every now and then Declan looks over to me and smiles, which makes me giggle. He's right, the stress doesn't last long. As I frolic along, I feel weightless, I feel exuberant, I feel . . . free.

"This way," Declan tells me before we turn and weave our way through the wooden vines of a berry bush. "It's a shortcut."

I look up at the pink berries that are as big as basketballs, and when we come to an opening and make our way out, I see Carnegie. And next to him is a bright red caterpillar.

"Pike?"

"You're awake!"

"Pike!"

I slink as quickly as I can to him, and he does the same.

"I never thought I'd see you again," I tell him.

"You can't get rid of me," he jokes as he nudges his stumpy head into the side of my tubular body. "You know, when you promised you'd do anything to get us a better life, I didn't think we'd have to be fucking caterpillars to get it."

We both laugh and Declan joins in as he sidles up next to me.

"Language, young man," Carnegie nags in his dapper British accent.

I worm my way closer to my lifelong friend. "Carnegie . . ."

"It's been far too long, my dear."

"What is all this?"

"Why, this is your afterlife. Nothing will ever hurt you again, because pain no longer exists. This is where dreams are reality."

"I told you it would all be okay, darling," Declan reaffirms.

I release a pleased sigh and lean my head against Declan.

Carnegie looks to us, asking, "So, this is love?"

Gazing into Declan's eyes, I respond, "This is love."

Declan and I continue to nuzzle each other tenderly while Carnegie and Pike are off by the pond's edge. Movement catches my eye, and when I turn to a tall bush next to me, an orange caterpillar appears. It stops and looks at me curiously, and then the beady eyes widen.

"Princess?"

My body sparks in bewilderment. "Dad?"

He rushes over to me, his tiny mouth fighting for the biggest smile.

"What are you doing h—"

Oh, my God. He's dead.

And suddenly, I see his smile drop when realization hits him that I'm dead too.

He stops moving, and when his eyes slip away from mine, he looks to Declan. "What happened to you two?"

I hold my breath, not wanting my father to feel any guilt that

I chose to pay the pay the price for his past—that Declan did too. "You tell me first."

He scoots a little closer before saying, "The brother of one of the guys I handed over to the feds ran me off the road right after I left the beach the last day we were together. He gave me a choice. He told me I could live and that he would kill you instead or he could just kill me." My mouth gapes in shock. "Obviously, I gave up my own life."

"There was never a choice," Declan tells him.

"What do you mean?"

"That same man paid me and your daughter a visit with the same ultimatum."

My dad's eyes dart back to me, and I tell him, "I told him not to hurt you and to kill me instead."

"You sacrificed your life for me?"

I nod.

"Sweetheart . . ."

"It's okay, Dad," I assure him. "Can I ask you something though?"

"Anything."

"What was your biggest wish when you were living?"

The corners of his mouth lift. "You," he says. "I always wished to have you in my life."

My heart floats like a feather. "And my wish was always you, Dad." My eyes mist over in pure delight. "Our wishes came true." I turn to face Declan and tell him in amazement, "This is my every wish come true."

The three of us look at one another as the truth crystallizes. We are a web of wishes come true. We no longer have to creep in the shadows of those who wish us harm. We are finally free from all that has ever haunted us. I know Declan and I would have never been able to find this kind of freedom among the living. It only exists here.

I look around at the magnificently colored flowers that wisp in the breeze above us, I see Pike riding on the back of a dragonfly—happy and whimsical, and then there's Carnegie, who never has to be alone again because he has us now. I laugh as he watches in merriment at my brother flying around. And my dad, overflowing with boundless mirth as he kisses the top of my head.

"This is all I ever wanted," he tells me.

I then turn to face Declan—amazed that our love was so powerful that not even death could part us. And then we kiss a kiss that's never existed until now. It's serene and vivacious and loving and entirely magical.

This is everything dreams are made of.

This is my fairytale.

from the author

Thank you for reading Hush book #3 in the Black Lotus series.
If you enjoyed this book, please consider leaving a spoiler-free
review.

Want to join other E.K. Blair fans for book talk, giveaways, and
inside peeks into Blair's upcoming books?
Join The Little Black Hearts fan group here at
www.facebook.com/groups/bangdiscussion

acknowledgements

THIS SERIES WAS a labor of love, and this book in particular! It took many people who love and support me to help me see this story come to fruition. I wouldn't be able to do what I do if it weren't for the following people.

To my fans, I cannot thank you enough for continuing to love my characters and support my stories. Your loyalty means the world to me. The greatest joy is being able to cut my heart open, pour my blood on the pages, and hand it over to you.

Sally Gillespie, you are one of my biggest blessings! The time you sacrifice for me is simply incredible. Thank you for helping me in the creation of this story. I had a blast working with you on the book. We've blushed, we've laughed, and we've cried more times than I can count, but we did it! You are my backbone, and I'd fall to pieces without you.

Bethany Castaneda, thank you for all the little things you do that are huge things for me! You save me so much time and so many headaches. Whenever I call, you are always there for me. And no matter what, I can always count on you for a good laugh. You keep this boat afloat, and I am so grateful to have you as part of my team.

Jennifer Juers, thank you for your honesty and time. I love that you don't sugarcoat anything! You never try to appease me; you only want to help me even if it means telling me the cold, hard truth. The time you put in to making this book the best it can be is invaluable! You are my secret weapon.

Mary Elizabeth, damn Daniel! Thank you for inspiring me to be a better writer. Your support, guidance, and friendship are so precious to me.

Ashley Williams, wow! Just WOW! How do I even thank you properly? The hours upon hours you have devoted to this book are downright incredible! You make my words strong, even though you bust my balls to do so. From the early mornings to the late nights, and everything in between, you have been there with me every step of the way through this book. I am looking forward to sharing this experience with you for many books to come. You are an amazing editor and friend!

Lisa Lisa Lisa, my partner in crime, there's no one I'd rather fight with than you! I cannot say it enough, you are truly a gem. Thank you for always believing in me, for always pushing me to be a better writer, and for not beating around the bush. You give it to me honestly, and even though I dig my heels in the ground because I'm stubborn, I really appreciate all that you do for me. I love you, and I miss you, and you should totally move next door to me so we can always be together!

Thank you, Denise Tung, for working your magic and organizing all the promos and reviews. I couldn't do this without you!

Erik Schottstaedt, once again, you've crafted another beautiful photo for my cover. Thank you for creating the whole look of this series.

Bloggers, there are too many of you to name, but each and every one of you are equally important. Thank you for your undying support.

To my husband, none of this would be possible without you. You're the best Mr. Mom I know. Thank you for taking care of the children, the house, the laundry, the dinners, and so much more to allow me the time and privacy I need to write. I love you, babes!

And finally, thank you to Elizabeth, Declan, and Pike. Living inside of your souls for the past two years has been an amazing experience. We've been on quite a journey together. I'm heartbroken to say goodbye and to put you up on my bookshelf after all we have been through. I will miss each of you in very different ways the way each of you have touched my heart in different ways. You have allowed me to discover pieces of myself I never knew were inside me, pieces that I needed to know were there. I'm going to miss you. I'll look for you all in my dreams when I find my way into the forest—into the fairytale.

Ways to Connect
www.ekblair.com
Facebook: www.facebook.com/EKBlairAuthor
Twitter: @EK_Blair_Author
Instagram: instagram.com/authorekblair

Other Titles by E.K. Blair

Fading (book 1)
Freeing (book 2)
Falling (book 3)

Bang (Black Lotus, book 1)
Echo (Black Lotus, book 2)

89090922R00190

Made in the USA
Columbia, SC
08 February 2018